JOURNEY TO THE SUN

A Novel of Prehistoric North America

JOURNEY TO THE SUN

A Novel of Prehistoric North America
Ernest L. Schusky

Rutledge Books, Inc.

Danbury, CT

Front cover artwork by Victoria Vebell

Cover design by John Laub

Interior design by Al Robinson

Copyright © 2001 by Ernest L. Schusky

Rutledge Books, Inc.
107 Mill Plain Road, Danbury, CT 06811
1-800-278-8533
www.rutledgebooks.com

Manufactured in the United States of America

Cataloging in Publication Data
Schusky, Ernest L.

Journey to the sun: a novel of prehistoric north america

ISBN: 1-58244-123-5

1. Fiction.

Library of Congress Card Number: 00-109913

DEDICATION

Mary Sue Schusky

Mark and Read Schusky

CHAPTER ONE

"I'll never fit in here. Now he hates me," Warns of Enemy sobbed.

"Hush, little sister. It's the first time our husband hit you. It wasn't your fault. He's anxious because he's found no game." Dancing Eyes patted her sister's arm.

"No one likes me. They all make fun of my accent and my light complexion. Why can't I learn Shoshoni the way you did? You're even dark enough to pass as one of them."

"It's all right. They don't make fun, they only joke."

"It's more than that. Even our daughter is ashamed of me."

"No, that's not true. Maybe when she was younger. Hush now, she'll be back soon."

Songbird bit her lip. She hadn't meant to eavesdrop on her mothers. She felt ashamed when she remembered she had teased Warns of Enemy about her accent—but at least she hadn't called her "cloud skin." Songbird was proud to have her father's dark complexion. The tall, light Washo women were oddities among the Shoshoni.

Songbird wondered where her father would find a husband

for her. She hoped he'd be Shoshoni. She didn't have a close sister to be a co-wife, only distant sisters. She imagined a stranger as a co-wife, and doubted she could ever get along with her. If she were her husband's first wife it would be all right, but she hoped to be an only wife. Many Shoshoni married only one woman. She resolved to look for a young man at the next Bear ceremony and convince her father that he'd make a good husband.

Above all, she dreaded the idea of moving to a new land and experiencing her mothers' fate. It would be horrible to marry a foreigner and have to speak another language. Nor could she bear to leave a land as beautiful as her home.

She glanced from the green oasis of their summer camp to the gray and brown flatland with its scraggly brush hinting of green where roots reached water. The flatness stretched to the horizon at broken intervals to mark an ancient, dry lake bed. Mountains lined the basin edges to form a purple and black ring. The cratered homeland was part of a greater basin that also sheltered Ute and Paiute. Because her father and mothers knew the land so well, they usually collected enough to eat with little effort.

But this year was different. Songbird's father found neither deer nor antelope. He was lucky to return with a jack rabbit or gopher. The last real flesh her mothers had cured was the bear her father killed in early winter. Songbird's mouth watered at the thought of its sweet fat. She relished even the chewy strings of its dried meat.

"You've brought much wood, my daughter," her father said, startling her as he came up behind her. "You'll make someone a good wife."

"You'll find me a Shoshoni husband, won't you?" she said anxiously.

Pocatello drew back in surprise at the urgency in his daughter's voice. Her fourteen years of age meant he could wait a while before he searched for a husband for her. He joked, "We can't afford to lose a good worker like you."

Then, as if for the benefit of his wives, he said loudly, "Except your mothers may grow lazy with you doing all the work."

Dancing Eyes and Warns of Enemy scurried from behind the brush lean-to to join their husband. Pocatello looked downcast at Warns of Enemy and said to Songbird, "We must look for a husband who will never beat you. Good husbands never beat their wives." Songbird recognized an apology in her father's words, and she saw Warns of Enemy hide a smile behind her hand.

He turned to Songbird and said, "Perhaps at the locust drive I'll find a young man for you, one who is kind and thoughtful."

To his wives, he said, "I saw signs of locust in the far valley to the east. I'll invite the nearby bands to drive them. I should return in eight or ten days."

Warns of Enemy hurried to prepare what dried food her husband could carry, and showed him the moccasins she had completed the day before. She basked in his smile of gratitude.

Pocatello nodded a departure when he left and turned to Songbird. "I'll invite any group with a single young man." Then he laughed. "Or any old men who need a second wife."

Songbird winced. Her father joked now, but in three or four years, he would look for an elder if he hadn't found a man her age.

While Pocatello searched for other bands, Songbird and her mothers traveled the streambed of the valley to gather every seed and root they could find. They scoured even the desert flatland to add to their supply because they wanted to be known as good hosts who fed everyone.

Drought throughout the basin made Songbird and her family long for meat but prepared them to settle for roasted locust. The charcoal-flavored meal teased the tongue, filled the belly, and stored well. Feasts brought everyone together, and lifted spirits when people sang and danced.

Songbird rejoiced as Pocatello's guests drifted into his camp. She watched the visitors erect a handful of windbreaks along the trickle of a streambed. The new arrivals greeted relatives and caught up on gossip.

In the bustle, Songbird hardly heard the accented words of her younger mother. "Come daughter," Warns of Enemy called with a gesture of her head. "We'll gather firewood along the creek." Dancing Eyes encouraged Songbird in perfect Shoshoni, "Hurry, child, we'll need loads of firewood. Everyone will fill their bellies, so we'll do nothing but celebrate for days." Then she said sternly, "Except you. If you don't gather your share of wood, you'll have to grind all the locust."

Songbird knew she joked and returned the banter. "When you break your tumpline and can't haul firewood, don't expect me to carry your wood. Then I'll watch you grind meal."

When she and her mothers were out of earshot of the guests, she spoke in Washo. "Did you have this much fun in driving locust when you were young?"

The two sisters smiled. Dancing Eyes said, "We were never lucky enough to drive locust. They're not that far west. It takes moons to walk to our country. But, in spring, the fish in Tahoe Lake jumped into our baskets. When they left the lake to spawn, we netted them all day. We ate trout until we burst, and we dried mountains of it."

"Does trout taste like the fish father spears for us?"

"Oh, there's no comparison," Warns of Enemy blurted out, sounding homesick at the thought of trout's oily sweetness. "Even when dried, it's far better than the bony, tasteless suckers we have here."

Dancing Eyes switched to Shoshoni and changed the subject. "Come, let's see who can get the driest wood. We'll need hot fires in the brush."

The three joined the women visitors in a dry streambed. Their joking eased the chore of gleaning the driftwood tangled in the willow trees along the banks. They caught up on news of other families they hadn't seen all year as they talked of births, marriages, and deaths.

At a thicket of cottonwood, Songbird reached for a prize clump of wood only to encounter another hand on the other side of the brush. It belonged to a girl about her own age, her breasts hardly differing from those of boys.

The slender girl stood a little under the height of an armstretch. Her black hair, glistening in the sunlight, showed signs of recent braiding, but now it hung loose to her shoulders, parted in the middle to flow down both sides. Laughing black eyes punctuated her round face. Songbird saw the stranger had painted her cheeks with vertical, red wavy lines like her own designs, and they hardly showed against a creamy, chocolate complexion.

"You keep the wood," Songbird said.

"I'll carry it, but it is our wood, I think. Won't we likely start the same fire?" the girl said in a friendly, inviting way.

The tone of voice, more than the words, intrigued Songbird. She wanted to learn the girl's name, but it was impolite to ask.

So, she said with a smile, "Do you come from far away, sister? We didn't have to travel since we camp near here."

"We walked six days from the north, from the Grass Seed camp, my father's home. He hunted along the way because he's found no antelope all year, but he didn't see a single animal."

"It's the same with us," Songbird said. "My father hasn't killed big game all summer. We had a bear in early winter, but nothing after that. If it weren't for rabbits, we'd be vegetarians."

"I know. I thought we'd starve this spring before we could dig roots, but now we've had enough. If we don't dry meat though, what will we do this winter? Can you imagine eating nothing but locust meal?" The girl wrinkled her nose in disgust.

Her expression made Songbird laugh, and the two forgot the coming winter. Songbird knew it didn't help to worry. She tossed her head and said, "My father's father's brother moved north. He knew the Bear ritual. He was burly like a bear and dark, so people nicknamed him Black Bear."

"I know Black Bear," the girl said pertly. "My mother's father's sister married him. So, you and I are cousins, but I'd like to be your sister. I'm the only child in our household so the only other sisters I have are my mother's sister's two daughters, and they live days from us."

"I'm the only child in my camp," Songbird said eagerly. "At least, so far. My younger mother thinks she's pregnant. It will be her first birth," she added with a giggle. "She seems confused."

The two girls covered their mouths with their hands as they laughed aloud at the joy of another relative.

The two discovered other distant relatives they shared while gathering wood. By the time they finished, the two knew each other well. When their net carrying bags were full, they swung them to their backs, and shifted the weight to the tumpline across their foreheads. They smiled a parting, just as Pocatello came down the streambed.

"Who's that girl?" he said.

"I just met her. She's from Black Bear's camp."

"I thought I was seeing double. Do you know how much you resemble her?"

"We use the same face painting. Is that what you mean?"

"That too. But you look very much alike. Your complexion. Your hair. You both are the same size."

Songbird smiled and asked about Black Bear's wife and sister-in-law. Her father grinned and said, "You want to know your friend's name, is that it?"

Songbird looked down. "Yes. I don't know who else to ask."

"I'll see if I can find out."

That night, when Pocatello came to the lean-to, he beckoned Songbird to come with him. While they walked he told her he had found Black Bear's lean-to and learned that her new friend was called Twisted Rabbit.

"I haven't heard that name before," Songbird said.

"I asked about it because it is unusual. Her father told me it's a nickname from when she was very young. She tried to help her mothers twist rabbit skins for a blanket. She threw a temper tantrum because she was so clumsy. One of her fathers called her Twisted Rabbit after that."

"I can't believe she'd get angry anymore."

"Probably not. If she's anything like her mother, you'll like her. The woman always has food ready for you. I'll find out if Twisted Rabbit has a grown-up name yet." His face brightened, and he winked. "Maybe her mother is widowed. I wouldn't mind marrying her, and maybe throw away one of your mothers. Then you and Twisted Rabbit could be sisters."

"Oh, Father, you're not funny," Songbird said, hiding a smile with her cupped hand.

The next day, a brilliant sun dried everything. Instead of gathering firewood, the families turned over browned brush lining deep gullies that cut the valley walls. A few green patches showed in a few bushes, but the sparse grass had turned yellow.

By midday, the yawning gullies brimmed with firewood as men joined women to break up dried brush from the year before. Under large, fluffy clouds that took on endless shapes, the women carried the wood they had gathered the day before to strategic points along the gullies.

Several men pretended to direct the work, but the seasoned women needed no orders. Given the respect that they showed each other, the directions of the self-appointed bosses amounted to little more than suggestions. Twisted Rabbit and Songbird found each other early, and they joked about possible husbands. That night, the two joined the others at a roaring fire where they danced in a circle around the men. The slow shuffle let them whisper about the boys they passed until they lost themselves to the hypnotic drumbeat. The night had nearly passed before Songbird went with Twisted Rabbit to her windbreak. They managed a few jokes about potential husbands before they fell asleep under the soft mantle of a rabbit-skin blanket.

The next morning, no one stirred until well after dawn. The sun's heat promised a good day for a fire. Even the large, black crows circling overhead seemed to anticipate a feast.

Since Songbird's family lived in the territory of the drive, Pocatello gathered the elders to counsel. They quickly reached a consensus on how to conduct the drive. Adults assembled at the valley mouth to spread across its width. The young went to the upper reaches and the ridges that lined the valley.

Songbird asked Twisted Rabbit if she liked any of the young men in her band. Twisted Rabbit said, "Is your father looking for a husband for you?"

"Not yet. No. I guess I don't know," Songbird said in confusion. "We joked about it yesterday."

"My father talks the same way. He's always mentioning old men who need a second wife." She grinned and then grew somber. "He scares me because he can pretend to be so serious."

"I think about my mothers a lot," Songbird said in the same tone. "They came far from the west, and they've never been home since they married. I couldn't stand to leave my people. I'd rather be a second wife than marry a foreigner."

The girls reached the top of a steep ridge where an old woman nodded to a ravine. They understood they were to drive back any locust that failed to seek cover in the brush-filled gullies below them. On a signal from below, they were to start fires near the rim of the ravine.

"I hope my ember lasts, Twisted Rabbit," Songbird said. "The spark burns faster than I thought it would."

Songbird didn't really worry about her ember. She mentioned it as a way to use Twisted Rabbit's name.

Twisted Rabbit's face brightened. "Mine, too, but it will last. They're shouting louder, aren't they, Songbird? The locust will be here soon."

Twisted Rabbit used Songbird's name casually, but Songbird caught the significance. Twisted Rabbit cared about her. Her face flushed with joy. Before they could say more, a few locust buzzed past. The two girls shouted and waved their arms, dashing across the rim where the old woman had assigned them.

Black clouds rose from the valley, spinning upwards in confusion as the locust sought shelter in the brush. Here and there, black and white flashes of magpies braved the shouts to feed on the locust.

When the elders reached the bottom of the ravines, they started fires. Rising smoke signaled the youth atop the gullies to ignite their brush. At the first brush pile, Twisted Rabbit and Songbird took powdered cedar bark from their belts and blew their glowing embers over the tinder. Sparks flew on the bark and burst into flame. Their nearly naked bodies flinched from the heat. Songbird felt hypnotized as she watched the fire jump from side to side along the ravine.

Despite the intense temperature, the green wood released a stifling smoke that found Twisted Rabbit's lungs. Her coughs broke Songbird's spell, and she grabbed her friend's hand to lead her away. As they backed away, the wrinkled, gray-haired woman at the top shouted for them to move to the next gully. Songbird had forgotten it in her concern for Twisted Rabbit. When the girl nodded that she had recovered, the two darted for the second ravine. Its sides were steeper than the first, and the brush poorly placed. The two searched for footholds to reach the firewood tinder. In the struggle, Songbird dropped her ember.

"How stupid of me," Songbird said, looking around frantically.

Twisted Rabbit said calmly, "I have mine. We'll be fine. I see a good place to start a fire, but it's farther down."

"I'll go while you catch your breath."

"No, I have the starter. Let's not argue."

Songbird hesitated. She wondered what Twisted Rabbit meant by, "let's not argue." Her mothers admonished her for her strong will and reminded her to put others first, so she let Twisted Rabbit climb down the ravine to a point where two large rocks blocked the way. A narrow passage between them allowed only a single person to squeeze by.

After Twisted Rabbit squirmed through, she dashed down the draw to stop at thick brush. She dropped her ember as she drew it from her pouch, but Songbird saw it glow when the girl blew on it. A strong, acrid scent of smoke touched Songbird's nose. Fire and smoke from farther below raced upward to sting her eyes.

"My cedar bark didn't start," Twisted Rabbit called. "But don't worry, there's grass here that'll do. I'll get it going." "Forget the fire, Twisted Rabbit. Come back," Songbird screamed. "We won't need it. The fire from below is burning so fast, the locust can't escape. Come on."

As soon as she shouted, Songbird knew Twisted Rabbit would ignore her. The girl would think of others before herself.

Songbird breathed with relief. She saw Twisted Rabbit ignite the grass, which exploded into flame. When Twisted Rabbit climbed up the steep gorge, rocks slipped under her. Her bark moccasin twisted sideways. Songbird heard a stifled cry of pain and plunged downward to help her friend.

As she squeezed between the two rocks, the heat from below struck her and smoke filled her nose. She raced to her friend's side to help the girl to her feet. The wrenched foot hung useless. When the two struggled to the narrow passageway, she tried to push Twisted Rabbit through, but the girl screamed, "No! Pull me through!"

Songbird had no time to think, she simply obeyed.

Savage heat and a ruthless cloud of smoke smothered the two, and Songbird lost her grip.

"I can't breathe, leave me, Songbird."

"No," Songbird choked as the thick smoke filled her lungs.

She clutched Twisted Rabbit's hand again. She pulled with all her might, but she edged the other girl only finger lengths' forward. Her lungs begged for air. Flames dashed upward in heat so intense that she almost gave up when Twisted Rabbit failed to move.

Songbird screamed as fire devoured her friend's apron. Her own apron smoldered. With no other protection, she fell backward between the two rocks. She felt a scorching pain sear her left cheek and realized her long, loose hair was on fire.

The pain, heat, and smoke left her senseless until an arm around her waist revived her. She struggled for a toehold with her moccasins, suddenly aware that one was lost, the other in flames.

Farther up the gully, her lungs filled with something other than smoke. The fresh air awakened her, and she glimpsed the gray hair of the woman who had directed them. Her next thought was of Twisted Rabbit.

"Where's my sister?" she choked out.

The old woman's silence told her that she hadn't been able to rescue Twisted Rabbit from the fire, but Songbird refused to believe it.

"We must go back."

The old woman gathered Songbird in her arms, as much to restrain her as to comfort her. Songbird was convulsed with grief. Salty tears stung the burns on her cheek, but she hardly felt them. She wondered how she could be so careless and clumsy, and why the fire hadn't killed her.

"It's all my fault because I dropped my ember. If I had gone to start the fire, I'd be the one who died." Her tears soaked the old woman's neck. "I never do anything right."

Songbird despaired that the confidence she once enjoyed was lost. She thought her knowledge of a second language made her special, but now nagging self-doubt choked her.

Her mothers added to her anxiety and grief. They spoke of ghosts of the dead as troublesome spirits who make life miserable. They urged their husband to move camp downstream, and they persuaded Twisted Rabbit's family to burn their lean-to. Songbird begged her father to let her stay, but he insisted she accompany her mothers.

A few band members laughed at the Washo's exaggerated fears, but most of them feared ghosts, too. They prepared to leave as soon as they gathered the locust. Twisted Rabbit's father came to Songbird to assure her that she wasn't to blame. He told her that people had started fires too early, but his reassurance did nothing to ease her guilt.

She felt uneasiness in the air as men rushed to help the women gather the roast locust and in their haste, overlook much food. Songbird also overheard people question Pocatello's ability to direct a drive.

Her mothers seemed convinced that Twisted Rabbit's ghost caused the poor harvest and the mean-spirited criticism of their husband. In their camp downstream, they urged Songbird to grind the insects quickly and hinted at another move. To keep her busy, they sent her to dig new storage pits. Once they had stored a supply of meal, they convinced their husband to leave for a distant valley.

Songbird sweated under heavy baskets of locusts as her family climbed a mountain trail toward a saddle. On the other side, a downward path zigzagged to another valley floor with an undependable stream that emerged into three or four brackish oases. Sparse grass provided late summer seed for them and feed for rabbits and an occasional deer.

The arid valley served as home for the family for less than a moon. Seldom had they moved so early in the summer but the grass was very scarce. As she looked around at her dry surroundings, Songbird hoped they might find a few roots.

She watched Dancing Eyes go directly to their former campsite though she saw no trace of the old lean-to. Her mother had spotted a large stone that she used as a cover for a storage pit.

"Look at the matting we left," Dancing Eyes exclaimed. "The stone protected the hole so well, it's just as we left it. There's even a little seed to mix with our meal." She showed even more enthusiasm when she found a grinding stone. "Look sister, it's a sign we did the right thing to move."

Songbird suspected her mother pretended to be pleased with the new camp. She figured that her mothers had felt the presence of Twisted Rabbit's ghost at the old place, and were delighted to have a mountain range for protection.

"Wouldn't it have been easier to grind all the insects back there?" Songbird said with a tone of resentment. "I thought I'd never make it up the mountain pass with all the extra weight." "You did well, daughter. We all had extra weight, but now we're in a fine home," Dancing Eyes said encouragingly.

"You know we left food behind. In a few days, I'll return to fetch it."

Songbird fantasized about Twisted Rabbit's ghost. Her friend's spirit would be welcome company, she thought. Her mothers' faces both turned pale, their eyes wide with shock.

"There's too much to do here, daughter," Dancing Eyes said. "The grass seed ripens. We must replace the matting in the pits and grind the last of the locust. Besides, herbs grow here that I can use for your burns. The ones on your feet are healing nicely, but your cheek is turning black. I need to treat it."

Warns of Enemy spoke matter-of-factly, placing her arms around Songbird's shoulders to comfort her. "We planned to leave food in those pits for late fall. So, you don't have to return." The obvious fright in her mothers' faces convinced her to stay.

A few days later, Songbird asked her father where ghosts went. Pocatello was resting from a futile search for deer and seemed glad to talk with her.

"Could we talk about the spirit of Twisted Rabbit, Father? My mothers are terrified of her ghost. She'd never hurt me. It's unfair that I have to stay here."

"Spirits become different personalities," he said, shaking his head. "Even kind people like your friend might seek revenge. It's the nature of spirits."

"It's hard to believe," Songbird said dubiously.

"Me, too," her father said sadly. "I liked the girl. We must stop using her name now."

As usual, her father's rebuke was indirect and kindly. How could she have used the name of a dead friend? she thought.

"I don't know what to think," Pocatello said. "My spirit helper gave me power to call rabbits, but it told me nothing of what happens when we die. You know the story of the Shin-au-av brothers, the sons of the first man? When they decided how they would work for their food and what happens in the after-life?"

"Grandfather told me once, but I don't remember it."

"Long ago," he paused in thought, "the younger Shin-au-av suggested that when people die, they return the next day. The older brother disagreed. He said the dead are no more. The younger brother didn't like that answer. When he discovered his brother's son in the woods, he shot him. The older brother searched a long time to find his dead son. When he returned home, the younger brother smirked, and reminded him of his rule. The older brother realized who had killed the boy. In his anger, he caused the earth to rock."

Pocatello hesitated, then said, "Many people end the story here, suggesting the dead don't return, but my grandfather believed the father of the two brothers allowed the dead to come back as ghosts. He didn't think all ghosts cause trouble, but he feared the dead. Pocatello paused and said, "Those Washo, though, are terrified of them." He shook his head in concern for his wives.

"I'm sorry for their fear," Songbird said earnestly. "But, I feel like you do about the dead."

.   .   .

In the days ahead, the family harvested the valley's grass seed, husked and winnowed it, and began the tedious grinding. Songbird took her turn at the metate, and her mothers let her weave most of the mats.

A visit of Pocatello's distant brother diverted Songbird more than work. The dark, lean man looked like Pocatello except for his limp. Because of the injury, he depended upon trapping small animals and learning their ways. He related that he had never received a vision to give power for calling rabbits so he sought a Rabbit Boss.

He said to Pocatello, "How good to find a Rabbit Boss. I heard about your locust drive. How is your other hunting?"

"It's not been good. I've killed no big game since early winter. How are things to the west?"

"No better. Luck brought me an antelope in one of my traps, but it was small and skinny. We ate it without drying any of the meat," he said haplessly.

"My women have done better than I," Pocatello said. "They've stored roots at our winter camp and harvested the valley's grass. You could join our camp to share our food."

Songbird wondered if the visitor noted the reluctance in her father's tone. The visitor responded with his own invitation.

"Bring a little food to the valley west of the south range, about six days' walk. People avoid it because its springs are bitter, but this year the winter runoff was sweet. The grass feeds many rabbits. A good Rabbit Boss would call enough to feed us through the winter." He paused a moment as he looked at Pocatello respectfully. "You're the best Rabbit Boss I know, and I beg your help."

Songbird grimaced at the prospect of eating stringy rabbit for the winter. They needed the furs for their winter blankets, but even fresh flesh was tough. When dried, the meat chewed like leather.

"It's been a few years since I called the rabbits," Pocatello said modestly. "But we have no choice. Our rabbit nets are in the low country. We need three or four days to get them, and from there I guess six days more to your valley."

"I've invited another band. The leader has a long net, but he lacks rabbit power. I'll invite a fourth band, too."

"I hope they have nets. Do you have one?"

"Our long one of a hundred paces got burned last year, but my wife and daughter are repairing it. They've used most of their own hair to reinforce it because the milkweed fibers are brittle this year."

"That should do. We'll finish up here tomorrow and start for our winter home. We'll meet you in about ten days."

The next morning, Songbird's mothers packed their carrying baskets. When they finished, they swung their heavy burdens to their shoulders. Songbird cried in pain when her tumpline slipped from her forehead to cut across her burnt cheek. She bit her lip to keep from whimpering, but she could not hold back the tears. She said bravely, "I'm all right. The tumpline just surprised me."

"You've a good heart. I know it hurts. I'm sorry my herbs failed. I couldn't find all the plants," Dancing Eyes said.

"Oh," Warns of Enemy blurted, "the tumpline cut into the scab. You're bleeding. It's going to leave a terrible scar."

"We don't know what will happen," Dancing Eyes said calmly with a stern glance at her younger sister. "You're young enough that the skin may grow back. We'll have to wait and see."

Songbird's spirits sank. She knew her face would be disfigured. No one would marry her now. In despair, she didn't care. She only wished the fierce pain would leave.

By late afternoon, the steep path challenged Songbird's endurance, and her tired bones overrode her pain. The downhill trek started well, but the weight on her tumpline yanked this way and that. Her worn sandals hardly protected her feet.

That evening on the valley floor, her mothers settled at its far end to distance themselves from Twisted Rabbit's ghost. They didn't bother with a windbreak, and Songbird knew her mothers would be anxious to leave at first light.

Tired and dejected, her father entered the camp late, after a futile search for deer. The few ducks hanging from the fiber belt that supported his breechcloth would break the diet of rabbit and seed gruel of the past moon, but a worried wrinkle in his normally confident face marred his good looks. The scar that blazed across his chest, the result of a Ute arrow, attested to his bravery and made him more handsome. Such a man surely would find a suitable husband for her, Songbird mused.

A few days later, the weary band entered their winter camp and collapsed. Once recovered, Songbird's father helped the women unwind their net which extended fifty paces and an arm's length in height. The women patched broken places with their hair, but since Dancing Eyes seldom put things off, the net needed little work. They were ready to leave for the bitter springs.

The mountain ranges turned from blue to gray and black by noon. Sparse brush and patches of grass near the scarce water broke the flat desert floor of sand and rock. In places, dried water beds shone white from alkali left by evaporation. Visitors thought the country uninhabitable, but for the Shoshoni it was home. The land regularly provided enough food to anyone satisfied with what the earth offered, but, on rare occasions, chance combined a shortage of deer, antelope, and other game.

Songbird's father knew all the low passes. She saw that a second gathering of bands revived his spirits. They hiked steadily and reached the bitter springs within five days. Everyone there greeted them with a feast. A large fire burned into the night, and people started the moccasin game.

Two teams formed opposing lines. All the men and women took turns hiding a stone in one of two moccasins. Each player's team sang loudly to distract the opposition. Songbird seldom got a second chance to hide her stone, but Dancing Eyes was a master gambler hiding her pebble in a blink while the other hand convinced opponents she'd left it elsewhere. When she lost a turn, she explained her tricks to Songbird.

In the morning, Songbird watched the women inspect their nets to determine the best way to fasten them together. She saw her father join other men to scout the valley. The grass was unusually high, but from its movement, she knew jackrabbit skittered here and there.

When the men returned, Pocatello said to his family, "The rabbits have multiplied, but it's a poor valley. I'll need all the power I have. Every rabbit must come when they hear me."

That afternoon, Songbird watched him bend small saplings to make half a sphere, an arm's length in height. When he placed granite stones in a fire and scooped a hole in the center of the lodge, she knew he was preparing a sweat lodge. He covered it with mats and invited the other men to join him. After they entered, Songbird listened to them sing, and saw her father carry red hot rocks to the hole. He returned for a basket of water, and she heard steam hissing on the rocks. The singers increased the tempo of their song.

That night, Songbird overheard her father tell her mothers he must leave for a distant peak to seek his spirit helper. The next day, when Pocatello returned, he lacked his customary smile. Songbird noticed he looked anxious, and he hesitated when he directed the women to stretch out their nets. She searched his face for a spark of his old confidence but found nothing. Her mothers called her to join them at the valley's far side. The men assumed strategic places along the length of the net. Then they tested their throwing sticks.

Pocatello stood before the nets to call the rabbits in his singsong litany. The notes commanded them to come to the nets. The practice of mesmerizing antelope by song was common, but only a few men knew how to call rabbits. The song carried far up the valley to command the attention of every rabbit. When the women heard the sound, they beat the brush to help the rabbits respond.

Songbird had been in only two other drives, but she realized the women were too far apart as frightened rabbits darted among them. The women flailed their arms and shouted louder. Rabbits scurried downhill mostly, but often one broke between two women followed by others.

By noon, the women slowed their pace while men scurried to club rabbits. They seldom had time for their throwing sticks, so rabbits that jumped the net escaped. Songbird saw two places where frightened rabbits had dislodged props to render the net useless. As the women approached, rabbits turned back. Less experienced with their clubs, many women missed their prey. For every three they killed, one escaped. Songbird knew that they could ill afford the loss.

When the frenzy of the hunt ceased, Songbird joined others to search for dazed and injured rabbits. She clubbed as many as she could carry, and piled them at the family lean-to. Her mothers already had completed a second trip. Songbird calculated the furs could replace their worn winter robes, but the meat wouldn't be enough.

The next day, everyone skinned and dried rabbits. When Songbird returned with wood to smoke the meat, she watched her mothers strip the fur and slice the flesh. They were so engaged they failed to notice her.

"It couldn't be our husband's fault. It had to be that ghost," Warns of Enemy said fearfully.

"You may be right," Dancing Eyes replied. "She seemed so

fond of Songbird, but you never know about ghosts. I bet she's angry at being burned."

"I can't believe she followed us so far. It isn't fair," Warns of Enemy complained.

"Well, she's got her revenge. Maybe she'll leave us alone now."

Warns of Enemy got in a last word. "She's wrecked our husband's reputation as a Rabbit Boss. No one will ever ask his help again."

Songbird stood dejected. She couldn't believe that her beloved friend caused such misfortune. But, if she didn't do it, then her father must have lost his power. She didn't want to think he had failed. She sucked in her breath as she thought of the locust hunt. She had heard people gossip that her father had started the fires too early and caused Twisted Rabbit's death. Now his rabbit drive had failed. The pain in her heart surpassed the pain on her cheek.

CHAPTER TWO

Snow swirled an early winter warning, and ice stopped the trickle of water where Songbird's family camped. She gathered wood for a fire to melt ice, then a second storm covered the basin floor in white. She joined her father to search for tracks, but the land yielded only rabbits and gophers. Even they burrowed farther into the ground to escape the cold.

A warm spell followed the early freeze. Over gruel one night, Pocatello spoke solemnly, "This year is the worst I can remember. Most of my life we've had enough to eat, but it's clear we can't all survive this winter."

"It's that ghost's fault," Warns of Enemy said bitterly.

Pocatello's glare silenced her. "Blame won't solve anything. We've got to act. You need extra food while you're pregnant and afterward to nurse the baby."

He turned to Songbird. "We simply don't have enough, my daughter."

"I'll join Twisted Rabbit, Father. I'll run to the west until I drop and die."

"Don't speak of death. We're not that desperate, but I've failed again. I must take you north to a Kutenai friend who'll find a husband for you. He's a chief who will select a good man and give me venison to bring home. Enough for three of us."

Songbird's heart sank. She faced her worse fear, marriage to a stranger in a distant land. She'd hardly heard of the Kutenai. She'd have to learn their language, and everyone would laugh at her.

In two days, Songbird and her father left. She carried a basketful of locust; her father held his bow and shield. For a moon, they traveled in Shoshoni country and found relatives who welcomed them. They would share a meal, but the year had been cruel throughout the basin, and no more could be offered.

The last Shoshoni band they met had pemmican. The dried meat pounded with berries strengthened them for the climb to the high pass in the mountains that separated Shoshoni from Kutenai. The saddle soared to a height that often caused frostbite, and Songbird counted every breath as they mounted the ridge before heading into a steep, narrow valley.

As they descended, Songbird was reminded of a giant mortar because the sides were so steep and the valley so compressed. At its end, they found the band that her father knew. Their leader had heard they were coming, so a feast awaited the weary travellers.

In a few days of visiting, Songbird rivaled her father's knowledge of Kutenai because he relied on sign language while she spoke, listened closely, and learned to sign. When her father signed to his friend, Chief Kustata, that he sought a husband for Songbird, her heart wrenched.

Pocatello said to her, "He's asked for four days to find a

suitable husband. Actually, it's a matter for his wives and sisters. They'll make the choice, and he'll pretend he did."

On the fifth day, Kustata called them to his lodge. It stretched fifty paces with five cook fires down the length of its center. Songbird felt small and insignificant. Kustata sat before her, surrounded by the women of his family. Several murmured as they stared at her. Others surrounded a fire at the far end where a large pot boiled. The smell of meat and turnips reached Songbird's nose. Although she had eaten her fill the past few days, the aroma made her mouth water.

A young girl passed bowls of the broth, heavy with meat, to Songbird and her father, then to the others. After they ate, Kustata said, "My friend, I have considered the generous offer of your daughter as a wife. She is as welcome as you are." He smiled at Pocatello and said, "She might help you learn our language. I've heard her speak. You rely too much on signs."

Pocatello responded with a joke begun in Kutenai but finished with a flourish of his hands. His gestures brought a burst of laughter from his hosts.

Kustata replied in a serious vein. "You will give your daughter to Eloquent One, a guide chief and good provider. He observes a period of mourning, but his wife has been dead half a year so he'll be ready to marry in six moons."

Songbird understood enough of the speech to suspect her husband to be old. He might have other wives. She also worried that the women who stared at her focused on her scars. She guessed that her looks affected Kustata's decision.

"I have informed Eloquent One, and he has agreed. The two mothers of his dead wife will help your daughter learn to cook and to speak our language. He'll give you all the pemmican you can carry for your trip home."

Songbird missed her father as soon as he left, but Eloquent One's lodge was comfortable. Her future husband seemed kind and helpful. He was stoop-shouldered although his hair had no trace of gray. She guessed he was no more than forty years of age. His two mothers-in-law were aloof, and Songbird suspected they joked about her scars. The new language tripped her tongue, and the sounds twisted in her ears. She struggled to make sense of it, embarrassed by Eloquent One's mothers-in-law who laughed at her pronunciation. Its words were nothing like Shoshoni or Washo.

In a few days, she asked simple questions and understood direct answers. Eloquent One proved to be a sympathetic instructor. By use of signs and patient explanation, he told Songbird how her father came to know the Kutenai.

"He came north to visit our neighbors, the Okanogan, because his grandfather beguiled him with stories of abundant game and fish. He enjoyed the fishing and hunting and mastered signs while he grew soft. The Okanogan, too. They weren't prepared for our raid, and we overpowered them. Your father cried out in Shoshoni. We thought he said, 'I want to see the sun.' When enemies say that, we take them prisoner, and treat them well. It's a practical tactic that encourages surrender. That's how Kustata adopted your father," he said with approval.

He chuckled as he continued, "Your father was amazed at the fish that jumped into our nets, and he thought our caribou practically begged to be killed." After a pause, he said, "He also met the Dhegiha, an unusual people from the east, who claim their home to be the Center of the World. Your father never understood how they could think they were so superior, simply because they traveled the world to trade exotic goods. He did admit the gifts were unlike anything he'd ever seen.

"One man told him that the Dhegiha controlled the journey of the sun from south to north each year, so all people may enjoy summer, when food abounds. The man boasted that their Sun, the Dhegiha chief, performed a ritual to control the journey of the sun. Your father really laughed when he told me that."

.   .   .

A few days later, when the mothers-in-law continued their endless ridicule, Songbird wished her father had never found the Kutenai. She was about to marry a stranger because of his adventure. On second thought, she realized the friendship would save her mothers and a newborn brother or sister.

She set out to please Eloquent One, working as hard as possible to learn Kutenai. She repeated new words to herself and concentrated on everything anyone said.

Songbird's, progress soared at the end of winter when Beloved Enemy, the mother of Eloquent One, returned from visiting other children. When the older woman saw how Songbird worked and studied, she welcomed her as a daughter-in-law. The friendship made the lodge a different world.

However, the mothers-in-law of Eloquent One, Woman Alone and Rattlesnake Eyes, kept treating Songbird with contempt and ridiculing her accent. They claimed the sounds of her name were impossible for Kutenai tongues to speak so they nicknamed her "Burnt Cheek."

Beloved Enemy hesitated to confront the two women, but she called Burnt Cheek to her side one evening to console her.

The two sat alone before a cook fire that warmed the lodge, and, with a kindly gesture, Beloved Enemy offered to tell a story.

The flame deepened Beloved Enemy's wrinkles as she began her tale. "It's a fable about the long ago." Burnt Cheek listened closely but understood nothing. She feared her study had been for naught.

"What language is it, mother-in-law?" Beloved Enemy's kindness made Burnt Cheek want to learn everything about her.

"It's Mandan. They live several moons to the east on the Missouri River. A few venture up here to the river's headwaters to trade with Kutenai. I came here as you did. My brothers gave me to Bull Robe to ally our peoples. So I know how hard it is to be far from home, but Bull Robe's been good to me."

Burnt Cheek couldn't contain her joy at finding such a comrade. "Will you speak more Mandan? What's your childhood name? Did you receive a new name, here, as I have?"

"The Mandan called me Works Alone. Bull Robe's mother was named that, too. He used it to confuse us. That's how he joked. When his mother tired of his antics, she insisted he give me a new name. He thought a long time before naming me Beloved Enemy. It had the right sounds, and it changed my luck. I became pregnant with Eloquent One."

"I like your story, Works Alone. May I use your name just once to test its sound? Mother-in-law seems so stiff."

"Call me grandrelative until you marry my son. Grandparents and grandchildren call each other grandrelative," Beloved Enemy explained. "Would you like to hear a Mandan song? I only remember my childhood songs." She started the lullaby without waiting for an answer.

Burnt Cheek listened in enchantment to the woman's voice. Then a phrase and its melody startled her. It was Washo.

Interrupting, though she knew it rude, Burnt Cheek begged Beloved Enemy to repeat the phrase. On the third time, Burnt Cheek joined in. "You learn quickly," Beloved Enemy beamed.

"It's a song my mothers taught me. Their language is Washo. Will you speak more Mandan?"

Beloved Enemy spoke slowly, pointing at objects as she named them. Wrinkles at her lips deepened and covered other wrinkles as she grinned when Burnt Cheek's face glinted with recognition.

The similarities between Mandan and Washo, though rare, inspired Burnt Cheek to learn more. The study eased the loneliness, and Beloved Enemy's smile lessened Burnt Cheek's pity for her self. Her rapid learning dispelled Beloved Enemy's fears that a fourth language might be too much.

One day when Burnt Cheek asked about Mandan terms for parts of the lodge, Beloved Enemy shrugged and smiled. She explained that a Mandan earth lodge differed from a Kutenai longhouse so much that terms couldn't be translated.

"We'll practice household terms in a few days, grandrelative. Chief Kustata told Eloquent One that he is to inform the camp we move to the fishing station. A Chinook wind visited its warmth on us yesterday to advise us that spring comes."

.   .   .

Soon another Chinook wind brought more unusual warmth. The break in the cold would allow them to relocate near a choice salmon stream.

"Watch Left Hand and Bird Woman closely," Beloved Enemy advised. "Good Woman, too. They're your age. They won't say much because Rattlesnake Eyes will be shouting orders. Respect the nag and her co-wife. After you marry, they should leave our lodge."

Burnt Cheek smiled and said, "I have watched Left Hand at the middle fire. She's a hard worker and always busy."

"She's also kind and generous. Most of all, she's blessed with a special power," Beloved Enemy tilted her head mysteriously. "When we build a new lodge, you'll learn more about the other women here. Now we must stay busy with our own cook fires, but people avoid us mostly because they don't like Rattlesnake Eyes and Woman Alone."

The women of the lodge spent the morning removing mats from its sides. Burnt Cheek quickly learned to untie the knots that held them, despite Rattlesnake Eyes' ridicule about her clumsy fingers. Young men helped to remove the horizontal poles that connected the two tripods at both ends of the lodge.

Eloquent One and Bull Robe accompanied Kustata to the new campsite to locate the lodges that would surround the chief's home. Men and women scooped out an earthen floor a few hands' length in depth to give the floor of the lodge protection from the colder winds. They dug fire pits down the center for each family of the lodge.

At the old lodge, Works Alone, the elderly mother of Bull Robe, headed the lodge. Beloved Enemy cooked at the first fire with her son, Eloquent One. Other descendants of Works Alone cooked at the second and third fires.

The women dismantled their lodge in one day and rebuilt it near the river. In the meantime, the men built fishing platforms to spear the first trout or salmon to swim upstream. Burnt Cheek worked steadily beside Left Hand from the third fire. They had little chance to talk until the third day when they chatted freely.

Left Hand smiled and said, "You learn Kutenai quickly, my

sister-in-law. May I call you sister-in-law? Else I don't know how to address you."

"I like sister-in-law. You made the work easy. I hope you teach me to speak as easily as you showed me how to tie knots."

"You speak better than any stranger I ever met. Foreigners say it's a difficult language so we use signs. A few of the Dhegiha traders work hard to learn Kutenai, but they mangle the sounds. They're a strange lot. All they think about is their trade goods."

"Do you try to learn Dhegiha?"

"No, I've no interest." Left Hand scowled. "But perhaps you can teach me Shoshoni," she said, as her face brightened.

"It's easy." After offering a few simple phrases, Burnt Cheek was chagrined at Left Hand's accent. Soon Burnt Cheek did the learning. Left Hand seemed to enjoy her role as instructor and hesitated to try the strange sounds of Shoshoni.

Instead, she asked about customs. "Do many Shoshoni women seek guardian spirits?"

"No, the vision quest is for men. Do Kutenai women acquire spirit helpers?"

"Oh yes, many do," Left Hand said. "Perhaps not many, but it's common."

"Do any women in our lodge have spirit helpers?"

"At least one does," Left Hand answered. "It's not something we talk about."

"I'll bet it's Beloved Enemy," Burnt Cheek guessed.

Left Hand laughed. "No, Mandan women don't seek visions. Anyway, she was too old when she joined us."

Burnt Cheek worried for a moment about offending Left Hand if she kept guessing, but she couldn't help saying, "Walks from Cave appears wise, but she says so little, I don't know. Works Alone seems special. Is it Works Alone?"

Left Hand hid her grin with her hand, "I guess I can tell a sister-in-law without offending my guardian. I have the power."

Burnt Cheek winced as she recalled that Beloved Enemy had told her that Left Hand was special. Why didn't her mind work faster? she asked herself. She hid her self-reproach by saying, "Can you tell me more about the power, my sister-in-law?"

"An owl visited me. She gave me power to cure wounds, and the women of the Owl Dance Society invited me to join them."

"I haven't heard of the Owl Society. Do you hunt owls?"

Again Left Hand smiled. "No, indeed not. Owl protects us. When you learn more Kutenai, I can explain further about this part of our religion. Now we better join our families. Tomorrow I expect to have salmon. Join us at our fire."

Burnt Cheek's heart beat faster at the invitation. When Left Hand rose and walked away, her gait resembled Twisted Rabbit's walk. Burnt Cheek felt both remorse and warmth. She wondered if she could share with Left Hand the way she had with Twisted Rabbit.

Burnt Cheek greeted Beloved Enemy with a smile and said, "Your niece invited me for salmon. She's as friendly as you said."

Rattlesnake Eyes glared at the news and complained, "You haven't brought enough roots nor wood. We can't let the fire go out just because you met someone. There's no time for gossip."

Woman Alone matched her sister's anger. "You can't visit other fires before you've married our son-in-law. I suppose you don't care what people say? Or you can't understand them," she added sarcastically.

Burnt Cheek blushed in shame and wondered when she

would ever learn, but Beloved Enemy recognized the women's envy and said, "No one's going to talk about my niece and whom she invites to her cook fire. My future daughter-in-law works hard and can visit my niece."

. . .

Burnt Cheek was amazed that salmon could be as red as fresh venison yet taste so differently. Its juicy oil shone between the flakes of flesh, then coated her tongue. She couldn't decide which was best, the distinct sweetness of the oily meat or the smoky residue from the roasting. The richness reminded her of the bear fat the Shoshoni relished.

One morning, Burnt Cheek joined Left Hand to fish. She realized Rattlesnake Eyes and Woman Alone resented the growing friendship, but Beloved Enemy had assured her that any good Kutenai would never think to impose her or his will on another.

"Do the Shoshoni catch many salmon?" Left Hand asked in her quiet way.

"My father showed me how to fish for suckers, but I didn't enjoy it. I just liked being with him, he joked so much."

"Then I have much to teach you," Left Hand said. "Instead of repairing the old traps, I should have built a new one."

"Can't we still do it? I'd like to learn."

"Of course. Your future husband will see you are becoming Kutenai. You have amazed everyone with how well you learn our language. Your accent is almost as good as Beloved Enemy's."

"Is it all right? I don't have to think much about it anymore. Don't you hear an accent?" Burnt Cheek asked fearfully.

"Only if I listen closely. I know how my tongue mangles Shoshoni, so I haven't tried it much. I thought you were going to teach me." Both girls laughed at the accusation.

Left Hand picked up a trap and told Burnt Cheek the words for its parts. The cylinder of willow branches had one end closed. A funnel fitted the other end. Its wide end served as a mouth. The narrow end stopped at the middle of the cylinder.

"I can see how a fish will be trapped. But why do they swim into the funnel? Does someone sing to lure the salmon?"

Left Hand smiled and said, "I don't think fish can hear. Come, I'll show you at the stream. Grab those branches."

The two young women hurried to a tumbling brook. Left Hand carried one large trap under her arm, and two smaller ones in each hand. Burnt Cheek had her arms so full of branches that she failed to see the stream until one foot splashed into it. The cold surprise made her drop the bundle.

Left Hand laughed. "Don't try to spear the salmon. We mean to trap them."

"I thought I'd drop the bundle on them and drown them." Burnt Cheek took pride joking in Kutenai, even if Left Hand only half grinned.

"Do you see the streaks of silver just below the water?"

Flashes gleamed at the stream's surface, elsewhere fins broke through. The water teemed with fish.

"Bring the branches," Left Hand called. "We'll stick them upright across the stream to force the fish to swim to the trap that we place in the middle."

Burnt Cheek mused at the ingenuity of the trap, with its simple but efficient design. Once they completed the fence, only moments passed before a fish swam into the trap. Several others followed before Left Hand emptied it.

"We'll be busy drying fish all summer." Left Hand tossed her head and laughed.

"I don't know," Burnt Cheek said. "How can you stand the cold? My legs are freezing." Burnt Cheek often went barefoot in the snow, but the icy water penetrated like bone needles, causing as much pain as the brushfire. She couldn't believe that Left Hand stood there laughing.

"Did your mothers prepare you to endure the cold at your menstruation?" Left Hand asked in a serious way.

"They taught me to work hard so I'd make a good wife."

"But what about endurance? Or to follow a straight path?"

"No, I don't know anything about that," Burnt Cheek dropped her head.

Left Hand considered the answer while Burnt Cheek emptied the trap. The warmth of her new friendship failed to protect her legs, but mercifully Left Hand announced that they had caught all the fish they could carry. They started home loaded with fish and traps.

"Exactly how did your mothers prepare you?" Left Hand asked. "Perhaps your rites fail to protect you from cold water."

"They isolated me four days in a small hut and instructed me in Shoshoni customs."

"Hmmm. That may be the problem. We require seven days. I assume you ate little? Were your fingers and toes bound?"

Burnt Cheek recalled her hunger, but she hadn't been tied. "I just sat in the hut, except when I ground meal. I worked hard to shape my habits."

"It's worth a try," Left Hand said encouragingly. "At your next period, let's ask my mother to watch over you. My grandma, Works Alone, is wise. She can advise us. She used to foretell the future until she lost her power."

"What happened?"

"You get only so much power. You use it up in helping people. Doesn't that happen with Shoshoni?"

"I don't think so, but I never knew any women with power."

"Well, we Kutenai have medicine people, both men and women. Most of us find a guardian spirit so all of us have some power."

"Does it just come, or do you seek it?"

"After children are seven or eight, they are taught so they can understand. They fast and go into the woods alone. If a guardian spirit fails to visit them, they try again at puberty."

"Is it too late for me." Burnt Cheek wasn't sure she wanted to know. The thought of a guardian frightened her.

"I don't know. You may be too old or maybe the power only visits Kutenai." Back at camp, Left Hand loaded Burnt Cheek with fish. "Here, impress those two hags at your fire and make Beloved Enemy stuff herself. Come over tonight, and we'll ask Works Alone about you seeking a guardian."

When the two consulted Works Alone, she mumbled that her power was expended, but in response to Left Hand's persistence, the woman meditated. She spread cedar bark and herbs on the fire to fill the air with incense, then she sang a melody that mesmerized the three of them. They drifted in and out of the real world.

When the air cleared, Works Alone said, "My guardian smiled at me one more time. She told me the menstrual ritual couldn't hurt our new lodge mate."

A few days later, Burnt Cheek anticipated her period. Left Hand and her sister, Bird Woman, prepared an isolated menstrual hut, with a path of poles from it to a spring so she would never touch the ground during her seclusion. Works Alone then showed Bird Woman how to tie Burnt Cheek's fingers.

Works Alone admonished Burnt Cheek, "Now you will always help your relatives. Your soul will be as straight as your fingers and toes. Follow a straight path. Think about these things," she said, as they left Burnt Cheek alone.

During the seven days of isolation, Burnt Cheek sat on a log platform. When she went for a drink, her feet never touched the ground. She passed the time reflecting on Kutenai customs and practiced Kutenai words.

Not until the sixth day did her stomach beg for food, and her fingers plead for relief. While rubbing her hands against her stomach, she experienced dizziness. In woozy semi-consciousness, she concentrated to stay balanced on the logs. It would be terrible to touch the ground with the end of the ordeal so close, she thought. How terrible to rip the blanket of twisted rabbit skin. What skin? she wondered, and where was Twisted Rabbit? Burnt Cheek felt a presence. Had Left Hand come early? She heard a sound like wings beating on the hut. Burnt Cheek threw off a mat. Huge eyes of two owls peered into her soul. Their wings beat, but they did not fly until they flew directly at her. Their talons closed on her shoulders, but caused no pain. She felt them carry her into the pitch blackness of the night sky with no idea that flying could be so wonderful.

The first streaks of dawn ended the flight. Burnt Cheek worried about landing, but suddenly she was back on the platform, the cramps of her stomach and fingers ended.

"My sister-in-law, here is warm mush. You have done well. Eat slowly." Left Hand scooped the well-cooked roots into Burnt Cheek's mouth as Bird Woman slit the bonds. Burnt Cheek seized the wooden bowl of mashed roots and finished them quickly. "It's the best food I've ever tasted. Is there more?"

The tall, slim Bird Woman smiled. "You must eat slowly after fasting. Works Alone is making fish soup for you. Even Rattlesnake Eyes has prepared a treat. Come."

By evening, Burnt Cheek felt the effects of the fast's end. Her stomach swelled, though she slowly sipped Beloved Enemy's soup. She ate a little of Rattlesnake Eye's stew until her stomach rebelled. Burnt Cheek praised the stew before joining Left Hand's fire where the two found privacy.

"How was it, sister? Did your fingers ache? That was the worst for me. I forget the hunger but never my fingers."

"My hands only hurt the last day. The hunger bothered me most. But now I'm sure I'll stay warm." Burnt Cheek's confidence lasted only a moment before she added worriedly, "Won't I?"

Left Hand took her hand to comfort her. "You have more endurance, I'm sure."

Burnt Cheek hesitated but finally asked her friend, "Did any spirit helper come to you at menstruation?"

"No, I did not seek one."

"Do visions ever come when a person is not seeking them?"

"I don't know. Perhaps." Left Hand hesitated at first, then as if she realized Burnt Cheek was perplexed, she said, "What happened in the hut?"

"Just before you came, while it was night, wings beat against the roof. I should have been afraid, but I wasn't. When I threw back a mat, two owls stared at me." Burnt Cheek saw the owls clearly in her mind, and they still perched in front of her. "They flew onto my shoulders. I felt their claws, but they didn't hurt. When they flew, I flew with them. The sensation thrilled me. I soared wherever I wanted to go until they returned me to the hut. I'm sure it wasn't a dream. What does it mean?"

"You did fly," Left Hand said firmly. "Owl gave you power. I have flown, too. Quite a few Kutenai women do. I never told you much about the Owl Dance Society because it is secret."

"You, too, have flown? How wonderful!" Burnt Cheek was overjoyed.

Left Hand smiled and said, "Now I can tell you about the Owl Dance Society. Works Alone is our chief. That strip of otter fur tied in her hair is the chiefly symbol. Owl protects all the women in her lodge."

"Is your mother in the society?"

"No. Owl never visited her. But Good Woman and her mother belong. Have you noticed that no one in our lodge is ever ill? Owl's power gives good health."

"Did you become a member after you dreamed of owl?"

"No, the members decide. But Works Alone invited me shortly after I told her of my experience."

"Can a foreigner be admitted?" The hope in Burnt Cheek's voice was clear.

"I believe they'll invite you." Left Hand took Burnt Cheek's hands. "Owl's choice is obvious."

.   .   .

When Left Hand told Works Alone about Burnt Cheek's dream, the old woman agreed she had been shown special favor. She asked Left Hand to get Gifted Tongue, and the three women went to Fish Weir Woman's lodge where her helper sat, repairing salmon traps. The three joined in the task, and the eight hands nimbly wove new willow branches.

After Works Alone explained her visit, Fish Weir Woman gave careful thought to her answer. "I don't remember a foreigner ever dancing with us. The Shoshoni girl might have heard of our society from Left Hand. I doubt owl would visit anyone except Kutenai."

Works Alone said how much she valued Fish Weir Woman's opinion and praised her for never flinching from her duty to whip members into formation during the dance. She commiserated with the difficulty of whipping sisters, even in ritual.

While Works Alone and Fish Weir Woman spoke quietly to each other, Left Hand drew Burnt Cheek aside. She told her that Works Alone could count on her helper's loyalty. Burnt Cheek was delighted but frightened. She knew she must perform without flaw.

Burnt Cheek thought of nothing else until owl inspired Works Alone to announce a meeting. Left Hand came to fetch Burnt Cheek. "Tonight the Owl Dance starts. Wear the white dress, the deerskin that we bleached, and that you fringed so well."

"It hasn't any designs. Shouldn't we paint it?"

"We don't need to. The whiteness and the fringe are more important than designs."

Burnt Cheek scrubbed her moccasins to whiten them. She wanted to wear her dress leggings because of their fringe, but it was too warm. She combed her long, black hair, surprised at the tangles that snagged her bone tooth comb. The two braids she wove must be even to look Kutenai.

She had barely finished when Left Hand led her from the lodge. "Fish Weir Woman calls. It's a night to celebrate. Works Alone left already in her otter skin. I like your hair," Left Hand said breathlessly.

Gifted Tongue saw that the women assembled before the lodge of Kustata. A chorus formed around two drummers, and the rhythm found the women's feet. White dresses flowed into a swaying stream, its waves lapping to the timing of the drum. The beat and song assumed a life of their own. The lodges vibrated with the pulse of owl. The dance and music seized Burnt Cheek with the force of an unknown power.

Works Alone's high-pitched keening startled Burnt Cheek. She started the dance. The gray-haired woman twirled so gracefully that she made Burnt Cheek wonder if she floated. The other women formed a line with Fish Weir Woman at the rear. She carried a bundle of willow branches in her left hand while her right hand whipped the air with one. When Burnt Cheek merged into the line, she felt a lash on her bare legs that stung like a bee.

Works Alone circled the chief's lodge, and all the women followed. They went around another lodge and another. As the dancers circled more lodges and passed through others, Burnt Cheek melted into the line. She heard nothing except the music and felt nothing except the rhythm.

The hypnotic rhythm flowed through them as the women entered all the lodges again and again. Burnt Cheek left the ordinary world as Works Alone headed for a pine grove and owl's domain. Fish Weir Women lashed the women to meld them into a line so powerful it went through the first tree just as it went through a lodge. Burnt Cheek never hesitated before a tree but glided through it following the woman before her. Works Alone pulled the line westward while Fish Weir Woman pushed from behind to enter an extraordinary world.

Burnt Cheek sensed that they had entered owl's realm. The line of women rose into the air, pulled to the west by Works Alone and whipped forward by Fish Weir Woman. Burnt Cheek felt owl everywhere, with a power that lifted the line upward. How beautiful to look down on the earth, she thought. She needed no wings, her will floated her, going ever higher. She merged with the will of the line to feel part of a whole but also to be the whole. Nothing in her life ever felt so good.

Suddenly Burnt Cheek felt another power. East called stronger than west. She could no longer follow the other women. She turned and soared above the line executing a slow curve, back to their origin. But not her origin. The unexpected pull toward the east overwhelmed her, tugging her toward sun's domain not owl's. She must journey to the sun.

Suddenly the drums stopped, and everyone was back on earth.

It was over. Could it ever be over? she thought. She could never forget the experience. The feeling of wholeness in the Owl Dance Society astounded her as much as flying. Yet, something had called her away from the group. What interfered? she wondered anxiously. Maybe no one noticed she had broken rank.

.   .   .

"Why did you do that, cousin?" Distress rang in Left Hand's tone, and the use of cousin instead of sister stung Burnt Cheek. "Fish Weir Women said you fled to the Shoshoni. Didn't you feel her whip? She did all she could to keep you in line."

"Oh, cousin, does everyone know? Was it so obvious? What have I done?" Burnt Cheek started to cry. "I didn't try to go home. Shoshoni country is south. I was pulled east. I don't know why. I want more than anything to be a member of the Owl Dance Society. But I couldn't resist the pull. What do I do?"

CHAPTER THREE

Left Hand came to Burnt Cheek's lodge to tell her about the aftermath of the Owl Dance meeting. "Fish Weir Woman was adamant. She said you could never be a member if you won't follow our ways."

"But I will. If I have a second chance, I will."

"Let me finish. I explained you had lived with us less than a year, and that you have trouble with our language. Fish Weir Woman insisted that owl has always instructed us to fly west. We can't be united if we fly in all directions."

"I'll fly west next time, I will."

"We'll have to wait. When owl grants flight to a woman, we have never turned her away. But, Fish Weir Woman says that owl flies in the night with the setting sun. Still, she said you might be able to join later."

"I do wish I could begin again, but I know I'll have to wait." Burnt Cheek choked back a sob.

Left Hand took Burnt Cheek's hands in hers and told her everything would work out. She lifted one of her hands to stroke Burnt Cheek's face, then left her alone.

Before Burnt Cheek could feel too sorry for herself, a young man's shout interrupted. He ran into camp. Sweat bathed his lean body. He gasped for breath as he called out, "The Dhegiha come. One of their scouts reached my outpost. He promised we will be weighed down with gifts."

Kustata loomed at the door of his lodge. The youth fell silent as if he suddenly remembered he should have reported to the chief before broadcasting news to the camp, but Kustata did not rebuke him publicly.

Instead, he said for everyone to hear, "Go find the guide chiefs. Tell them to meet me in my lodge."

Shortly, many women gathered outside Burnt Cheek's lodge. Even Rattlesnake Eyes grinned in anticipation, although she had frowned at Burnt Cheek when she saw her talking with Left Hand. Now, the clamor from the expectant women who joked and teased enlivened Rattlesnake Eyes and made Burnt Cheek forget the Owl Dance. She got caught up in the speculations about the number of Dhegiha canoes and which of their chiefs led the traders.

Good Woman said, "Crazy Bull gives the best speeches, but he seldom gives the best gifts. He lacks favor with the Sun."

Burnt Cheek listened to Left Hand whisper that the traders talked about their religion and boasted of their wealth but rarely talked of anything else. It made her suspicious of them.

Aloud, Left Hand joined the banter, "I hope it's Tied to Sun. He speaks well, and he gives the best gifts."

Good Woman retorted in jest, "You want it to be Tied by Sun because he's so good-looking. I saw the way you looked at him the last time."

Burnt Cheek thought Left Hand blushed as she said, "I didn't look any more than other women." Burnt Cheek guessed her friend maneuvered to change the subject by asking, "Why do you think it's 'Tied by Sun'? I interpreted the signs as 'Tied to Sun.'"

"We may never figure out the meanings of all their signs," Good Woman said. "Anyway, you're just trying to change the subject. Admit it, you'd like to see such a good-looking man again."

"Wouldn't we all?" Left Hand said with a laugh. "He is handsome, but I hope he doesn't wear those Long Nosed God earplugs. What did he call that god? I didn't mind the nose, but if anyone stared at his ears, he'd get a sermon."

"You're right," Good Woman said with a grimace. "Anyway, what's important is what they bring. Do you think our husbands will get any copper ornaments? I can't keep my eyes off Eloquent One's necklace with its incised circle and cross." She looked at Burnt Cheek and said, "What do you think of it?"

"It is interesting." Burnt Cheek sucked at her lip. Before she had to say more, Left Hand nodded that they enter their lodge. Burnt Cheek took a deep breath and wondered if she would ever fit in. She had thought copper was a kind of shell, but apparently it was a special material. Worse, she had no idea what necklace of her future husband Good Woman was talking about.

She breathed with relief when Left Hand stayed beside her at the fire to tend a boiling pot. She watched the other women putter at their fires, while they waited for the guide chiefs to announce news of preparations for the Dhegiha.

Left Hand explained what to expect. "We have plenty of roots and dried fish. The men will kill caribou, or maybe an elk, and spear fresh salmon. The Dhegiha will flaunt their wealth after we feast them and give copper or jewelry of carved mica. They also sculpt stone beautifully. I like the graceful animals they carve into pipe bowls."

"Why do they come so far to give gifts?" Burnt Cheek said with a puzzled look.

"We give them all they can eat and enough for their return trip. They really come for grizzly bear teeth and claws. Our hunters haven't been as lucky as usual this year so some men traveled to the place of hot waters where they find yellow stones and mine obsidian. The Dhegiha love that shiny, black stone."

Burnt Cheek had experienced giveaways of food and rabbit skins among the Shoshoni, while among the Kutenai she had seen visitors bring their best weaving or grizzly teeth. They would exchange them for weaving and more grizzly teeth amidst constant feasting. The celebration brought everyone closer together. Left Hand's description of Dhegiha gifts suggested a different kind of exchange. The strangers brought goods the Kutenai never had while they sought goods they lacked. Burnt Cheek was hard-pressed to understand such an odd custom.

The next day, Burnt Cheek and Left Hand joined everyone else to await the Dhegiha. Rumors flew, and people joked in anticipation. A shout went up when the first Dhegiha appeared. Burnt Cheek was surprised to see that they dressed only in loincloths like those of the Kutenai. Only their stone earplugs and necklaces of exotic materials identified them as Dhegiha.

A slim young man with several necklaces raised an arm. The crowd grew silent, and Left Hand whispered that he aspired to be an orator. He spoke in Dhegiha and used signs while another Dhegiha translated. Burnt Cheek could not understand the heavily accented Kutenai, and Left Hand also seemed to rely on the signs.

"As you know," the speaker signed, "the Dhegiha travel from the mouth of the Missouri River all over the world, from the mountains in the east to your western mountains. From the four corners of the world, we gather precious material for the Center of the World where artisans create the finest art ever seen."

Burnt Cheek wondered how the orator could make such a claim when the Dhegiha had never visited the Shoshoni, but she forgot her doubts when he introduced the Dhegiha leader. "Today, the great Tied to Sun demonstrates the great skills of the Dhegiha in traveling the great rivers to bring the greatest of gifts."

Burnt Cheek wondered if the orator meant to be so redundant in his speech, or if the limited expression of signs led to his many uses of great. She concentrated on the sounds and heard a few familiar ones. The speaker's signs failed to coincide with his spoken words so she couldn't be sure of meanings. She did know that the words were not Shoshoni, Washo, or Kutenai. She probed her mind as she tried to follow the Dhegiha oration. When the speaker slowed for emphasis, he put sign and speech together. The words resembled Mandan.

The climax of the speech announced Tied to Sun's arrival. From the direction of the river came drumbeats and a low-pitched song that relied more on percussion than melody. It peaked when Tied to Sun appeared.

Eight men carried a man sitting atop a litter. A canopy shaded him. Burnt Cheek guessed it had to be made of doeskin because of the way it fluttered in the slightest breeze. The same material covered the man's chest in poncho fashion. Its red and blue designs zigzagged in unusual shapes over a white background.

"What kind of skin is he wearing?" Burnt Cheek asked Left Hand in guarded tones.

"It isn't skin. They call it cloth. It's woven, the way we make baskets, but with skinny fibers they call cotton. It's as fine as milkweed. They don't weave it with their fingers as we do our nets. They squeeze it together on what they call a loom. They include cloth among their gifts, but it isn't practical for us. Kustata wears his mantle only to greet the Dhegiha."

"What do the designs mean on the cloth? I've never seen such symbols," Burnt Cheek said.

"I don't know because I don't understand their language. Since no women come with them, it's hard to talk to them. A few men will sleep with our women, but the ones they call nobles, like Tied to Sun, say that their religion forbids such hospitality." Left Hand's raised brow questioned Dhegiha customs.

"What is that thing he's carried on? Can't he walk?" Burnt Cheek guessed Left Hand's smile meant her question was naive.

"It's called a litter. They claim he has so much power it may rub off and contaminate us until we get used to it." Burnt Cheek joined Left Hand in hiding a grin.

Left Hand said, "I don't mean to ridicule their beliefs, but they think they are so superior. I see no reason to believe it, except their art is extraordinary."

"Have any Kutenai ever visited their homeland?"

"I don't know anyone who has. Why should we go, when they come here?"

Both women were distracted for the moment by a procession of Dhegiha weighted with parfleche bags. Designs similar to those of Tied to Sun's mantle covered the leather wraps.

"What's in the bags?" Burnt Cheek asked. "Surely, they knew we would feed them."

Again Left Hand smiled. "They hold the Dhegiha gifts. Tied

to Sun will give more than usual. Do you think that Good Woman is right, that he's attractive?"

It was Burnt Cheek's turn to smile. "Good Woman thought you found him attractive, sister. Is he?"

"Oh, she just teased," Left Hand said with a blush. "I'm an old, married woman."

"How many winters have you experienced?" Burnt Cheek asked.

"About twenty, I guess. And you?"

"About fifteen. Do you think I'll be a good wife to Eloquent One?"

"I'm sure, and he'll be a good husband. He respected his first wife, and they seldom quarreled. Do your work and respect him. Besides, you both like languages. You'll have a good marriage." As Left Hand left for her fire, Burnt Cheek fantasized a return to Shoshoni country to find a husband. Then she focused on reality.

.   .   .

"Come out, you Kutenai," the Dhegiha orator shouted. "See what gifts the Center of the World brings. Let the magnificence of the Sun dazzle you. The Sun's envoy will bestow wealth from the whole world. You feasted us. Now you'll find what eminent guests you entertain. It's a day never to forget."

"Their orator outdoes himself," Left Hand said appreciatively. "He signs well."

"He no longer calls everything great," Burnt Cheek said with a grin. "For such a thin man, he has a mighty voice." Then she concentrated, comparing Dhegiha with Mandan. She heard eight or ten familiar words.

"Do you think the translator's handsome?" Left Hand asked.

"I thought all your interest was in Tied to Sun," Burnt Cheek said to show she could joke in Kutenai. Left Hand smiled and pretended not to hear her. She glanced at the children who ran around as they became bored with the speech.

Left Hand resumed her joking. "Of course, my interest is in Tied to Sun, but I'm thinking of you. The translator dresses like our men. He is what the Dhegiha call a commoner. In their thinking he would be our equal. I could ask Eloquent One to invite the translator to our lodge for the night. You could keep him warm while you learned Dhegiha."

Burnt Cheek answered back, "Perhaps he can persuade Tied to Sun to come, too, and you could keep him warm."

The appearance of Tied to Sun ended the teasing, and the children stopped their play. Dhegiha drums sounded the approach of Kustata and his guest as they left the center lodge. Kustata wore a necklace that Tied to Sun apparently had given him the night before. Copper plates among brilliant white shell beads reflected the morning sun. Although it was a striking piece, Tied to Sun's own necklace outshone it. Large, thick white shell beads separated bear claws, and a copper eagle hung at the bottom. As Tied to Sun walked, the eagle swayed in flight, soaring in its own sky over Tied to Sun's blue mantle.

Burnt Cheek had never seen such splendor. As she stared at the flying eagle, Left Hand said, "Don't overlook the earplugs because of the necklace. They are his Long Nosed Gods."

The earplugs danced in the sunlight. From a distance, Burnt Cheek could not detect what material artisans had used to fashion them. Since she had never seen mica, she didn't recognize its gleam. Bits of it were worked into copper to give the earplugs a glimmering effect. Despite the freakish looks of the long, conical noses, the heads beamed with an awesome essence.

Two Dhegiha commoners spread pieces of cloth before Kustata's lodge. Eloquent One and other guide chiefs sat at Kustata's side in anticipation. Their younger brothers lined up behind them. Drums throbbed to a crescendo to herald the presentation, and Dhegiha singers exalted Tied to Sun's generosity. Burnt Cheek watched him display finely chipped projectile points of all sizes.

The Kutenai chiefs fingered the points, seeming to revere the exquisite flaking. Burnt Cheek watched Tied to Sun study his hosts as if to judge each one's importance and their interest in his goods. She could see why Left Hand found him attractive. His long black braids fell over a broad, bronzed chest. His rugged face spoke of determination. The only defect seemed to be in his eyes, which on occasion flashed with disdain.

When he spoke, his tone matched his eyes. "These points required many days' work by our finest artisans. Here are points of Gifted Hand and his ward mates, Kansa People. The Kansa have chipped flint from time's beginning. They make the best points the world has ever seen. They fashion arrow shafts from the straightest reeds in the Mississippi Valley."

Next, he opened finely woven baskets and the painted parfleche bags. Burnt Cheek observed how his eyes shone with delight as he contemplated how the Kutenai would be obliged to provide him with raw materials. He drew out a prized possession that puzzled Burnt Cheek. She wondered why anyone would sculpt a life-sized hand. Still, the delicate piece of twinkling, translucent mica fascinated her.

"Worthy friends, I enjoy bestowing this wealth. Just as I gave you our best projectile points, I give you this jewel. No other mica compares to it. Have you ever seen such translucence? Its color matches my flesh. Omaha artisans breathed life into it. Can you not see a pulse beat?"

As Tied to Sun turned the hand, it seemed to take on life. The hand throbbed in different angles of light. Burnt Cheek saw the delicate, thin fingers and thumb beat as if with a pulse. When Tied to Sun returned the hand to the parfleche bag, he brought out a thin, shimmering fish the size of his hand.

"Consider this mica fish. It swims in our lakes and canals. You can see it eating. The artist made it dance for joy."

Burnt Cheek wondered if it was artistic skill or Tied to Sun's oratory that held the Kutenai spellbound. None of them stirred. An awed silence continued until Tied to Sun concluded the presentation with a sheet of copper transformed into an eagle. The metal gleamed in the sun while the bird flew above Tied to Sun's hand. The wings beat against the wind.

"Beloved allies, this eagle visited its maker in his dreams. Its copper came from the Great Northern Sea, the sea superior to all others." Tied to Sun paused for dramatic effect and to take a deep breath. "See how it bathes in the sun's essence. Can you deny it lives? An expert of the Ponca Ward fashioned it. He's the greatest copper artist in the world."

Tied to Sun called out the guide chiefs for gifts. He began with the youngest ones. While he lauded his gifts, he emphasized his ties to each recipient, recalling how his fathers had traded with their fathers. When he had bestowed most of his gifts, Left Hand whispered with a worried look, "He has bypassed Eloquent One. I can't imagine why he would ignore him."

"What could my future husband have done to offend him?" Burnt Cheek asked.

The two women soon had an answer. As the recipients narrowed down to the oldest chiefs, Tied to Sun singled out Eloquent One for special attention. He used all his oratorical skills, head nods and hand gestures combined with a bellow. "My brother-in-law, my old acquaintance," he roared at Eloquent One, "How long we have known each other. I present you with this living hand. I hope you treasure it, as I treasure you like a loyal relative."

"What's going on?" Burnt Cheek said to Left Hand.

Left Hand's brow wrinkled in puzzlement. "I don't know. They seldom address us as kin. Oh, they call us brothers and sisters like everyone does. But I don't remember a Dhegiha ever calling an individual a brother-in-law as he did Eloquent One."

"What sisters does Eloquent One have to give Tied to Sun?" Burnt Cheek asked, surprised and hurt that no one had told her of his unmarried sisters.

"The ones I know are all married," Left Hand said. "Maybe Tied to Sun intends to give his sister to Eloquent One. I don't remember any Dhegiha leader ever taking a wife from us. But why would he give a wife to Eloquent One? Maybe you are about to have a co-wife once Eloquent One ends his mourning."

Burnt Cheek thought Left Hand only half-teased, "Are you serious? My co-wife would be Dhegiha? How could we talk to each other? We'd be complete strangers."

"I'm sorry. It would be hard to share a husband with a wife from a different tribe. Let's wait and see. The Dhegiha have never yet given us a wife. Maybe we misread the signs. That's it," she said warmly. "He didn't mean brother-in-law."

Burnt Cheek wished she shared Left Hand's confidence about mistaking the signs. She kept thinking of her assurance that the Dhegiha had never given brides, but Tied to Sun had bestowed a prized gift on Eloquent One. He must expect a special favor.

.   .   .

Eloquent One turned the mica hand in the light of the lodge fire that evening. He tried many angles that reflected light to catch his eye. Eventually, he laid it on a flat stone palette to protect its delicacy. Without oratory, Burnt Cheek was less awed. Still, it glimmered like no other art she ever saw. What vision directed such delicate work? she wondered.

"I have good tidings, lodge mates," Eloquent One began. "Last night in council, the Dhegiha visitors told us that they met a Shoshoni downstream who had visited Pocatello's camp. He told them that her father returned home safely, with only a touch of frostbite." Almost as an afterthought, he said to Burnt Cheek, "He also reported that one of your mothers gave birth."

"How wonderful," Burnt Cheek exclaimed. "Do I have a sister or a brother?"

"The Dhegiha signed your mother gave birth. I know no more about it."

How like men, Burnt Cheek sighed to herself. They don't care if the baby was a girl or boy. But how callous of me, she thought. My father's alive and well. That's what matters.

When she looked at Eloquent One, she saw he was troubled. She wanted to comfort him but didn't know how. Before she could say anything, he said to her with a catch in his voice, "You'll come with me to Kustata's lodge tonight."

Burnt Cheek saw Woman Alone and Rattlesnake Eyes glower at her. She guessed that the thought of the chief welcoming her to his lodge angered them. Burnt Cheek welcomed Beloved

Enemy's smile that countered the frowns. Obviously, the old woman was happy for her future daughter-in-law.

When Burnt Cheek went with Eloquent One to Kustata's lodge, she was surprised to see so many people packed into it. Only one fire burned, the other pits had been covered to accommodate all the people. She appreciated that the lower mats on the lodge were removed to encourage the mild evening breeze.

Burnt Cheek flushed as Eloquent One seated her close to Kustata and Tied to Sun. Kustata's wives hastened to bring them food. Large chunks of meat swam among a blend of wild onions, turnips, and herbs, to tease Burnt Cheek's tongue.

She watched Kustata sign to Tied to Sun while they waited patiently for her and Eloquent One to finish eating. He praised Tied to Sun's gifts and his oratory. Tied to Sun flourished his signs, much the way he spoke. It made his meanings difficult to follow. Burnt Cheek believed he reviewed the long-standing ties between people at the Center of the World and the Kutenai.

Tied to Sun rose. His broad smile and flashing eyes made him even more handsome, Burnt Cheek thought. He waited until he had all eyes on him, then spoke. Clearly, he had rehearsed, and Burnt Cheek wondered why no one had helped him with his accent.

"The Sun wants all peoples of the world to share his knowledge of the sun's power. He knows all peoples benefit when they exchange gifts, when they offer their best and the Sun sends them his best. It is essential that we Dhegiha communicate with all peoples. Signs are good enough for gift giving, but they do not suffice to tell about the power of the Sun. We require interpreters for the Sun's message."

With a condescending nod to his Dhegiha interpreter, he continued. "Weasel, here, learned Mandan, so he serves us on our upriver journey. He learned a little Kutenai from a Mandan, but I know how incompetent he is."

Tied to Sun drew a deep breath and said forcefully. "It will please us to have a Kutenai join us and learn Dhegiha at the Center of the World. She will be even more valuable if she speaks other languages."

For the first time, Tied to Sun looked at Burnt Cheek. She studied the handsome features of the stranger for a moment before lowering her eyes. She wondered if he had caught her staring. His look flustered her, then her heart fluttered as she realized he spoke of her. Fear gnawed at her stomach. This stranger meant to take her from her new friends and relatives to be a wife in a land no one knew.

She realized her worst fear when he said, "The Shoshoni warrior we met told us not only of this woman's father but also taught me much about the Shoshoni people. I had thought them to be a break-away band of Kutenai, but now I know they are a different people who live over a vast territory. The Dhegiha can leave no land unexplored. I will be the first to explore it and claim it for the Sun."

His boastful tone moderated in an after thought. "Your chief has recognized the importance of an interpreter for this mission, and his guide chief has been generous to arrange it for me."

Burnt Cheek had all she could do to hold back the tears. She hardly felt Eloquent One take her arm to lead her to Tied to Sun. The three retreated to a corner of the lodge where they could talk above the murmuring of the Kutenai who speculated on what Tied to Sun meant by showing his gratitude to Kustata.

Eloquent One confirmed Burnt Cheek's dread when he led her to Tied to Sun. "Here is your future wife, great Dhegiha chief. She is a hard worker with a talent for languages. She signs well and is nearly fluent in Kutenai."

"Well, woman," Tied to Sun said, "How would you like to learn Dhegiha and travel to the Center of the World?"

"Could I not serve you here, great chief? It's here I can use Kutenai and Shoshoni. I also speak Washo, the language of my mothers. They grew up far to the west."

"Did you ever visit your mothers' people?" Tied to Sun asked, his face radiating curiosity.

"No, they lived several moon's walk away on a lake they called Tahoe."

"Does their country have the black, shiny rock we call obsidian or the mica I showed? Have you seen copper before?" Tied to Sun couldn't restrain his interest.

"The only tools I've seen were of wood or flint." Burnt Cheek thought how to denigrate the value of the languages she knew. "I doubt that the Shoshoni or Washo have anything you want. They are very poor people who get by on roots and insects. Last year my father killed only a bear. You have no reason to visit them, I assure you."

"That is for me to decide, woman." Tied to Sun nearly shouted his arrogance. The outburst shocked Burnt Cheek, but he seemed to compose himself to resume speaking as an equal. Burnt Cheek could never guess how he postured for people he regarded as savages.

"I need your help, my future wife. You strike me as very intelligent, and I want to make a place for you in my lodge."

Kustata confirmed the upcoming marriage. "You are like a daughter to me since your father is so much like my brother. I know you will be a good wife for our ally. Eloquent One and I have talked. He approves your marriage. He is indebted to

Tied to Sun for his gifts. Think about it tonight. You must decide."

Burnt Cheek was too stunned to reply, as Eloquent One ushered her to the door. She wished for her mothers' advice. Left Hand would help but could never contradict a decision of Kustata. She returned to her lodge in a daze. For once, Rattlesnake Eyes and Woman Alone ignored her, unable to comprehend her marriage to a Dhegiha chief.

Burnt Cheek dozed in tormented sleep until owl called her. Startled and scared, she felt talons grip her shoulders at the same moment that she felt wings beating the air. The piercing eyes of her guardians blazed as she soared into the air with them. They bore her toward the sun.

CHAPTER FOUR

For once, Burnt Cheek was grateful to Rattlesnake Eyes. The bossy woman had organized a berry-picking expedition that gave Burnt Cheek an opportunity to speak with Left Hand in private. Few fall berries remained except in protected valley floors where aspen held golden leaves that stood out against lustrous green pines. The contrast drew her and Left Hand into the current of colors while they sat near a berry patch.

"At last we can talk," Burnt Cheek said. "It's been eight days. Woman Alone keeps me busy since my marriage to Tied to Sun to prove I'm a good wife. She acts like a mother-in-law, but now she'll never be my mother-in-law. At least I haven't time to feel sorry for myself."

Burnt Cheek's anguish alarmed Left Hand. She asked sympathetically, "What's happened? Does your husband beat you? I knew it a mistake to marry a Dhegiha stranger."

"Oh no, it's nothing like that. I shouldn't complain, really." Burnt Cheek shook her head sadly.

"You wouldn't complain without reason," Left Hand said. "Go ahead, tell me."

Burnt Cheek shed a tear, then almost babbled in confusion. "I don't know if I'm married or not. I thought we were married the night Kustata feasted us. Everyone acted as if we married."

"Of course you are," Left Hand said. "Tied to Sun came to our lodge to sleep with you. I saw him there after you two married. Why don't you think you're married?" Left Hand's puzzled brow shot up.

"Because all he did was sleep with me. He's done nothing to make me pregnant. My face disgusts him. I'm too ugly to bear his children."

"Did he tell you that?"

"No, not exactly. He said we needed a Dhegiha ceremony to be truly married. His clan mates must witness it. I have no idea what he means by clan. We communicate mostly by signs. It's so confusing at night. When he tries to teach me Dhegiha, we speak Kutenai and you know how little he speaks."

"It's difficult. I've never heard of marriage without sex. But everyone assumes you're married, I'm sure."

"What happens if we don't consummate our marriage? What if there's no chance of children?" Burnt Cheek said desperately in hushed tones.

"I guess you wait until you reach the Dhegiha camp. It'll be hard to just sleep with him. He is handsome. Have you coaxed him to do more than sleep?" Left Hand giggled. Burnt Cheek knew Left Hand didn't intend to joke about such a serious matter, but realized that her friend must find humor in the Dhegiha's bizarre behavior.

"I've tried combing my hair over my scars. In the dark I

don't think he sees the burn. When I've rubbed against him, he turns away. I'm just too disfigured." Burnt Cheek fought to hold back tears.

"You must be mistaken, sister. After all, he asked to marry you. No one thought to give you away. Give him a chance. Kutenai men don't always come to live with their wives. Some wives go to their husband's parents' lodge. Rattlesnake Eyes' sister married into a different camp—if she had not, you would have had another shrew at your fire."

Burnt Cheek smiled at her friend's attempt to comfort her, but her voice shook when she spoke. "I'm about to go off to who knows where, when I thought I had a home here. I'm to leave with a stranger who may or may not be my husband, and whom I can't talk to except with signs. I've asked if I have co-wives, and didn't understand his answer. I believe he said he's married, but he denied I'm a co-wife. Maybe he believes we aren't married yet because we're not sleeping together. Well, of course we sleep together, but not really. Now he's left for a moon to visit other camps. I think he married me, if I am married, only to have an interpreter."

Left Hand held the bride's hand, and said unconvincingly, "I don't believe he's using you except to ally the Dhegiha with us. Many marriages are that way. Your marriage to Eloquent One would have been like that."

"But that's different," Burnt Cheek replied. "It's friends becoming more friendly. Tied to Sun only seeks to take advantage. Do you think he'll go to the Shoshoni out of friendship? That's the only good thing about my marriage. I may have a chance to go home."

"He's certain to take you to Shoshoni country," Left Hand encouraged. "Maybe it's my imagination that he thinks he's so high and mighty. He's acted like one of us since he's been here, or at least like Chief Kustata."

"But why did he arrive on a litter and wear such fancy clothes and jewels if he didn't feel above us? It had to be more than male vanity."

"I don't know what to tell you," Left Hand said. "I don't see how anyone could believe they are superior to us, but I think they do." After a moment of thought, Left Hand smiled and said, "They are friendly. Go with him. If it doesn't work out, you can return next spring. You'll always have a home here."

"I feel better, knowing you want me. The prospect of a year among strangers isn't reassuring, but you're right. I can leave him if it doesn't work."

Burnt Cheek found a smile and continued, "Maybe the Center of the World will be as delightful as it is here. Tied to Sun tells me it is in a large river bottom, where they cultivate plants, whatever cultivate means. They seem to put seeds in the ground and then dig out other plants. I think that's what cultivate means. I don't know why they don't gather their food the way everyone else does." Doubt struck again, and she was crestfallen, "Oh, sister, it's going to be so different: the foods, houses, customs. And their gods. I understand so little about them. I can't go."

"I'll talk to Eloquent One," Left Hand said. "He'll go with us to Kustata. We can end the marriage. Kutenai won't force anyone to do what they don't want."

Rattlesnake Eyes interrupted the two women with a shout. "You've fallen too far behind. We've got all the berries we can use. It's time to go."

After they reached their lodge, Burnt Cheek no longer felt like discussing her plight, and Left Hand had no further advice.

Burnt Cheek stored half the berries for fall treats. She put the other half aside to pound into the dried meat that would serve as a staple until spring.

. . .

When Tied to Sun returned from the neighboring villages, the first frost struck, and the aspen lost their last bits of gold. Burnt Cheek fantasized about burrowing into her lodge to hibernate, but she knew her husband planned to depart.

She decided her destiny was to accompany him. Owl had revealed the future. Tied to Sun might not make her happy, but he was her Kutenai husband now and had promised to become her Dhegiha husband soon. She determined to master Dhegiha and work hard at her marriage.

The night was cold. Burnt Cheek snuggled close to Tied to Sun and massaged his neck while she rubbed her legs against his. She whispered to him that their lodge mates were asleep.

He avoided her attempt at seduction by rising up to sit and announce both in signs and speech, "Tomorrow we leave, my Kutenai wife. Kustata has filled our bags with food. Confer with Weasel about what you want packed. You will accompany me in my canoe to practice Dhegiha and teach me Kutenai. I'm speaking it much better." He puffed out his chest in pride. "More than a moon here has given me much practice. What do you think?"

Tied to Sun's words encouraged Burnt Cheek. She heard a pompous note but no condescension, and it excited her when he called her wife. He seemed genuinely interested in her opinion, so she fudged in her estimate. "You speak extremely well, my husband. In another moon or two you would talk like a native."

"A few moons should suffice to learn such a primitive language. Yet, I encounter new words all the time, and new meanings for old words. It's certainly not as simple to learn as Dhegiha, even though we express ourselves infinitely better."

Burnt Cheek heard the arrogance in his voice and winced. She shook her head and wondered what manner of man her husband was.

.   .   .

The fleet of canoes shot along in the rapids of the upper Missouri until they reached its broad valley. Burnt Cheek had never seen so much water, and wondered if her father had. She swallowed against the wave of homesickness the thought of her father brought to her.

She plunged into language lessons to forget her family. Her husband sat in mid-canoe facing forward, while Burnt Cheek sat with her back to the bow. The two Dhegiha paddlers stroked only enough to be able to steer in the current.

"I'll point to objects in the canoe and along the shore, and tell you the Dhegiha word for them. Then you repeat the Kutenai word. I will then sign a verb so we can make sentences."

Burnt Cheek concentrated with every ounce of her intellect to play his game. She seldom missed forming a sentence. Sweat poured from her brow, even in the cold, as she focused on storing vocabulary.

Tied to Sun played at the lessons. "I know that Kutenai word. You don't need to tell me. What is the Shoshoni word?"

Burnt Cheek bit her lip to keep from laughing at his accent when he attempted Shoshoni. As she signed rarer words of Kutenai, Tied to Sun failed to form sentences. Clearly, he became frustrated, and she returned to common verbs. After a while, he did most of the teaching and said, "You see how easy Dhegiha is. Anyone can learn it quickly. But a savage language like Kutenai is almost impossible to learn."

Burnt Cheek could do nothing but nod in agreement. At least his attitude gave her the opportunity to learn Dhegiha. After a moon of instruction, Tied to Sun varied his lessons, feeling Burnt Cheek capable of more complex explanations.

"You have done well, my Kutenai wife." Tied to Sun both signed and spoke in Dhegiha. Burnt Cheek glowed at his use of the term wife but wondered why he always qualified it as Kutenai wife.

"Today, I will teach you the words we use for relatives, the natural way. The Kutenai misuse kinship terms, a result of their savagery, I suppose. In the civilized way, you must first understand clans. Each clan lives in its own ward in the city. When a woman marries, she comes to the husband's house. Naturally, their children belong to his clan. The wife always remains a member of her father's clan, unlike Kutenai savages. So the clan has a male core of fathers, sons, and son's sons. All their sisters are their clan mates, but when they marry, they go to live with their husbands. So a clan has sisters in all wards, but the important relatives, the males who pass on clan membership, all live in the same ward. The clan organizes all our life. It owns the farm fields, and it finds wives for us by giving our sisters to other clans for wives."

Burnt Cheek listened attentively to the bizarre life Tied to Sun described, then said innocently, "But my Kutenai husband, who did you exchange for me. Will you bring a sister on next year's visit?"

"Taking wives from foreigners is different. I'm describing how common Dhegiha live."

"Are you common, Tied to Sun?"

"Never use my name, woman," Tied to Sun bellowed in exasperation. "It costs me power to hear it. Address me as lord or Kutenai husband."

"I don't understand the word lord my Kutenai husband. Will you explain it?" Burnt Cheek did grasp that the term suggested the superiority she so detested.

"I'll explain later, after I teach you our kinship terms. Remember, people in the clan are all important. Mother and her relatives are related but in a different way because they come from different clans. Did I tell you that everyone must marry outside their clans? So a man calls his mother's brother mother's brother, as expected. Now pay attention. The son of his mother's brother will also be his mother's brother. Do you see?"

Burnt Cheek looked at him blankly.

He sighed in exasperation but continued, "Mother's brother's son is in mother's clan. So one lumps all the males of mother's clan together. The term for them is mother's brother, just like all the women in the clan are mothers. It's the natural way."

Burnt Cheek nodded agreement although she regarded it as unnatural and puzzling. How could people of different generations be called by the same kinship term? Still she tried to follow Tied to Sun's logic. With a little help, she thought, she might master the details.

As more days passed, Burnt Cheek's learning accelerated. She glowed when Tied to Sun radiated pleasure, but she wasn't sure if it was her progress or his conceit at how well he taught that made him smile. After one lesson, which she performed without a flaw, he said, "My Kutenai wife, I'm contemplating a Dhegiha name for you. Burnt Cheek translates poorly, nor do we need to call attention to your ugly face. I have been thinking.

Henceforth, I will call you Gifted Tongue. Its sound is melodious and diverts attention from your looks."

Burnt Cheek churned with mixed feelings. Tied to Sun could never overlook the scar. She held back a tear. Yet, he recognized her talent with language, maybe even the hard work it required to concentrate on each sound, to learn new meanings, and to ask the right questions. Most of all, she liked the wonderful gift of a name he had bestowed. Even from her scant knowledge of Dhegiha, she recognized the lilt of the sounds in Gifted Tongue. She rolled the words over in her mind, and the sounds delighted her voice as she practiced them in a whisper.

. . .

Gifted Tongue's eagerness to learn tired Tied to Sun so he joined a hunting party that fanned out along the shore. She was left with Weasel to instruct her in Mandan. She sensed that he disdained to teach a woman anything, but since she might marry Tied to Sun, he mustered his mind to action. She did not tell him that she had learned a little Mandan from Beloved Enemy, and he was overwhelmed with her response. Begrudgingly, he said, "Your new name fits you well. You learn faster than anyone I've ever seen." She was tempted to confess, but reconsidered and continued to impress him.

When Weasel's imagination failed him in further instruction, she drilled herself, but soon tired of the exercise. She thought to pry into Dhegiha ways that Tied to Sun had hidden. "Tied to Sun explained kinship, but I'm slow-witted. Perhaps you can teach me?"

Perplexed, Weasel stuck to his assigned task, pretending his pupil asked about Mandan practices. "Mandan kinship is baffling because they have it all backwards."

"What do you mean? How could it be backward? Like a woman calling her man wife?"

"No, they're not that stupid. In fact, for savages the Mandan are quite advanced. They farm almost as well as we do, or at least they try. Their ceremonies impress me, too. I guess it's just in kinship that they're so backward."

"What about their kinship?" Gifted Tongue prodded craftily.

"You know how Dhegiha call mother's brother, and mother's brother son, and the son's son, by the same term because they're all in mother's clan? Did Tied to Sun teach you that?"

"Yes, he did. It's all the men of the mother's clan who are alike, so there's one term for them."

"That's right. They're all in-laws, hardly relatives the way clan mates are. Clan members are your true relatives. The relatives in your wife's clan are barely related to you."

"So how do the Mandan turn that around?" Gifted Tongue said.

"Instead of mother's brother and his son and son's son having one term, it's father's sister and her daughter and daughter's daughter who have one term. They lump a line of females together instead of a line of males. They reverse it."

"Maybe the Mandan have clans where females are the vital links. Maybe children belong to their mother's clans instead of father's clan?" Having grown up with no knowledge of clans, Gifted Tongue perceived how they operated, even if she did not realize that the clan arranged marriages, held property in common, settled disputes, and performed religious rites.

Weasel, however, was so imbued with the idea that only

men could pass on clan membership that he dismissed her insight. "No, that's impossible. A son can only inherit from his father. How could women ever be important? They couldn't teach their sons the clan ceremonies."

Weasel's sharp tone told Gifted Tongue that no answer could satisfy him, yet she guessed the truth. "What if the mother's brother taught his sister's son whatever he needed to know?"

Her question stumped Weasel, who could not deny her logic. He seemed to mull over the possibility in his mind, but couldn't admit that she might have guessed more about the Mandan than he had learned.

With Weasel's continual drill, Gifted Tongue dreamed in Mandan a few days before Tied to Sun announced they neared their villages. She took the dream as an omen to study harder, both Mandan and Dhegiha.

The next morning she said to Weasel, in Dhegiha, "I understand that among Dhegiha when a woman marries, she goes to live with her husband's people. Is that right?"

"Yes, of course. Her children must grow up in the heart of their clan. Where else could a wife go?"

"What if she stayed home? Isn't that the Mandan custom? Why couldn't a Mandan husband join his wife's home? Then the children would belong to their mother's clan."

She shaped her analysis so simply that even Weasel had to appreciate its accuracy. "I guess it's possible. You can ask the Mandan. We'll stay with them until the spring thaw. You'll have plenty of time to practice the language and learn about their clans."

No one had told her they would spend the winter with the Mandan. How like her husband not to mention it, she thought.

She had needlessly worried about enduring the winter on the open plains.

"I need to learn more about the Center of the World, too," she continued in Dhegiha, occasionally resorting to sign language. "My Kutenai husband started teaching me about relatives. What is the Dhegiha term for wife?"

"There's no one word for wife." Gifted Tongue saw that her use of Dhegiha made Weasel's task so simple he responded without thinking. "The term used by commoners is commoner wife. Of course, we must find wives outside our clan so we have in-laws in all the other clans because our sisters marry men in those clans, and we marry the sisters of those men."

He continued without pause, "It differs for the exalted clans. The falcons are the top clan. They select a Sun. The bear and turtle clans are in between them and the commoner clans, like my own. The bears and turtles are nobles. A bear should marry a turtle or a falcon, but a noble may settle for a wife from a commoner clan. Such a wife is also called a commoner wife by a noble. The nobles honor us commoners when they marry one of our sisters. Although she can never be in their clan, her children are, because children always belong to their fathers' clans."

"What if a noble married a woman who was not Dhegiha?" Gifted Tongue spoke in a tone she hoped showed only an interest in learning vocabulary.

"It seldom happens, but she's called a servant wife." Weasel winced at his answer, and shifted to Mandan to describe a marriage ceremony. Burnt Cheek guessed that Tied to Sun had instructed Weasel not to divulge anything about her place in his family.

After a period of silence, Weasel asked, "Has Tied to Sun explained Dhegiha marriage practices to you?"

"Oh yes, but your review helps. He promised me a Dhegiha marriage at the Center of the World." She assured him he had not revealed more than he should, and she remained so composed that Weasel could never guess at the turmoil racing in her head.

What kind of life faced a servant wife? Gifted Tongue even wondered how she would be related to her own children. A hundred other questions strained her mind. She pledged to herself by winter's end to speak better Mandan than Weasel and to know far more about Mandan culture. She'd make Tied to Sun not only need her but love her.

CHAPTER FIVE

Tied to Sun bellowed his disgust into the morning sun as the canoes rounded a bend and suddenly found a Mandan village. He had spent a cold, uncomfortable night a short distance from a welcome haven. Why hadn't his men recalled the landmarks? he grumbled irritably. Refusing any responsibility himself, he yelled at Weasel, "Get my litter. We'll forego the herald. The Mandan know my station from the spring ceremony, and they'd better remember my gifts."

After the outburst of anger, Gifted Tongue saw that he regained his self-control. He struggled to create a diplomatic veneer to conceal the frustration of so many days in a canoe and an unnecessary night on the freezing, desolate prairie. She wondered how she could help her husband announce his renown. She did not wait long to be disappointed.

"Help the servants with the parfleche bags, woman," Tied to Sun barked. "I'll need time to explain your presence. Practice your Mandan with the women, but don't talk to any men unless I'm with you."

Gifted Tongue quivered at the suggestion Tied to Sun might be jealous, but she guessed he simply might not want her to upset his carefully cultivated relations.

A deep drum bass announced the arrival of the Dhegiha while bearers joined pieces of cedar to form a litter. The procession left while Gifted Tongue trailed behind with servants to pack the bags. The party climbed a small bank to find tattered brown stalks harvested moons earlier. Gifted Tongue asked Weasel what the unusual plants were.

"These are cornfields that provide their winter food. Fields like these surround the Center of the World, although ours are much more productive."

"You mean they have to plant the seeds? Why don't they just gather whatever they need?"

Weasel frowned in contempt, as if the question was ridiculous, and Gifted Tongue knew he wouldn't answer. In silence, they reached the highest terrace and found the village spread along its edge. Large rectangular earth lodges filled the skyline. Beloved Enemy's description of her home barely prepared Gifted Tongue for the striking difference from Kutenai villages. She could only imagine the large mounds to have been thrown up by giant prairie dogs. They looked too large to be comfortable. Weasel left before she could inspect them, and then a line of women descended on her. She girded herself for a barrage of Mandan, hoping a few women used signs. The first words she heard were Kutenai. "Your white dress is Kutenai. Welcome, sister."

"How good to find a Kutenai sister," Gifted Tongue exclaimed. She immediately took to the woman's dancing eyes and pleasant smile.

"It's been so long since I've spoken Kutenai, I must sound strange. I can't think of the words I need."

"Why are you here, sister?" Gifted Tongue asked. "You're moons from home."

"My brothers brought me here when hunger struck the Kutenai. The fish failed to spawn. Even the caribou disappeared. It was an unusual year. My brothers found me a Mandan husband. So here I am."

Gifted Tongue recognized that they were more than Kutenai sisters. They shared marriage to a foreigner. The woman would be a wonderful companion through the winter.

"Stay in my lodge, sister. Crow's Heart, my husband, and his sister and her husband are visiting relatives downriver. Our son and my mother-in-law are the only ones here, so we're lonely. The corn harvest was poor because we planted late, but we have enough. We'll spend the winter talking Kutenai, or I can teach you Mandan. I must tell you it's hard on the tongue." The woman said as a way of identifying herself, "You need only ask for the lodge of Scatterscorn, and anyone will point it out."

"I'm not sure where to stay," Gifted Tongue said. "I must wait until my husband tells me."

"You mean you are married to a Dhegiha?" Scatterscorn said doubtfully.

"Yes, I am the wife of Tied to Sun."

"Oh." The woman's puzzled look told Gifted Tongue such a marriage surprised her.

"We married a few moons ago among the Kutenai. Do you think that strange?"

"No . . . well, yes. Once or twice a Dhegiha has married a Mandan woman, but they never took their wives with them. Scatterscorn wrinkled her nose in hesitation, then said, "It seemed to me that the Dhegiha regarded it as a marriage of convenience, just so they'd have brothers-in-law among us."

"My marriage may be no more than that," Gifted Tongue said. "Tied To Sun claims we will marry again at the Center of the World in a Dhegiha ceremony. Then we would be truly married."

"Oh, that's good. It explains everything. The Center of the World must be exciting. The Dhegiha describe it that way although one of our men who visited there thought the homes were uncomfortable and everything too crowded."

By this time, the Mandan women could no longer control their curiosity, and their excited voices insisted that Scatterscorn translate. Her brief interpretation accelerated the buzzing as the women speculated on who would host the Kutenai stranger. They knew Tied to Sun could stay with either the war chief, Black Wolf, or the peace chief, but rivalry between Crow's Paunch and Bear Looks Out kept the peace chieftainship open.

Questions flew as the women queried Gifted Tongue while they attempted to establish a place for her. Suddenly, the buzzing hushed with the appearance of Tied to Sun. Gifted Tongue felt him behind her before she saw him. His eyes flashed anger. "Why do you cause trouble, woman? I expected you to be a curiosity, but you've whipped up a crisis. I want no trouble from you."

"I found a Kutenai sister, my Kutenai husband. She only wanted me to stay in her lodge while we talked of the mountains."

Tied to Sun smiled, betraying a hint of gratitude, "You do well, woman. Make a place for yourself with your sister. That way, I won't have to explain that I have a Kutenai wife. If you need me, come to Black Wolf's lodge."

Gifted Tongue's heart raced. She was elated to stay with Scatterscorn, but how could she win her husband's heart when she was in a different lodge? "I am glad to serve you, my

Kutenai husband. If you need me for anything, please send for me." He seemed to ignore the longing she knew was in her eyes as he quickly turned away to leave.

Scatterscorn touched her arm and invited her inside her lodge. A large smoke hole over a central fireplace lighted the inside. As her eyes adjusted, she saw matted beds lining both sides of the lodge, what she thought were backrests, numerous skins in various stages of preparation, and strings of what must be corn piled at random. At the rear of the lodge was a pipe rack, shields, and what she guessed were ritual trappings.

After they sat down near the entrance, Gifted Tongue asked, "Won't people know your home by your husband's name?"

"Oh no," Scatterscorn laughed. "My husband has no lodge. Among the Mandan the rules are strict. The lodge belongs to the wife so the husband comes to live with her. Since I'm an outsider, I lived with Crow's Heart, but his home was known to be his mother's. She's called Otter. She'll be home soon, after she calms her husband's relatives. When we quarreled in our downstream village, half of us moved up here this spring, a little late to plant. But we managed. The squash did well although the corn and beans weren't the best. We left because the soil was so sandy that our cache pits kept caving in. But the old women there were too stubborn to do anything. Well, not all of them. A few came with us. Mother Earth is ideal here for storage pits. It's been a hectic summer clearing new fields and building lodges. We only need to finish a ceremonial lodge."

Gifted Tongue marveled at Scatterscorn's incessant talk. She might regret spending the winter with such a chatterer, she thought. No, she decided, she would learn far more Mandan with someone who could explain things in Kutenai.

Only after they settled in Scatterscorn's lodge did her host notice Gifted Tongue's accent. "My sister, you seem to have an accent. At first I thought I forgot what our language sounded like. Are you from the far western Kutenai?"

"No, sister, I'm an easterner. But I was born Shoshoni. It was my first language. I learned Kutenai after menstruation."

"You speak so well I would never guess that it wasn't your first language. It's a tiny difference. I'm going to enjoy the winter with you. You can tell me about the Shoshoni, too."

Gifted Tongue did not expect nor want to be the center of attention for the winter, but before she could think about it, the warmth and softness of a bison robe wrapped her in sleep.

.   .   .

For a moon, Gifted Tongue and Scatterscorn practiced Mandan, with occasional Kutenai explanation. Without realizing it, they soon spoke only Mandan, and Gifted Tongue steadily progressed.

One cold morning, when a hard frost shone on the prairie grass, Scatterscorn led Gifted Tongue to a terrace between the lodges and cornfields. At a low mound, she pulled back matting laid over poles.

"We've been slow to complete this last cache. Too much corn is piled up in our lodge. You must think I'm a terrible house-keeper. The field mice are eating more than their share. They'll be fat as fall bison if we don't finish this pit."

Gifted Tongue prepared to jump down, eager to work, but at the edge, she gasped. The cache was two persons' height.

"You look surprised, sister. Oh, you've probably never seen a Mandan cache. I forgot. The Kutenai had little to store. Well, all that dried fish. But we have so much corn and beans, and the dried squash, we need much more storage space."

Scatterscorn reached into the pit for a notched pole and said, "Here's a ladder. You can see why the right kind of soil is necessary. If we dig out the sides a little more, we'll have a giant underground pot. The earth cover keeps the corn from freezing." As they climbed down the ladder, she said, "Our winters are colder than in the mountains. The first winter I thought I would freeze to death."

Scatterscorn picked up a bison shoulder blade hoe to dig as rapidly as she talked. Gifted Tongue couldn't help thinking of a mole at work before realizing that she should scoop the loose dirt into an old, worn basket. Sweat covered her, despite the cold, as she repeatedly climbed the ladder to empty it. When the sun reached overhead, Scatterscorn declared that the cache was finished.

"We'll have mush and a little pemmican before we haul the corn here. Two other lodges use the cache. Those women, my adopted clan sisters, store more than I do. You'll like Dances Along who lives next door. She's cheerful, and always does more than her share. Juneberries lives behind us. We get along well, but she complains a lot. And she's such a talker. Hard to get a word in when she starts up."

Gifted Tongue smiled at the thought of the two together.

After their pemmican and mush, Scatterscorn took Gifted Tongue to the lodge of Dances Along, who put aside the quills she'd softened for her brother's moccasins. Her cheerful countenance hid her years, but Gifted Tongue recognized a generation's difference. The three talked briefly to put off packing their corn to the cache.

"Have you seen Juneberries today?" Scatterscorn asked.

"I took her some sweet squash this morning. She complained

yesterday that nothing tasted good. Maybe when our bison kin give themselves to us, fresh meat will perk her up," Dances Along forced a grin.

"Or maybe if the sun comes out at night, she'll perk up." Scatterscorn said teasingly.

"You shouldn't joke about your sister. She's a good woman. That husband of hers hasn't done anything to make life better for her. Gone half the time."

"To escape her constant griping," Scatterscorn muttered under her breath.

Dances Along said to Gifted Tongue, "That's better than all the time, the way my sister left. I haven't seen her since my menstruation time. No word in twenty years. I don't know if she's dead or alive."

"Think of all your other sisters," Scatterscorn hastened to say. "And how good they have been."

"You're right. I've been blessed with good sisters and brothers. But the only other child of the woman who gave birth to me is gone. I do wish I knew if she's alive."

Gifted Tongue thought of her own mothers. In a few years, she would not know if they were alive. Scatterscorn broke the gloom. "Let's get Juneberries, and we'll fill the cache." When the three women reached Juneberries' lodge, Dances Along raised her voice, and Juneberries hustled to the lodge door to greet them. They had barely begun to warm themselves at the lodge fire, when Juneberries started.

"It's good of you to come. I thought I would meet your guest sooner. But I know you had more important things to do."

Gifted Tongue recognized a distinct whining tone in Mandan that differed from Kutenai. "My Kutenai sister has been resting from her long trip and has been learning Mandan. Speak slowly for her," Scatterscorn said. Gifted Tongue thought slowly might mean without a whine.

Juneberries spoke loudly, "I hope you like it here. The winter may not be too cold, if we're lucky. Much of the hard work is finished, except we have all this corn to store."

"That's why we've come." Scatterscorn interrupted before Juneberries could add further grievances. "Gifted Tongue helped finish the cache this morning, so we can fill it."

"Why didn't you call me? I would have helped. Are you sure it won't collapse? Remember what we lost last year?"

"The cache is in good shape," Scatterscorn said emphatically. "We should start filling it."

She lifted a string of corn, and Gifted Tongue jumped to her side. The two shouldered several strings before the other women started. Gifted Tongue admired the ingenuity with which the corn husks of ten or twelve ears were woven together in a string.

The four women nearly emptied their lodges of corn by dusk with the strings rapidly filling the cache. No one attempted to separate the contributions of different lodges. Gifted Tongue realized that each family was free to use whatever they needed.

They topped off the cache the next morning. Juneberries complained of aching joints and left for home while Dances Along and Scatterscorn showed Gifted Tongue how to seal the cache with mats and sod. When the three returned to Scatterscorn's lodge, they found that Otter had cooked a special treat of squash, herbs, and dried meat.

"You did well, daughters-in-law. I thought I would have to help you since that lazy son and daughter of mine weren't here. At least they had the sense to find hard-working spouses." The gleam in Otter's eyes told Gifted Tongue that the woman wasn't serious about her children. She guessed the elder felt lucky that her son's family lived with her as well as her daughter's.

Overtly, Otter continued to harp on her children. "You two should rest a day before we begin the ceremonial lodge. It'll go faster without Good Robe and Crow's Heart getting in your way."

Scatterscorn said reproachfully, "Good Robe is one of the best at building a lodge, mother-in-law. Our guest is going to get wrong ideas, the way you talk."

"Her engineering skill is useless if she isn't here," Otter said with a toss of her head. "She's always deserting me. She won't be able to help that husband of hers with his leg. It's up to the shaman down there to heal it."

Scatterscorn spoke to Gifted Tongue in Kutenai. "She always complains when her daughter's away. But she's not serious. It's her way of flattering me. She's a wonderful mother-in-law."

"I've heard the stranger speak Mandan," Otter said disapprovingly. "You're speaking Kutenai so I won't understand, aren't you?"

Gifted Tongue wasn't sure if Otter joked this time. The old woman's wisdom easily disguised her motives. But when she said that the ceremonial lodge should be started the next day, it was clear what she meant.

Scatterscorn said, "I'll talk tonight with women of other clans, my mother-in-law. Black Wolf has suggested we should start, but it's not his business. He's a good war chief, but a peace chief should decide on the ceremonial lodge." Scatterscorn said to Gifted Tongue, "The people can't decide between Crow's Paunch and Bear Looks Out. Crow's Paunch is in the east moiety. He should take it. But Bear Looks Out is the best orator."

"He'd be my choice," Otter said. "But being in the west moiety, like Black Wolf, could make trouble. We've had problems when both chiefs weren't from opposite moieties." Otter turned to Gifted Tongue and said, "I don't suppose anyone's told you about our moiety groups. Half the clans belong to the east moiety, the other half belong to the west. Each should be represented by a chief, but it doesn't always work out that way."

Otter's wisdom convinced Scatterscorn to campaign for Crow's Paunch. She explained to Gifted Tongue, "A council of elder men are supposed to decide, but if we women reach a consensus, we'll sway the men."

Gifted Tongue accompanied her host to various lodges that night to become initiated into Mandan politics. Scatterscorn used her introduction as an excuse to campaign for Crow's Paunch. The two were pleased to find that most of the older women thought as her mother-in-law did, and their visit prompted the women to boost Crow's Paunch with their brothers.

Several days later, while the men still debated, the women gathered to select a site for the ceremonial lodge. Since the other lodges were already built, the location for the new lodge was obvious. Gifted Tongue watched Otter point to positions for the four postholes that would serve as the foundation.

"Otter will force the men to reach a consensus," Scatterscorn told Gifted Tongue. They both smiled when Crow's Paunch hustled toward the gathered women.

He spoke as if he had weighed the matter at length. "This site will be ideal for the ceremonial lodge. It is central to our village, and I have a good feeling for it. You may begin."

Otter nodded assent. Gifted Tongue thought she saw many women smirk at the chief's decision. The next day was sunny and the women scooped out a large rectangle in the thawed soil. Gifted Tongue guessed it to be eight persons' length by six, far larger than any Kutenai lodge. Otter directed, but was clearly reluctant to do so since she had never masterminded a ceremonial lodge. With her hoe, she marked four points of a square at the center of the pit and honored four older women to dig at each spot. Meanwhile, younger women hauled in four large trees that the men had felled, each trunk with a large crotch at its top.

Otter suggested a proper depth for the four holes and pointed where to cut the poles to achieve an exact height. Scatterscorn explained to Gifted Tongue that the old woman had only a finger's length leeway. "The four posts require an exact height. The logs in the crotches hold poles to form a perimeter wall, and the lower side of the lodge slopes down from it. If the pitch is not exactly right, the support poles won't stay."

After lengthy deliberation, Otter notched the trees exactly where she wanted them cut, and the elders began the work, rotating their task among clan mates. At mid-morning, they slipped the poles into each hole, and Gifted Tongue saw Otter sigh with relief. She knew the foundation would work.

.   .   .

Otter had invited Gifted Tongue and Scatterscorn to her lodge where she fed them a corn gruel mixed with beans. A hint of bison floated in the aroma that pleased Gifted Tongue's nose almost as much as her stomach. The crowded lodge was a warm haven against a blowing, cold day.

"I have asked Dances Along to join us, my daughters," Otter whispered the name. Looking at Gifted Tongue, she said, "She'll tell you the legend so you'll understand the White Bison Cow Society's ceremony which you are going to see soon."

Gifted Tongue studied the gray-haired woman, her wrinkles a clue to her wisdom. Despite her age, Dances Along sat straight and grinned good naturedly. Gifted Tongue tried to remember where she had seen the familiar demeanor.

"It seems as if I met you before I came here," Gifted Tongue said, deeply puzzled. "Were you ever among the Kutenai?"

"No, but I have a fondness for anyone from the Kutenai country," Dances Along said gravely. "I've wanted to talk with you because I have a sister there I haven't heard of in years. Her name is Works Alone. Did you meet her?"

Gifted Tongue recognized the name of Eloquent One's mother, but knew that she was born a Kutenai. She wondered about the problems of translating names, but offered that the only Works Alone she knew was a native Kutenai. Suddenly, it struck her.

"But of course. It's Beloved Enemy. It must be."

"How can that be?" Scatterscorn asked.

Gifted Tongue said to Dances Along, "The woman who taught me Mandan resembles you. That's why I thought I had met you. She married Bull Robe, my almost father-in-law. His mother's name is Works Alone, so the Kutenai gave your sister a new name to avoid confusion. Wasn't she younger than you?"

"Yes, by six or seven years." Dances Along's smile stretched the length of her face. "So friend, you were almost my daughter-in-law. What do I call you?"

"Beloved Enemy wanted me to call her grandrelative. Can I call you that?"

"I would like it."

The warmth generated by the new relationship inspired Dances Along to recount the founding of the White Bison Cow Society.

She began solemnly, "At the world's beginning, a man sought a vision. He fasted for four days and each day he heard a voice call, 'Put a child with them.' On the fourth day, a young woman approached with two children. She said, 'I am the bison; I give you these two children. Prepare a feast, and I will return with the herd.' The vision seeker returned home, told his dream, and people prepared a feast." Dances Along paused dramatically and continued. "A party of strange women brought two youngsters and taught the Mandan the White Bison Cow Ceremony. When they left, both children struggled to go with them. One succeeded, but the Mandan kept the other. Now each winter the bison women return to visit their child, and they bring their herd with them."

Dances Along smiled at Gifted Tongue's rapt attention. "So that is why we have the ceremony. The dancing brings cold weather when the bison seek wooded valleys. They come right to camp. Two years ago after the dancing, a cow walked up to the lodge door. The rest of the herd followed."

"Will you dance soon, grandrelative?" Gifted Tongue asked.

"Tomorrow. Because we are a small group now, the ceremony won't be elaborate. Usually Goose Society women would buy membership, but this year, no one's eligible."

Gifted Tongue's puzzled look prompted Dances Along to say, "We Mandan have a series of age grades. The men have six groups, the women four. The first two for women prepare girls for adult life. When their children are grown, they can buy membership in the Goose Society. Their payment proves their sincerity. The ceremonies of the Goose Society ensure the return of geese, who bring spring. After menopause, the Goose members can enter the White Bison Cow Society."

The next day, before the ceremony began, women purified themselves in a sweat lodge. Gifted Tongue and Scatterscorn cooked pots of mush for everyone. When it cooled, they rolled the gruel into corn balls. Each variety of corn produced a different morsel that Scatterscorn and Gifted Tongue sampled until they were stuffed.

The following morning, the White Bison Cow women sang inviting songs while they danced at the lodge entrance. Gifted Tongue watched as they entered the lodge, followed by the elders. Black Wolf and Tied to Sun trailed behind them. Just before he bent to enter the lodge tunnel, Tied to Sun looked at her. She couldn't interpret his glance, but at least he hadn't ignored her.

The lodge was nearly filled by the time Scatterscorn led Gifted Tongue to a seat at the left. Before them, five men beat a large drum and led the singing. With the whole village in attendance, the lodge looked shrunken.

Light from the entrance showed Dances Along kneeling opposite them. Scatterscorn explained that she was keeper of the ceremony. As her eyes adjusted, Gifted Tongue noted a bison skull at the back of the lodge, close to where a girl of not more than four or five years of age sat in the place of honor. She, too, was dressed in white and seemed anxious about her honored place. Tied to Sun sat near her with Black Wolf.

The dancers circled slowly. The grace of the old women flowed in each movement. Their fringed, buckskin dresses accented the rhythm of the drum as they swung in one direction, then the other. Their flowing black hair, held only by a band of white bison hide, flew back and forth to the beat.

Gifted Tongue recognized few dancers because the left sides of their faces were painted red, the right side blue. Only when someone ventured into the light of the overhead opening did she identify anyone. She didn't recognize a matron dressed in white, whose dress looked Kutenai. When Scatterscorn saw her puzzled look, she explained that the Mandan considered the rare albino bison sacred and used its hide for special ceremonies.

When the dancing stopped, Otter and Dances Along served corn balls to everyone. After a drumroll silenced the lodge, Dances Along fed the bison skull. Then she circled the lodge with an incense burner. The sweet smoke permeated the lodge. Its gray cloud passed over the bison skull, the singers, and the honored child, who no longer seemed anxious.

After everyone ate a second time, the line of dancing women approached the revered girl. Three leaders danced an invitation before taking her to the center of the lodge. The child matched the women's grace, proudly keeping step until morning.

Gifted Tongue and Scatterscorn returned to their lodge. As they laid down to sleep, Scatterscorn explained that the little girl represented the child left by the Bison people. She would entice her relatives to return to camp.

After two nights of dancing, a chilling cold struck, brought by the dancers' devotion. In such weather, the bison would leave their home on the plains to find shelter along the riverbed. Gifted Tongue forced herself back to the ceremony on the third day, despite the cold that reminded her of the icy Kutenai fishing streams. That night, her throat grew raw, her nose ran, but the worst part was that she shivered uncontrollably even under a second bison robe.

She forced herself up the next morning to attend the last day of the ceremony and to welcome the approach of the bison. She never thought to miss the final night, despite Scatterscorn's pleas for her to remain in bed.

The climactic fourth night saw the dancers in full splendor. Singers never missed a beat, tones sparkled, and the dancers reached a vigorous pace while the small bison girl in white excelled in her steps. The balls of corn never tasted better, and the incense never smelled sweeter.

Gifted Tongue floated on a cloud of incense, propelled by drumbeats. When she reached the heavens, she smiled to see that her owl guardians awaited her. As she approached, they scowled in disgust and flew at her face flapping in fury. Did they threaten to leave her? she thought frantically. She thrashed to avoid the beating their wings promised, and she cringed to avoid their talons. They drew back. Behind her, a white bison snorted its warning. It charged. She couldn't tell if it was going to save her from the owls or kill her. It stopped directly over her while the owls circled overhead. The bison's fiery breath burned her lungs. When her guardians swooped down, their fanning wings brought relief, but she burned again as she fell beside Twisted Rabbit. She didn't know if flames from the brushfire consumed her or if it were the bison's breath. Once again her owls struck. One drove its talons into the bison's nose, and it roared in retreat. The other owl fanned her forehead. Through her disjointed senses, she heard a voice.

"Her fever has broken. You have worked another miracle. The name of Whirlwind will be known forever. Your herbs and prayers are perfect medicine."

The voice of Tied to Sun awoke her. She stared at him for some time before recognizing him. His presence was less real than the owls and white bison. She spoke, but no one understood Shoshoni. As she slowly returned to her senses, she wondered if it was worth the bother to speak.

When the fever inside receded, she rejoiced that Tied to Sun had saved her life. He did care for her, she thought warmly.

"My husband," she began in Dhegiha, "you saved my life. I am indebted."

"It was no trouble. Whirlwind knows medicine from around the world and the supernatural world as well. Your friend had herbs, too. They may have helped. I went to no bother, so don't worry. It's good to see you looking better, my Kutenai wife."

Gifted Tongue breathed deeply in contentment at hearing her husband's words but when he spoke again, her heart sank.

"I have invested too much in you for you to go and die on me," he said abruptly, as he left.

CHAPTER SIX

Since sunrise, Gifted Tongue had helped Weasel and the bearers load parfleche bags of dried bison for the trip downriver. Despite the early spring cold, she wiped sweat from her eyes. After one heavy bag, she glanced at the upper terrace.

She shivered at the sight. The rising, red sun behind Tied to Sun revealed only his silhouette, but she recognized his tall, rugged features. What chilled her was the tall, broad figure beside him, in a flowing dress. The woman swirled her hair in an alluring gesture.

Gifted Tongue had convinced herself that she would not be jealous of Tied to Sun's wives, but she wasn't ready for this woman. She imagined her husband spending the winter with her. On second glance, the figure lacked some undefined feminine quality. As the two drew closer, she saw that Tied to Sun's companion had gray hair. She hoped the woman might be a relative. Her sharp features suggested masculinity, but when she smiled at a joke of Tied to Sun's, she cupped her lips with her hand in a woman's modesty. A fine quill pattern on her dress spoke of a skilled feminine hand, as did the fringe of her dress.

Weasel guessed at Gifted Tongue's curiosity. "It's Whirlwind with your husband. He spent the winter with the Mandan sharing herbal knowledge. He's an eminent Dhegiha shaman."

Weasel's use of he reverberated in Gifted Tongue's mind. Weasel said, "Whirlwind is a berdache, a man who dresses as a woman." Gifted Tongue had known berdache among the Shoshoni, and felt a touch of jealousy since some berdache slept with men.

"He looks too elderly to travel so far by himself. How many winters has he seen?" Gifted Tongue said, with a tinge of hope.

"Only forty or so. He's not yet an elder. They say that on his vision quest, a whirlwind carried him all over the world, even to Rock's home at the center of the earth. From there it took him above to Blue Dome." Gifted Tongue's mouth dropped, and Weasel said, "Someone will explain the Rock and Blue Dome to you who knows the story better than I do. The point is that Whirlwind was carried everywhere and shown the world's medicines."

"Is he a good friend of my husband? Does he use his power for him?"

"He uses his power for whomever needs it. Beware though, his power is dangerous. You should know, too, that the priests don't like shamans. Their ways are different."

Before Weasel could add more, Tied to Sun and Whirlwind descended from the terrace and walked to the nearly loaded canoes. With one hand, Whirlwind lifted two bags in one swoop onto a canoe.

"Don't aggravate yourself, my friend," Tied to Sun said in a grandiose manner. "The commoners and my Kutenai wife can finish loading."

"You forget that I, too, am a commoner, my lord. And I could be a wife, perhaps," he simpered.

"You are too proficient a shaman to be just a commoner."

"Don't you like the quillwork on my dress, my lord. Isn't it better than any that your wives do?" Whirlwind teased.

"It's the best I've seen," Tied to Sun said admiringly.

"But not the best I've done. Still, I like it."

The strange sparkle in Whirlwind's eyes fascinated Gifted Tongue. She first thought it hinted at contempt for her husband's airs, but he deferred to him as a woman does to a man. Or it could be the demeanor of a Dhegiha commoner, she thought. She realized there was much to learn about the Dhegiha.

The Dhegiha party loaded the last canoe by mid-morning. Scatterscorn led the Mandan women who came to see Gifted Tongue off. They signed their affection, while Black Wolf and Bear Looks Out stared impassively at their departing visitors.

. . .

The first few days of canoeing on the river, everyone watched for blocks of ice that could rip a canoe's hull in an instant. Submerged tree trunks caused further problems. In the spring flood, the canoes made rapid, if cautious, progress.

Soon the party settled into a routine. Tied to Sun ordered Gifted Tongue to share a canoe with Whirlwind so he could instruct her in the Dhegiha language and culture. Despite Weasel's warning about Whirlwind, Gifted Tongue leaped at the chance to break the trip's monotony.

She expected Whirlwind to lecture as her husband had. Instead, he rambled on as Scatterscorn might. He gossiped so much the first day that Gifted Tongue doubted she would learn anything of Dhegiha custom. But by day's end, she had practiced Dhegiha with few lapses into Mandan. She had learned more by chatting than any formal lesson could teach her.

She also discovered how close to death she came in Scatterscorn's lodge. Whirlwind said that her fever had lasted two moons. She missed the bison herd that the White Bison Calf Society lured to the village, and Whirlwind delighted in regaling her with how he helped the women butcher so many animals that they feasted the whole winter. He teased her that the work wasn't so hard that she needed to evade it with a fever.

The next day began innocently, too, but Whirlwind's questioning led Gifted Tongue to do the talking. He steered her toward her dreams during her long fever.

"I felt so secure when I saw my owls, but then they attacked me. Or, they meant to warn me. But with them there, I thought I'd recover, until a bison drove them off. It breathed fire that burned me. How could my owls resist it? But they did. One shielded me while the other drove the bison away."

Gifted Tongue hesitated, aware of how much she had been talking.

"What else? I want to know everything." She could feel his sincerity as he probed her memory.

"The breath of the bison burned like fire. I wanted to die, but when the owl fanned me, I felt I'd live. I recall voices, women's voices. One powerful woman." She hesitated, then breathed deeply at the revelation and said, "Was that you, sister, er, brother?"

"It was I, child. Call me grandrelative. In years I am not that old, but the Wakan chose to age me quickly."

Grandrelative, Gifted Tongue mused, when yesterday he seemed like a sister. She thought he made grandrelative such a comforting term that he must be the most remarkable person alive.

"Grandrelative, tell me about Wakan," she said. "I haven't heard the word."

"Wakan is the all-powerful force of the universe. The gods have Wakan, and sometimes people. It should be used for good, but once in a while an evil person uses it for personal gain. Then it is dangerous. It may work at cross purposes, too. Tell me your vision about owl, child."

"When the Kutenai isolated me for menstrual ritual, two owls came to me. I was older than usual because I had been brought up a Shoshoni. Do you know them?"

"I have visited them. The Kutenai have strong medicine. The Shoshoni are interesting. They were eager to learn my medicine," he said casually. Then he said intently, "Did owl come to your hut?"

"Yes. On the seventh day. My fingers were bound, and they ached. My stomach ached more. I heard beating on the hut. When I threw back a mat, two owls glared at me. Their power lifted me, and we soared. I felt wonderful. The experience didn't last long enough."

She realized that her glow and tone told Whirlwind how much she relished flying. Before she could tell him of the Owl Dance Society, he contrasted his own flight, one filled with terror and compulsion. It swept him along like a raging river for what seemed like years, and it forced him to learn the lessons of the gods wherever the current carried him. He shuddered at his memory of the vision.

"For now, child, I must be silent. We'll have time to talk as sisters, but now I must meditate on your experience with owl and bison."

She was disappointed that Whirlwind did not mention her dream again that day. Instead, when he spoke, he explained Dhegiha grammar and drilled her on pronunciation. Her able tongue pleased him.

She spent an anxious night, alone on shore as usual. Despite gathering wood and cooking, her tired body tossed as she dreamed in snatches of Dhegiha and fear of her husband's customs.

The next day in the canoe, the sun cheered her, but she worried when Whirlwind's kindly but piercing eyes studied her. He said, "I've thought about your vision. It reveals much about what Wakan grants you. Ask questions if you don't understand. Usually it's not good to interrupt, but you still learn Dhegiha so it won't be impolite."

She nodded that she understood.

He bent toward her and said, "Owl and bison are very different. One is of the earth, the other the sky. Father Sky and Mother Earth complement each other but are also opposites, male and female. Owl is of the night, bison is of the day. Day and night complement each other and are related as husband and wife, but they are also opposites. Your day and night creatures stand for opposition, Do you understand?"

Gifted Tongue nodded yes, but she said doubtfully, "I'm not sure about how day and night are opposed. Don't they follow each other?"

Whirlwind answered patiently, tossing his long hair to one side, "Sun and Moon follow each other and are female powers, but day and night are opposed. The Wakan between them is delicately balanced, and it is vital to keep it that way."

She looked puzzled, but said, "I think I understand, grandrelative."

Whirlwind nodded that he knew her difficulty. "You will understand better when I explain the origins of life and the universe. For now, I'm going to concentrate on one immortal who has a special interest in you. She shares her Wakan jealously, so you must be careful to balance it."

Gifted Tongue shivered at the thought.

"This immortal is Double Woman. She's the daughter of First Man and First Woman who lived Below. She was the most beautiful woman anyone ever saw, so beautiful that Wind fell in love with her. He persuaded First Man and Woman to give him their daughter even though Wind was a god. Wind and Double Woman lived happily and had four children, but then Double Woman grew bored.

"Another god conspired with her parents. He promised that if they helped, Day would marry Double Woman, even though she was pregnant with her fifth child. The affair shamed Night terribly, and she appealed to Sky. He judged the gods and immortals."

"Is the Sun at the Center of the World equated with Sky?" Gifted Tongue asked earnestly.

"A good question, my child. Once we get to the Center of the World you will find that the Sun's relatives try to connect them, but the Suns are mere mortals. They control human lives but not the gods nor the immortals."

She listened closely to this introduction to Dhegiha politics and religion.

"Sky decided to send Double Woman to the earth's surface where we live now. He made one side of her face ugly while the other side remained beautiful. Some people believe the two faces are on opposite sides of her head, others that they are left and right sides. I believe that one face is internal, the other external.

"Double Woman came to the earth's surface with extraordinary powers. She seduced men with her beauty, and caused problems for pregnant women, even the deaths of their infants. Double Woman also clouded peoples' minds. For herself and persons she selects, she gives a tremendous power of concentration. So if Double Woman chooses you as an immortal's mortal, she grants you these powers. When you find such power, use it for good."

Gifted Tongue churned the drama in her mind, conscious from the beginning of her own appearance. She wondered if her scars suggested a Double Woman connection to Whirlwind, or if she truly possessed the spirit powers he described.

He apparently guessed what the girl was thinking because he said, "Remember that I believe the two faces of Double Woman are internal and external. I have known beautiful women on the outside who were unbearably ugly inside. They were slothful, jealous, and eager to seduce men. On the other hand, I have met homely women who work hard, are cheerful, and help others. They would never cheat their husbands. These women are beautiful. A thoughtful man quickly discovers the internal beauty."

Gifted Tongue's awe of Whirlwind's knowledge made her hesitant to ask further questions. His sincerity made her doubt that he simply wanted her to forget her scarred face. She imagined that she could be beautiful if she developed the inner qualities that people admired.

She had concentrated so hard on his lesson that she almost overlooked the river's change of course. Their southeast drift had shifted due north. The change was so unusual, it awed her, and she asked Whirlwind about it with alarm. He smiled and said, "The river is reluctant to reach the southern ocean. It turns back because it wants to return home." He grinned mischievously, then smiled sympathetically and said, "Don't you want to go home sometimes?"

"I miss my father and mothers. I'd love to be going home, but I think owl revealed a different destiny for me."

"At least for now, my child, your destiny is with the Sun. But your powers don't say you must stay at the Center of the World forever."

"But shouldn't I remain with my husband?"

"You can't know the future. Many things can happen. Your husband travels. He may take you home someday."

Gifted Tongue thought for a moment, then said, "But the river can't return to its source, can it?"

"No, my child. It makes a large bend northward before dropping straight south to form a peninsula on the west bank. When travelers are rushed, they portage here to save a few days. I'll show you where they come out on the other side when we get there. But Tied to Sun is in no hurry so we'll stay with the river." He paused and said considerately, "In less than a moon, you'll master Dhegiha. You do have a gifted tongue."

.   .   .

Gifted Tongue sensed the anticipation that surrounded the Dhegiha paddlers when they stretched with extra effort. She looked over to Whirlwind to find him scrutinizing the shoreline.

"What is it, grandrelative?" she said, after looking at the shoreline herself.

"We're nearing home, my child. We'll soon reach Dakota

Post, a town north of the city. It controls the upper reaches of the bottomlands. Our Sun says the bottoms are the richest farm fields in the world. Quapaw Post guards the southern end. Sun tells us we are one happy family, but he pits the leader of the northern outpost against the southern leader. He encourages the two to compete for his favor."

"I've seen husbands do that with their wives, but I've never known it among leaders," Gifted Tongue said.

"Politics at the Center of the World differ from everywhere else. Other peoples treat each other as equals, and they respect each other. Here the exalted clans are thought to be above everyone else. The Sun is the supreme leader of the Falcon clan, the most exalted one. The Bear and Turtle clans are also exalted, but not as much as the Falcons. Their members call themselves nobles. Your husband is one of the nobility."

"What do you think of the nobility, grandrelative?"

"Do you mean, what do I think of Tied to Sun, child?"

She dropped her head in embarrassment at the ease with which he saw through her question.

"There are good and bad nobles, as among the commoners. I will not comment on the Sun and his clan."

Gifted Tongue noted that he had not commented on Tied To Sun either. Before she could ask about him again, the paddlers doubled their efforts as the canoes shot into the Mississippi River. She gasped at the sight of so much water.

Whirlwind smiled gently and said, "We call this river the father of waters. I've never seen so much water come together anyplace else in the world."

The sight of the two rivers joining held Gifted Tongue's breath. The paddlers stroked with even more effort, and the canoes shot across the broad expanse to dart into a small stream of quiet water. Whirlwind explained that the canal they entered was a natural slough, but the workers of Dakota outpost had deepened it. Moments later, she saw a high hill rising from the expanse of flat river bottom. Smaller hills flanked it. She asked him how the hills got into a river bottom.

He grinned and said, "The people of the Sun think the gods will notice them better if their temples are on top of mounds. They hold major rites on the highest mound. The priests prepare the Honored Dead in houses built on the smaller mounds."

"But it must take so much work, grandrelative. Why do their gods demand so much?"

"I'm not sure I understand the gods. The priests don't want the commoners to know everything. They certainly don't share knowledge with shamans such as I."

When Whirlwind beached their canoe at Dakota Post, Weasel ran from his canoe to tell Gifted Tongue that her husband wanted her to help unload and to remain at the shore where he could find her. She asked Weasel if she could help her husband, but he turned his back on her to shout orders at the bearers.

Whirlwind said to her, "Tied to Sun does not want Next to Sun to see him with a new wife nor with me." He added with a sly laugh, "Wives are a sore point between them, and shamans are never in favor with the Sun and his lieutenants. You should know that the leader of Quapaw Post, the southern town, is also called Next to Sun to remind them that they are in line to secede Sun when he dies. How could they help but cut each others' throats, even if they are supposed to act like brothers?"

"Why does my husband go to see Next to Sun?"

"He will present him with obsidian wrapped in a Mandan bison robe. It must kill him to be generous with this Next to

Sun." Before Whirlwind could elaborate, they saw Tied to Sun and his party return. As Tied to Sun approached, he smiled. "Next to Sun visits the Center of the World. I left my gifts without seeing him. The Long Nosed God smiles on me." To Whirlwind, he said, "I am sure you instructed my Kutenai wife well, my friend. I will share a canoe with her now to show her the wonders of the Center. Do not be a stranger in my house."

"You are generous, my lord. May the Long Nosed God continue to watch over you. Send for me whenever I can help you or your Kutenai wife. She is a fast learner."

Gifted Tongue's heart skipped a beat when Whirlwind left. She didn't know when she would see him again.

Tied to Sun's party paddled back to the Mississippi, but soon turned into another canal that wound toward mounds much higher than those at Dakota outpost. On the highest mound an awesome temple reigned over the floodplain. Tied to Sun called it the pyramid of the sun, and explained that the mortal Sun resided in the large temple atop the pyramid. He brimmed with enthusiasm when they approached stretches of posts connected at the top by poles with branches laid on them for shade.

"You see all the ramadas," he said with pride. "They are only one of many places where the Dhegiha trade with the world. Of course, much trade is among local clans, but the ramadas remind me that here is where the Center of the World facilitates world-wide trade." Gifted Tongue guessed at the meaning of "facilitate," wondering why her husband always needed to use a pretentious word in his speech.

"It's a good time to initiate you into the intricacies of our trade center. The commoners will have brought food and pottery, and most of the artisans will be here to display their work. This time of year, foreign exchange parties often arrive. They'll bring exciting gifts to Dhegiha friends, but we always give more than we receive because we're the Center of the World."

The crowd of people at the exchange disturbed Gifted Tongue. They crowded together as tightly as Mandan in a ceremonial lodge, but here, no ritual demanded attendance. Instead, hundreds of voices drowned out talk. It was a crowd of chaos. She wished to leave, but Tied to Sun insisted that she see the variety of beans available so early in the summer. He delighted even more in showing her the work of artisans.

"Consider these rounded red pots. Remember the gourds I showed you? The potters have copied their shape. Travelers gladly accept these pots, even though they break easily. Look at this stone-work. Imagine the skill it took to sculpt a woman kneeling on a rattlesnake. Look at the gourd vine curl up her back. The piece portrays a legend about the squash goddess."

The carving amazed Gifted Tongue. She couldn't imagine how people could work stone in such detail, nor why they would take such trouble. After she saw dozens of other rock carvings, her awe faded. Tied to Sun touched her arm. She warmed to his hand, but then realized he only wanted to show her another ramada.

"Not much here in mica," he said. "Remember my mica gifts to the Kutenai? I gave away some of the best work that mica artisans ever achieved." Tied to Sun's enthusiasm revealed his love of travel and trade. She wondered what her future would be like with a man so obsessed with the pursuit of wealth.

As they returned to their canoes, she noticed the dense cloud of smoke that hung over the city. Acrid fumes struck her nose. She asked Tied to Sun what was burning. "It's only the cook fires," he said, trying to dismiss the nuisance. "A little wind clears it out quickly."

He led her back to the shore where Weasel watched over two canoes while the rest of the party dispersed for their homes. Tied to Sun directed her to the bow, while he kneeled at the stern to show off more of the city.

"See how the pyramid of the sun catches the rays of the setting sun. The sun reaches out to touch its earthly cousin."

Gifted Tongue blinked. The sun sparkled on reddish earth plastered to a small wall at the top of the hill. A thatched building, larger than any she had ever seen, towered over the mound. From the tone in Tied to Sun's voice, she assumed that the scene demanded awe. She noted its importance to her husband, but she could only wonder why anyone would work so hard to prepare a ritual site. It must have taken years, she thought, or even generations.

"It's amazing how it catches the sunlight, my Kutenai husband. Is it a dance lodge?"

"No, the Sun resides in it," Tied to Sun explained impatiently. "The priests dance in the plaza before the temple. They also have vital rites to perform there on occasion."

"Isn't it a chore for the Sun to climb that hill? Why doesn't he live at the bottom?" Gifted Tongue asked innocently.

Tied to Sun shook his head in disgust. "You have learned so little. I thought Whirlwind would have taught you better. It's not a hill but a pyramid. People built it. Servants bring the Sun whatever he needs. He seldom descends except to visit nobles who live within the stockade walls, on exalted land. He hunts when he wants to, but mostly he communes with the gods."

"Then he commands much Wakan?" Gifted Tongue asked.

"No. Well, not exactly. We believe supernatural power is something like Wakan so we use the word for the benefit of commoners. That way they better understand the true religion.

What the Sun controls is the power of the sun, all its force. It's that force, not Wakan, that keeps everything in balance," Tied to Sun said. "I'm surprised Whirlwind didn't explain that much."

"If Whirlwind only controls Wakan and not the sun, why do you admire him so?" she asked astutely.

Tied to Sun's frown showed irritation. "He's especially perceptive, very wise for his years. He visits and learns from all over the world. Don't ask so many questions."

She remained silent while he stroked hard toward a dock east of the pyramid. Beyond the docking area, she saw a row of upright tree trunks set together in a line stretching south beyond her view.

She couldn't contain her curiosity. "Why have people put all those trees in the ground?"

"That's the stockade that separates nobility from commoners. I live near those homes ahead. Outside the stockade there are four wards. The northeast ward is called Omaha. That's where you'll live. The southeast ward is Ponca. Osage live in the southwest ward, the Kansa in the northwest.

Did Tied to Sun mean the stockade would separate them? Gifted Tongue wondered. On the journey downriver, the two had usually shared a bed although Tied to Sun remained withdrawn.

"I reside within the stockade, my Kutenai wife, with my noble wife. You will reside with my commoner wife who will teach you Dhegiha custom. Especially how to farm. You won't have to work as hard as most commoners, but I know you won't want to be idle. We supply the Sun with food, as well as ourselves, and he sustains the priests. In times of trouble he feeds everyone."

Gifted Tongue shrewdly guessed that Tied to Sun did not include himself in the "we" that did the farming.

"You may salute my noble wife later," he said. Gifted Tongue wondered if her husband meant she had to show special respect with a gesture, or why he chose a more abstract word than greet.

He continued, "Her name is Roaring Woman because she was born during a storm. Pay no attention to the jokes about how she tries to live up to her name. You won't associate with her often. You'll like Rising Moon. She's not much older than you, a Dhegiha commoner. Her father persuaded me to marry her. He does excellent mica work. I was glad to favor him, even if his daughter is a commoner."

Gifted Tongue sucked in her breath at her uncertain future. What if she couldn't stand her co-wife? she thought. What if the woman hated her? Where could she turn? Certainly not to Tied to Sun. She thought worriedly of Whirlwind and wondered where he had gone.

Tied to Sun pointed forward with his chin and stepped ahead to lead her along the outside of the stockade wall. Clusters of tall, thatched houses reached upward. She wondered where people found enough grass for the steep-roofed buildings. They seemed like high piles of grass until she noticed short side walls that looked built of mud. On a few houses, patches of horizontal sticks peeped through, and she saw that the walls were woven of branches and then plastered with earth. She couldn't understand why the doors were so small. The insides must be darker than Mandan earth lodges. Already, she missed the openness of her Shoshoni shelters.

Her nose filled with countless odors. The smoke of cooking fires overrode everything, but an occasional waft of stew delighted her. More often, her nose rebelled at what she later learned was called trash, something she had never smelled before.

She almost ran into Tied to Sun when he halted because she was trying to memorize the maze of paths from the canoe dock. "Here is your new home, woman. I've outfitted it well, for a commoner family," he said haughtily. "Here is your co-wife."

Gifted Tongue's first impression of Rising Moon allayed her fears. A pleasant smile beamed from a friendly round face. Her eyes sparkled, especially when Tied to Sun turned to her to say, "My Dhegiha wife, I bring a Kutenai woman to help you. I intend to make her my servant wife. She is accomplished in languages and will travel with me. While I am here, she'll assist you in the fields. She's from savage country where they know nothing about farming. She learned a little from the Mandan savages, but we stayed with them during the winter so she never farmed. Where can she sleep?"

"The corncrib is empty enough for a bed. Will you visit her often, my lord?"

"The second house with the corn will do nicely. See that she's comfortable, woman. I must spend tonight with Roaring Woman. Then I'll be here. You know how much we want a child." Gifted Tongue's mind raced at Tied to Sun's announcement. Wouldn't he want a child by her? she thought. All Shoshoni or Kutenai wanted children, but it sounded as if her husband didn't have any. She wondered why he hadn't mentioned such a detail.

She hesitated as second thoughts struck. Among Shoshoni, Rising Moon's children would be her children as well, and the children she bore would be sons and daughters of Rising Moon. But she hadn't learned if that was Dhegiha custom, and she was afraid to ask this stranger who would be her co-wife.

She took a second look at Rising Moon. She had to look up at the slim woman with such pleasant features. Her wide grin accented her moon-like face, broken by sharp cheek bones. She wondered if her looks had anything to do with her name.

A plain, wrap-around skirt complemented a light cloth mantle printed with pale yellow and black designs that barely covered Rising Moon's well-formed breasts. Gifted Tongue guessed her co-wife to be three or four years older than she. What appeared to be four vertical lines of paint running from lips to chin proved to be tattoos upon closer examination.

She felt Rising Moon appraise her. She noticed that her eyes rested only briefly on the scars, and she wondered how much they repelled her. Probably, she felt no need to be jealous because their husband must be equally repelled. What Gifted Tongue couldn't know was that Rising Moon sensed Gifted Tongue's warmth and inner beauty but suspected Tied to Sun might not detect it.

So Rising Moon welcomed the strong, young back to help her in the fields, keep her company, and care for whatever children they had. When she said they would both be mothers to their offspring, Gifted Tongue sighed in relief to know the Dhegiha followed Kutenai and Shoshoni custom.

"Let me show you the second house," Rising Moon said on a cheerful note. "We have used it for storage, but it's much like this one. Is this how you built houses among your people?"

"I grew up a Shoshoni, in the desert. We moved often so our homes were windbreaks. Then my father gave me to a Kutenai chief to marry, but he still mourned. Before we could marry, Tied To Sun came along, and I was given to him. We had a Kutenai wedding. He said we would have a Dhegiha marriage here."

"Has he said anything about having children, about how important children are to him?"

"He's told me almost nothing about himself, and he did nothing to make me pregnant. I'd like to be, but my face disgusts him." Gifted Tongue brushed her hair over her scars. "The shaman, Whirlwind, came with us from the Mandan village where we wintered. He taught me a little about Dhegiha beliefs, but I feel as if I don't know the first thing."

Gifted Tongue's frankness and vulnerability seemed to move Rising Moon. She put her arm around Gifted Tongue's shoulder and touched her scars lightly. "You're attractive enough, never doubt it. Let's call each other sister, at least until you've had a Dhegiha wedding. Even then we can use the sister term because men may marry sisters."

"You make me feel at home. I'll help you any way I can."

"We'll worry about work tomorrow. You must have endless questions. What do you want to know about the Center of the World?" Rising Moon said as she took Gifted Tongue's hand, and they sat beside the cook fire.

Gifted Tongue did not know where to start, but then she thought of Whirlwind. "Do you know what ward Whirlwind lives in or anything else about him?"

"I don't think I know him."

Gifted Tongue thought Rising Moon tested her. She couldn't believe that the Dhegiha wouldn't know each other. Then as she considered that tens of thousands of people lived here, she realized that some of one's own people could be strangers. How unbearable, she shuddered.

She explained to Rising Moon, "Whirlwind has white hair even though he's only forty years or so. His vision swept him all over the world, an experience so terrifying it turned his hair gray."

"Oh yes, I've heard of him. Is he a berdache?"

"Yes. We talked for days in the canoe. At times he seemed like a sister, but mostly a kind teacher." She hesitated to delve into what she had learned of Double Woman, and Rising Moon changed the subject.

"Did he tell you about our husband and the nobility?"

"Very little, except that he is a lord and Whirlwind a commoner. I don't understand what a lord is. Tied to Sun told me how the city divides into wards. I think he called them Omaha, Osage, and Ponca. I forget the fourth."

"Kansa. Also remember Dakota, Quapaw, and the Chiwere Posts. Did he tell you about them?"

"We stopped at Dakota Post. He left presents for Next to Sun. He explained another Next to Sun ruled at Quapaw Post south of the city. I don't remember Chiwere. Where is it?"

"The Chiwere live in western towns on the other side of the Mississippi. They are like younger brothers of the Sun, distant brothers. The Chiwere speak with an odd accent. Sometimes I can hardly understand them."

"So much to remember," Gifted Tongue sighed. "I hope you'll be patient with me," she said ruefully.

Rising Moon's warm smile promised compassion as well as patience. She described more of their husband's background.

"Tied to Sun's father was an influential noble of the Bear clan. The Sun valued his advice so much, he gave him his choice of wives. His father chose a commoner, and her first child was Tied to Sun. Usually the exalted clans exchange sisters in marriage, but sometimes they honor a commoner clan by marrying one of their women."

Rising Moon hesitated, but Gifted Tongue asked her to continue. "Falcon men have to take wives from the Turtles and Bears. The women of their own clan are their sisters. They get the best women, so the nobles among the Bears and Turtles often seek women from the commoner clans. Marriage ties make up a lot of the city's politics."

Gifted Tongue looked puzzled. Rising Moon waited patiently, until she asked, "I understand that people must marry outside their clans, like the Mandan do, but I don't understand exalted clans. What are they?"

"My father wondered if exalted clans were truly a Dhegiha custom," Rising Moon continued. "He believed the Muskoki added them to our legends when they came from the southeast to settle among us. Tradition says the Dhegiha could not grow enough food and fought among themselves. The Muskoki introduced corn and brought peace. So the Dhegiha accepted their clans, the Bears and Turtles, as exalted. They became the nobility. The Falcons say they were always Dhegiha, but my father believed they were Muskoki, too. The eldest Falcon becomes the Sun. What my father couldn't understand was, why do the people of the exalted clans speak Dhegiha as well as anyone."

"How little I understand," Gifted Tongue said. "The idea of lords or a Sun is so new to me. All Shoshoni and Kutenai are equals. If a Mandan acquired more wealth than others, he gave it to the poor. People suspect a rich person is a witch."

"We commoners are like that. We don't accumulate wealth because the nobility takes any surplus. The Sun stores food to give to the poor in bad times, and he hosts foreign visitors who bring more wealth. So we're glad to support the Sun. But commoners resent the nobility because they do nothing for society. Our husband is better than most. His expeditions support the Sun at least, but his noble wife is worthless."

"Why did he marry her?" Gifted Tongue asked innocently.

"He was being too clever. When Tied to Sun was young, he

persuaded his father to give his daughter to Next to Sun at Dakota Post. Tied to Sun's sister was beautiful. She wove and worked pottery as well as older women do. So Dakota Next to Sun made Tied to Sun an envoy to the world, but all his boasting annoyed Dakota Next to Sun. About that time, Quapaw Next to Sun gave one of his junior wives to Dakota Next to Sun. She was attractive when young, but she got fat and the fatter she got, the angrier she got. She made life so bad for her Dakota husband that he gave her to Tied to Sun."

"How did she dare nag a Next to Sun?" Gifted Tongue asked.

"Her father was much respected, like Tied to Sun's father. Indeed, they were friends so the families thought well of the marriage. Except for Tied to Sun. He suspects she's infertile, and she constantly reminds him of his commoner mother even if his mother's heritage isn't supposed to count. But people talk."

"And what is it they say?" Tied to Sun's question startled the two women. From his tone, he had listened to their gossip. She gasped, wondering what he would do. Rising Moon cringed, as if expecting a blow. But Tied to Sun apparently had more important business. He frowned in a no-nonsense manner and barked brusquely.

"Roaring Woman prepares a celebration for tonight. Both of you go to her home. Help her with whatever she needs."

"And the celebration, my lord," Rising Moon dared to ask, "what is the occasion?"

"I am going to marry Gifted Tongue. It's time she became a true Dhegiha wife, at least my servant wife."

CHAPTER SEVEN

Gifted Tongue paused under a rising sun that already made her perspire. She wiped her forehead. The heat would have been bearable if it were not for the moisture laden air that teemed with water as if Mother Earth pressed rain from her bosom. The sweat on her hands burned the blisters from long days of hoeing. Rising Moon had told her calluses would protect her hands, but they formed slowly. Meanwhile, the blisters bled.

"Just one more row before we quit, co-wife. How are your hands?" Genuine concern echoed in Rising Moon's voice.

"The sweat stings. It makes me forget my aching back."

Rising Moon raised an eyebrow at the complaint. Having grown up hoeing corn, she didn't understand her co-wife's inexperience. She hoed faster to finish the last row, but Gifted Tongue kept pace. As the two hoes flailed at the weeds, Gifted Tongue forced her mind to thoughts of the coming evening, when she would marry. She realized marriage would not end her drudgery, but at last she would have a husband, and an evening where people noticed her.

At the end of the row, Rising Moon smiled warmly to say, "Let's move more pots to my house so that yours won't look so much like a storage shed. Then we must report to Roaring Woman. She should be awake by now."

The two women joked while they cleared the second house. It remained crowded, but it looked more like a home.

"Come sister," Rising Moon laughed. "We have time to bathe. You must be presentable to Roaring Woman."

The two washed and started for the stockade. A tremor shook Gifted Tongue. She had heard endless reports of the woman's mean spirit. She dreaded the encounter, but she could do nothing except follow Rising Moon into the domain of the nobles. Roaring Woman's home loomed large. She needed the space. Not only was she large around, but she was even taller than Rising Moon. Gifted Tongue looked up at her submissively.

Roaring Woman talked down to Gifted Tongue. "My husband wants a proper arrangement, one befitting a servant wife." Gifted Tongue was startled to hear her lisp. She pronounced the s in servant as a th. "Take my garment." Gifted Tongue guessed the woman avoided the s in dress. "It may be a little large for you, child. Have you ever worn a woven garment before? I expect you're unfamiliar with cloth. You look completely befuddled. Don't you like it?"

"It's nice, co-wife. I'm glad you found it." Gifted Tongue hesitated because the dress was worn and dirty. The blue designs printed on the dress were faded, simple zigzags. A stain trumpeted the dress' long use.

The sorry state of the fabric distracted Gifted Tongue so much that Roaring Woman's bellow nearly floored her.

"Never call me co-wife. You are not my equal in any way. I

am Tied to Sun's wife to you," she thundered. "Don't ever forget it. And what don't you like about my dress?" Her speech was relentless, punctuated by her lisp. "Do you think you're too good for it? Don't you know your place, girl?"

Throwing the dress at Rising Moon, Roaring Woman shouted, "Take it in a little for your co-wife, woman, or let her dress in your old rags. You wear it when your child begins to show. Now get out," she yelled. "No, wait, return here at dark when you hear the drums. There's to be a marriage between exalted clans, and my husband will use the occasion to claim his servant wife."

Rising Moon nodded to acknowledge the dismissal. She touched Gifted Tongue's arm to signal they should leave. Once home, Rising Moon's soap and needle worked a miracle to make the old dress presentable, and Gifted Tongue glowed when she tried it on.

"You've made it like new," she exclaimed.

"It's your figure that makes the dress acceptable," Rising Moon said sincerely.

That evening, as the two young women entered a stockade gate, torchlights surrounding the pyramid of the sun entranced Gifted Tongue. In daylight, she continued to wonder about the sanity of a people who labored so hard to build a hill simply to raise the height of a lodge. But in torchlight, the temple loomed as an awesome symbol to validate the ritual of the plaza.

Gifted Tongue guessed that the four drum groups represented the directions and the wards. They competed with each other from the four sides of the plaza, yet cooperation infused the songs as one group followed where another group led. She felt a magic radiate over the plaza, and wondered if it stretched from the temple of the sun to the large conical mound and pyramid opposite it. She remembered that Rising Moon had told her the two mounds represented the sky and earth deities.

Dancers filled the plaza. Men engaged in vigorous solo performances to warm up. Gifted Tongue had never seen such colors and could not imagine where feathers of red, gold, and green came from. Women dancers, who encircled the warriors, rocked in a slow, steady leftward progression The designs of their dresses were dazzling blues and reds.

Despite the array of colors and multitude of dancers, the familiar rhythm drew Gifted Tongue into the outside circle. She danced halfway round, mesmerized by the drumbeat, before she missed Rising Moon. She decided to find her later. For the moment, she felt at home and happy to dance while contemplating her marriage ceremony.

A harsh hissing suddenly clouded her senses. Roaring Woman towered over her, doing little to repress her anger. In a bawling whisper, she said, "I told you never to forget your place, girl. That garment doesn't make you a noble. Only nobles and Suns dance here. When commoners are allowed in the plaza, it's only to watch their betters. Do you think you can teach me to dance?" She whispered so harshly that she spat whenever she lisped. Gifted Tongue feared to wipe the spittle away.

"Of course not, wife of Tied to Sun. I didn't know the custom. The drums were so enticing."

"What?" Roaring Woman shrieked when she heard enticing. Gifted Tongue could not know that her command of vocabulary dismayed Roaring Woman as much as her youthful grace.

"Get back to the bench with your co-wife and watch how nobles dance."

Gifted Tongue's tears clouded her view of the plaza while

she searched desperately for Rising Moon. Rising Moon found her in the crowd.

"I'm sorry co-wife. I should have realized you didn't know our customs. We're considered visitors here. We can only watch the games and dances. We commoner wives, after we have children, sometimes are invited to dance."

That prospect did little to soothe Gifted Tongue. She couldn't dance at her own wedding. A mean thought crossed her mind to alleviate the pain. Roaring Woman was so fat she must be awkward. She could laugh at her expense.

Gifted Tongue said, "Roaring Woman told me to watch her. Do you see her? I can't believe how crowded the plaza is."

"She's coming toward us now. She's a little taller than most women. See her?"

Gifted Tongue swallowed hard, her hurt unrelieved by the ridicule she anticipated. Other dancers, as well as spectators, admired Roaring Woman's grace. In years of practice, the woman had learned to take advantage of her size, emphasizing all the movements of her body with unusual style. Gifted Tongue's jaw dropped to see such poise.

Late in the evening, Tied to Sun materialized to lead Gifted Tongue to a terse wedding ceremony. The Bear clan elder recited the duties of a servant wife without mention of a husband's duty. Apparently, her reward was for her children to became full fledged Bears. The concluding parade of Bear glories failed to impress her.

Yet, marriage to Tied to Sun must be her destiny. Hadn't owl pointed the way east? she recalled. She longed for another visit from owl to confirm her destiny. She feared that her guardian might never find her in such strange surroundings.

She looked at Tied to Sun with affection and longed for a

sign of fondness. In the dark, she could not see any response. He touched her arm as they headed back, and her heart leaped. At home, he placed his hand on her shoulder and directed her into her house, but he turned and entered Rising Moon's. Gifted Tongue not only had failed to dance at her own wedding, but her husband went to bed with her only friend.

.   .   .

None of the following nights ever matched the misery of her wedding night. The backbreaking farm work helped Gifted Tongue forget some of its pain. A summer rain gave respite, and the moist soil was easier to hoe. Rising Moon took her to a patch of newly cleared land and showed her how to plant amaranth.

"We seldom have to weed it because it grows quickly. You'd think it difficult to harvest such small seeds, but it's easy to collect and takes no trouble to cook. It stores well, too."

It was the last easy task. A fierce heat wave baked the soil, and the two women made innumerable trips for mud to add to the barren hills where their corn and beans failed to sprout.

Rising Moon reminded Gifted Tongue to plant four beans in each of the four directions to replace what failed to grow. She spoke harshly, and Gifted Tongue wondered if Rising Moon blamed her for failing to follow the custom earlier.

She asked, "Shouldn't I plant four corn seeds, too?

Rising Moon answered impatiently, "It's only beans that our gods gave us. The corn came from foreigners. But Sister Bean will curl up the corn stalks, so the corn is useful besides helping fill the belly."

While the two women rested, they snacked on corn mush with leftover beans. Rising Moon apologized for being brusque, but she worried about a multitude of household chores delayed by the replanting. If the Dhegiha had been selected by the gods with gifts of food, Gifted Tongue wondered, why did they have to work so much harder than Shoshoni or Kutenai.

"We must weed a little more before we go back to grind corn," Rising Moon said. As they got up, two young rabbits scurried from a bean patch. Rising Moon threw a clod of dirt at them. "At least we're not bothered with such pests much anymore. The youngsters don't give them a chance."

The young rabbits gave Gifted Tongue the chance to ask about children, a subject she had avoided since her wedding night.

"When I was married, the clan elder told me I would be honored by bearing Tied to Sun's child. How will I ever receive such honor, when our husband always sleeps with you?"

"Do your people know it is the man's semen that causes a child to grow?"

"Yes," Gifted Tongue said hesitantly. "The mingling of the mother's blood and the father's semen makes the baby."

"I guess our beliefs aren't too different. Do you know a man has a limited amount of semen? He must preserve it to help the fetus grow."

"No, no one told me," Gifted Tongue said dubiously. "Neither the Kutenai nor Shoshoni believe that."

"It's our belief. Tied to Sun never slept with me at first because he used all his semen for Roaring Woman, but she hadn't gotten pregnant with her first husband either. I think a priest diagnosed her as sterile or else her tongue drove our husband from her bed." The two women laughed. "Whatever his reason, he came to me. So Roaring Woman hates me because children are so important to him. Once I give birth, he'll honor you next, I'm sure."

"You make me feel better," Gifted Tongue said, wiping away a tear. "Maybe it isn't that my ugliness repels him."

"You do not repel him. He speaks of you with pride. How intelligent you are, and how quickly you learn. Already you speak Dhegiha like one of us." Excitedly she said, "You should not be a virgin long. I have missed two periods so I may be pregnant. I guess Roaring Woman knows. That must be why she yelled at me to use your dress to cover my swollen stomach."

Gifted Tongue recalled Roaring Woman's vehemence with the dress. She had thought all the anger was directed at her. The wrath was one more thing that she and Rising Moon shared.

.   .   .

Tied to Sun showed his interest in Rising Moon's condition by giving her and Gifted Tongue a dress. Since he did not ask directly if Rising Moon was pregnant, she gave a vague answer that disappointed him.

He turned to Gifted Tongue. "See this solid blue border at the bottom, topped by a zigzagging red line?" he asked as he displayed the dress. "Everyone will know your husband is a noble because blue is nobility's color," he said arrogantly. "The red represents the Sun. His superiority shows by being above the blue. But we are the foundation."

"The dress is beautiful." Gifted Tongue asked demurely, "Can I wear it now?"

"Yes, you must," Tied to Sun commanded. "I have come to show you the city. You may enter the stockade when I accompany you," he said haughtily. "Your dress demonstrates your affinity with the nobility." His tone mixed pride with arrogance, as if he were about to display a prized possession.

"I'm slow to learn Dhegiha. What does affinity mean?"

"You are not slow, wife. And you can call me lordly husband now. Affinity means a tie of marriage. Our wedding married you to the Bear clan, not just to me. If I were to die, another Bear noble is entitled to you. Don't worry, though, I'm not about to die. We have many journeys ahead of us," he smiled.

"Now let us see the city. Rising Moon has kept you so busy you probably fail to appreciate the Center of the World."

He led her toward the stockade of vertical logs, about two persons' high, to pause at one of the many bastions that interspersed the wall. "The Sun who designed the first stockade lived generations ago. He used the bastions to display his grandeur. When visitors approached, they were greeted by singers at the top of each bastion. It must have been quite an experience for them to see such elegance."

"Then the stockade is not for protection?" Gifted Tongue said.

"Legends proclaim that the first Dhegiha built stockades for defense, but I doubt the necessity. Who would ever attack the Center of the World? The legend says that the first Sun negotiated peace throughout the valley so the stockade and plaza became a sanctuary for the exalted clans." Gifted Tongue tried to share her husband's interest, but she wondered if the laborers who slaved at such construction benefited in any way.

Inside the stockade, they neared the steps of the largest pyramid where he warned ominously, "Never set foot on the pyramid of the sun. In fact, avoid all mounds unless I'm with you. From here, you see only the peak of the temple because it's at the back of the pyramid. The ceremonial plaza in front is for priestly sacrifice and other ritual. Look at the Sun's emblem post, you can see its top," his voice blustered with enthusiasm for the city's glory. "It's the tallest in the city, really in the whole world. On clear days, Dakota Next to Sun sees it. It reminds everyone of the Sun's grandeur."

Gifted Tongue thought of how few clear days the city experienced. The smoke of morning fires competed with foggy haze to obscure the sky. Only a rainstorm ever cleared the haze to make the sky even close to the blue of her homeland. She had yet to see the clouds swell into the huge, fluffy giants of white that her imagination had once formed into endless shapes.

"Now turn around," Tied to Sun commanded. "You must have heard the drums at last night's dancing? The plaza seems mundane now without the drama. But see how well swept it is already. No trace of all the people who danced and dined here. The servants were up and working at dawn."

Gifted Tongue noted that the spaces around the nobles' homes within the stockade had been swept, then recalled the servants' homes outside the stockade. She had not visited other wards, but her neighbors buried their trash in shallow pits or partially burned it. Dogs ate what they found or dug up, but no one cleaned up after the dogs. She had to watch where she stepped amid an odor that bombarded her nose.

"In a few days, we'll have a lacrosse game there," Tied to Sun pointed at the plaza with his lips. "The Dhegiha nobles are matched with the Chiwere nobles. We've won the last three games, so the Chiwere will be out for blood. We'll take great pride in being victorious four games in a row."

"I'm anxious to watch, my lordly husband. I've never seen lacrosse. Will you play?"

Her interest appeared to please Tied to Sun, and he answered without second thought. "Commoners are not welcome at our lacrosse. Anyway you will be busy with Rising Moon. The corn demands much work this time of year."

Gifted Tongue thought the cursed city always required work, at least from the commoners.

Tied to Sun returned to his lecture. "See the two mounds at the south edge of the plaza? One so well squared, with a building, the other conical shaped. The conical one is a burial mound, for the most important people. The other is a charnel house, for the work of priests."

"What kind of work, my lordly husband?" The thought of noble priests working intrigued her.

"Most often, they prepare the bones of the dead. I know your people don't care about the dead, but here the corpses of the lesser Suns have to be properly buried. The body is kept for a year, the flesh removed, and the bones bundled. Every detail must be executed exactly. Only the Sun is buried as he dies because his body is too holy to be touched."

Gifted Tongue wondered how commoners were disposed of and what would happen to her body. She guessed her remains likely became part of the city's stench so she didn't ask.

Tied to Sun led her across the front of the pyramid to a gate in the western stockade. It opened onto the northwest ward which had its own temple mound and plaza.

"This is the Kansa ward. They're industrious and built a large platform mound for their doctor's society. Each ward has a doctor's society. They specialize in different practices so the wards depend on each other. The Kansa are known for curing open wounds. Of course, I see noble priests when I'm ill."

Gifted Tongue enjoyed good health so she had not thought of illness. Among her own people, someone like Whirlwind cured everything, but there could never be enough shamans for such a crowded population, she knew. With so many people so close together, endless witchcraft must sicken multitudes. She wondered how she could possibly survive.

"Be careful along here," Tied to Sun said. "People have dumped their trash without thinking. How can they live in such filth?" Tied to Sun's contempt contorted his face. The stench deepened the wrinkles around his nose. A long stretch of food scraps and excrement lined the path, and Tied to Sun hurried through it. At the edge of the ward, he pointed to a circle of widely spaced, upright logs.

"See these posts? Do you have any idea what they are?"

Gifted Tongue paused to let her husband speak, but for once he waited for an answer. "Are they the beginning of another stockade, my lordly husband?"

Tied to Sun's condescension bordered on contempt. "You still think like a savage, my servant wife. But then you have never been exposed to astronomy. Do you know the word?"

Gifted Tongue shook her head humbly.

"Astronomy is knowledge of how the sun and moon move through the sky. Commoners believe they chase each other across the blue dome and under the earth, or something like that. The nobility know that the sun comes north to generate our summer. As Mother Earth gets too hot, we send him south. He rests to rejuvenate his power, so he is again hot when we bring him north for the growing season."

Glancing around to see that no one watched, he hurried Gifted Tongue to the pole at the center of the circle. It stood within a ring of forty-eight vertical poles. Each was five persons' height tall and spaced about two persons' lengths apart.

"I'll keep details simple," Tied to Sun said, as if talking to a child. "If you were on the platform at the top of this observation pole, you'd sight over the east pole and see the sun rise above it on the equinox. Only our priests have ever determined such a point, an exact midpoint in the sun's cycle. It begins our year in the Deer Moon. Now count four poles to the north. When the sun rises over it, he is exactly as far north as he will go. It is the Moon of Little Corn. We harvest the first beans and squash and prepare for the Green Corn Ceremony."

Gifted Tongue saw that he watched her closely. The hot, muggy air stifled her mind, but she concentrated and looked attentive.

"We feast on the green corn the way Mandan feast on bison. The flint corn and flour corn are harvested in the Moon of the Grape followed by Mulberry Moon. When the sun starts back to his winter resting place and is exactly halfway there, we honor him in the Moon of Corn. Popcorn is a special treat. After that, our animal relatives take over, Moon of Turkey, then Moon of Bison follows. In the Moon of Bear, the sun reaches his winter rest at winter solstice."

Gifted Tongue tried hard to imagine why anyone took such interest in the course of the sun. The Shoshoni and Kutenai never did. Winter simply followed summer. It always had, and it always would. But she nodded vigorously and acted interested.

"What happens when the year ends, noble husband?"

"It's the cold meal month. People mix acorn meal with the last corn. The nobles consume the last of the dried meat or fish if their servants are reliable. Too many complain about the icy water. Has Rising Moon shown you how to fish? Maybe you can show her some Kutenai tricks." His question ended his lesson.

She appreciated the break and reviewed the Dhegiha year

before she spoke. "We haven't had time to fish, my lordly husband. Today is the first rest I've had from battling the weeds. The corn and beans grow well after the heat wave."

"Yes, the harvests promise to be bountiful." He boasted as if he had worked the fields. "The nobility will fill every storage bin. Then we can bestow more than usual on the Sun. It's a good year when the storage bins overflow."

Gifted Tongue bit her lip but could not contain her curiosity. "What does the Sun do with all that wealth?"

Tied to Sun frowned but apparently forgave his savage wife's impudence to question Dhegiha practice. "In theory, the Sun owns it all. In practice, he delegates its distribution to the Next to Suns for ceremonial feasts and to host our visitors. If we didn't overwhelm visitors with gifts, they would fail to bring us valuables to repay our hospitality." As an afterthought, he added, "Of course, the Sun must also support the commoners when they have been careless with their harvest. You see?"

Gifted Tongue did not admit that she failed to see the system made any sense. All the commoners she met worked as hard as she and Rising Moon, and she suspected they did not eat as well since Roaring Woman sent leftovers to Rising Moon. Gifted Tongue doubted that the commoners could be any more careful. Most of all, she wondered why the Suns and nobles were so obsessed with displays of wealth. They hoarded food only to give it to visitors who then returned gifts.

She sighed, thinking of all she had to learn.

Tied to Sun studied her perplexed look. She wondered if he guessed at her reservations about his way of life and the toll it exacted on the commoners.

If he had sensed any of her doubts, he must have dismissed them as he tossed his braids over his shoulders. "Let us leave the

Sun Circle. Even I don't understand all its complexity. We will proceed to Osage ward. You remember that they reside in the southeast. They haven't built an imposing mound nor even a decent plaza, but I have to admit, they are the best lacrosse players in the city, and so is their doctoring cult."

Sidestepping a bloody vomit, Tied to Sun said harshly, "Be careful here. Someone has been sick, and no one's cleaned it up. The dogs haven't touched it. These people can be filthy. You'd think they don't care that a noble might visit them."

Gifted Tongue tried to forget her husband's contempt for his own people, but wondered how she could spend a lifetime with him.

He took her arm to get her attention, then pointed with his chin to another mound. "You see that low mound and the building with the patched roof? It's the charnel house of the Omaha doctors. They are too independent. Oh, two or three cooperate with the priests, but they seldom prepare the bone burial bundles properly, and they shirk their responsibilities to the Sun. But what can we do?" he said disdainfully.

When Tied to Sun left Osage ward to pass directly south of the Sky and Earth mounds that marked the southern edge of the plaza, Gifted Tongue was struck by his change of attitude. Awe showed in his face, and he spoke in hushed tones as they neared a pole that was taller than the center post of the sun circle.

"Sun priests use this post to mark the sacred boundaries of the city. See how Sky mound lies directly on a line between the pole and the marker pole on the pyramid of the sun? Not long ago, Beloved Leader directed the engineer priests to mark off the sacred axis of his city. Before his reign, the pyramid of the sun faced west. Legends say it once faced east." Tied to Sun paused, as if overwhelmed by the memory.

He continued. "Remember this post is taboo," he harshly whispered. "So never touch it. During your period," he wrinkled his nose at the thought, "stay far away. Rising Moon will show you the eastern marker. It's taboo, too."

"Now see the ridge mound extending westward from this marker post? It doesn't look very impressive compared to other mounds I've shown you, but it's the burial mound of Beloved Leader and Beloved by Falcon. It is very holy. Never come near it when you menstruate." Tied to Sun's voice struck dread in Gifted Tongue. From the way he talked, she imagined running into the post by accident and being struck dead.

"I will tell you briefly about Beloved Leader," he said reverently. "He was the greatest Sun to ever live. Next to Suns never envied him. He cemented relations with the Chiwere, and extended our trade north and south." Tied to Sun puffed out his chest and said, "He inspired me to extend our influence up the Missouri, and one of these days I'll travel beyond Kutenai. Everyone respected Beloved Leader."

For a moment, he looked downcast. "When he died, many persons followed him in death. I was away on a journey, but Whirlwind witnessed the burial. Most commoners were excluded, of course, but while young, Whirlwind had been a kind of wife to Beloved Leader. Obviously, Sun couldn't honor Whirlwind with marriage, but the berdache served him out of love. He was still a youngster and hadn't experienced the vision which aged him, but even then, people knew he possessed extraordinary powers."

Mention of Whirlwind stirred a feeling of loneliness in Gifted Tongue, and she wondered if she would see him again. Tied to Sun apparently took her anxious look as a sign of boredom.

"I'll terminate our tour, servant wife, in the Ponca ward. Speaking of Whirlwind, we may run into him. He shares a home with his two co-wives, though he may be anywhere. The three are commoner wives to a noble. Technically, Whirlwind is married to a noble since the Sun's death, but he goes as he chooses."

After a brief walk eastward, he introduced her to the southeast quarter. "The Ponca take more pride in their neighborhood. It doesn't smell at all like the Osage."

Gifted Tongue wondered if her nose tricked her. The whole city swam in a sea of repulsive odor making her long for the cleanliness of the Kutenai. Even the smells in the close quarters of the Mandan village were preferable to those of the city. She wondered if Tied to Sun truly discerned a difference among the wards, or if his prejudice affected his perception. She knew it blinded him to the advantages of Kutenai custom.

"You see, the Ponca are ingenious and industrious. Part of a slough ran along the edge of their quarter. When the priests rebuilt Sky mound, the Ponca contributed their share of earth by extending the slough to the canal that leads to the Mississippi. Remember the ramada where I showed you all the trade goods? The Ponca can load their canoes here and paddle to that ramada."

Apparently, Tied to Sun remembered her distracted look and tried to regain her attention. "Look at those two boys fishing in the canal. Let's see how they're doing."

As they approached, Gifted Tongue saw a look of concern on the older one's face, as he studied Tied to Sun's clothing. Tied to Sun said in a condescending but reassuring way, "Go ahead with your work, boy. No need to honor me. I'm showing this foreigner the city. Have you caught many fish?"

The older boy left his brother with the net, and went to a

basket. He held up two small catfish. Gifted Tongue flinched at the sight. How could anyone eat them, she wondered, as she recalled the beauty of salmon and trout.

Tied to Sun laughed in an attempt to encourage the boys. "Keep up the good work. Those two will hardly flavor your stew. By the way, do you know Whirlwind's home?"

The older boy kept his eyes downcast as he replied, "He lives about fifty paces up the slough, my lord. I saw his co-wives earlier, but I did not see him. He was called to help a woman in labor."

Tied to Sun's forehead wrinkled in regret. "The boy seems certain about Whirlwind's absence. Too bad I've missed him. But he always appears when you need his help."

Gifted Tongue regretted his absence even more. She concentrated on landmarks at each turn of the trail to make sure she could find his house on her own.

·   ·   ·

Gifted Tongue often thought of Whirlwind the next few days as she and Rising Moon toiled in the humid fields to harvest the last of the crops. At the end of one particularly hot day, when the two were drenched in sweat, their skin raw and cut from picking squash, Rising Moon shrieked in pain.

Gifted Tongue rushed to her side and said in anguish, "What is it, sister?"

Rising Moon's contorted features showed as much pain as her shriek. She whimpered, "I'm not sure. It may be the baby."

Gifted Tongue pushed aside Rising Moon's dress. A stream of blood flowed from between her legs. The sight terrified Gifted Tongue who intuitively knew Rising Moon was aborting. She stood helpless, not knowing what to do. Then she recalled what

Whirlwind had told her of Double Woman power. It was dangerous for pregnant women. She had never thought of Rising Moon until now. It was all her fault, just as she had killed Twisted Rabbit she had now killed Rising Moon's baby.

Rising Moon screamed again, and begged for help. Gifted Tongue concentrated. She ran for a neighbor who brought warm water. Together they bathed her. Then Gifted Tongue knew she must find Whirlwind.

CHAPTER EIGHT

After the tedious day of work, Gifted Tongue still found the strength to scoop up Rising Moon and half carry, half drag her home. She cooled her co-wife's brow with water left from a hurried morning's meal and wiped at her thighs. When she found more than blood between her legs, she had no idea what to do. The discovery of the tissue horrified her. She felt her Double Woman's power had struck Rising Moon and caused her to abort.

She shook off the paralysis of terror. She must inform her husband although she knew that Whirlwind could help the most. She dashed for the stockade to tell Tied to Sun. Her dirty clothes and bloodstained arms announced her commoner status at the gate. A noblewoman shouted a warning, but she dashed to Roaring Woman's house.

"Rising Moon fell in the fields and bleeds from her womb. I carried her home, but I don't know what to do. Where can I find Tied to Sun?" she said breathlessly.

Roaring Woman scowled, despite the urgency in Gifted

Tongue's question. "He meets with a cleric of the Long Nosed God. You're not permitted near them. I'll go. Hurry back to your co-wife. Do nothing more until our, I mean, my husband arrives. He'll have a doctor." Roaring Woman threw a final insult as she hastened from the door. "Don't try any of your savage ways on her."

Her dash from the door showed the grace of her legs. Gifted Tongue welcomed her concern but guessed the woman worried more about the baby. What Gifted Tongue didn't see was Roaring Moon's deliberate walk once she disappeared behind a row of houses.

When Gifted Tongue returned, she found Rising Moon unconscious but writhing in pain. The neighbor crouched at her side, cooling her forehead, talking as if loss of the baby was more regrettable than her being near death. The harried woman complained she had to care for grandchildren. Gifted Tongue said a priest was on his way and begged her to stay. Before the thin, bowed woman could answer, Gifted Tongue sprinted in search of Whirlwind.

She remembered each turn and barged into his house. A woman looked up startled but sympathized with Gifted Tongue's concern and tried to calm her. She said Whirlwind would return soon and urged patience. She insisted that Gifted Tongue try some mush, but her dry throat refused the corn. Ages seemed to pass, yet the mush had barely cooled when Whirlwind appeared.

He sensed Gifted Tongue's distress, put a hand on her arm, and said, "What is it, my child? I've never seen you so distraught."

She answered in a sob, "It's Rising Moon's baby. We were working in the fields when she collapsed. She's bleeding between her legs. She's unconscious but suffers greatly. I carried her home. A neighbor is with her. I've told Roaring Woman. She told me to stay with Rising Moon and to do nothing. But I know you can help."

"It will not be easy." Whirlwind chewed on his lower lip. "In the city, Tied to Sun must employ a Long Nosed God priest. They claim to excel with problem pregnancies. They compete with the Water Monster Society of the commoners. At least the Water Monster doctors use common sense. The Long Nosed God people do nothing but pray and chant. I'll come tonight after the Long Nose leaves. Tied to Sun trusts me."

"I understand. Can you come and watch?" Gifted Tongue asked anxiously.

"I have a patient nearby. I'll visit him and tell you more on the way."

While the two hurried back, Whirlwind explained in hushed tones. "You should know that a few society doctors make people ill so they'll be hired to cure, but shamans never do that. People only reward us with whatever they can give."

"That's the Shoshoni way, too. Do you think someone deliberately harmed Rising Moon?" she said in fear.

"No, not since she's married to a noble. The doctors would know that Tied to Sun has to consult a Long Nosed God priest. Of course, some doctor might not know who her husband is." To calm Gifted Tongue, he added, "You don't have to worry about being shot by doctors. You're too poor to pay for a cure."

"What do you mean, shot?" Gifted Tongue said nervously.

"The Water Monster doctors have tiny, spirit arrows in their bellies. They spit these at a person, then suck them out."

"What if someone shot Rising Moon. How can you treat her?"

"I can suck out arrows. I can throw arrows, too, but shaman seldom resort to such tactics. Generally, I use plants that gave me knowledge of their power."

As they rounded a house, they saw Tied to Sun with a masked figure carrying a turtle shell rattle and an owl feather fan. Tied to Sun stooped to enter Rising Moon's hut.

Whirlwind whispered that his patient lived within earshot and departed. She watched Tied to Sun carry his wife from the hut. The priest wore a painted wooden mask highlighted by a hide cone nose stretching out an arm's length. It resembled a grotesque beak more than a nose. She thought it ludicrous, and wondered how her husband could have faith in such a figure.

The priest fanned Rising Moon and danced around her, muttering a dreary, low-pitched song. His slow pace accelerated as Rising Moon regained consciousness. Bewildered, she mumbled incoherently while the priest claimed that she was cured and concluded with a prayer.

Sun there on high, you are a god.
Show yourself on a seat.
So I pray of you.
Whatever I do, only good I desire.

Moon, there on high, have pity upon me.
A good road give to me.
Pity and help me.
Whatever I do, only good I desire.

Sky, Father above.
You are seated there.

I pray to you.
Whatever I do, only good I desire.

Earth there.
I pray to you, Mother.
Pity and help me.
Whatever I do, only good I desire.

Winds of four quarters.
A good road give to me.
I pray to you.
Whatever I do, only good I desire.

Rock, oh Grandfather.
Seated there.
Like you I desire to be.
Firmly seated to remain, I beg of you.

Long Nosed God.
Resting at the Center of the World.
Pity and help the priesthood.
Protect us from arrows, I beg of you.

Judging from Tied to Sun's lack of composure, Gifted Tongue suspected that he knew Rising Moon still suffered. He said to her anxiously, "How are you feeling, my wife? Where does it hurt?"

Gifted Tongue was touched by his tenderness and concern, a side she had not seen before. She whispered to him, "Do you understand what she says, my lordly husband?"

"I thought she recognized me, but her answers are incoherent. I'm not sure she's conscious, despite what the priest said. He didn't say anything about the baby."

Gifted Tongue tried to cheer him. "I did not know what to do except tell Roaring Woman. I found Whirlwind, too. He returned with me. Perhaps he can help?"

"You did the right thing, my wife. I want him here. Did he tell you why he didn't come immediately?"

Despite the circumstances, her heart fluttered at his unqualified use of the term my wife.

"He said as a noble that you shouldn't be seen using a shaman."

"Good. You understand. Now get him."

Whirlwind appeared before she could leave. "I want to help, my lord. If you desire it."

"You know I do, friend. A Long Nosed priest danced and prayed. He helped a little, but I trust you to do more."

"From what your servant wife told me, someone may have shot an arrow into her, but it makes no sense. Let me examine her."

Whirlwind sucked all over Rising Moon's stomach, exploring her insides. Shaking his head, he said he found nothing. But his ministrations lulled Rising Moon into a deep sleep.

"What are we to do?" Gifted Tongue said desperately to Whirlwind, forgetting that it was her husband's place to ask.

Tied to Sun ignored her concern. To Whirlwind, he said, "Do whatever you can, my friend. If you save the baby, whatever I have is yours." With that, he rose and curtly left.

Gifted Tongue thought surely her husband must be equally concerned for his wife, but then realized that the hope of offspring sprang foremost in his mind. Whirlwind's frown showed the disgust he felt for Tied to Sun's obsession with a child. He shook his head and said to her, "I'll never understand the ways of the exalted clans."

He then questioned her, "Before you went to the fields, child, what were you eating?"

"We warmed up leftover corn and beans. We drank corn-meal mixed with water. A few sunflower and squash seeds. Everything was fresh, nothing spoiled."

"Are you certain all the food was fresh?"

"Oh, yes, Rising Moon never keeps food long. She's been especially careful since she became pregnant."

"Did you eat anything in the fields? Something a worker gave you?" Whirlwind watched her intently.

"Several days ago a neighbor shared dried squash and sun-flowers," Gifted Tongue recalled.

"Did she eat with you?"

"Yes, I remember a joke she told us. I didn't get the point until Rising Moon explained it."

"Think hard, grandrelative. The day before or the day that Rising Moon fell ill. Did you eat anything unusual?"

"No. Well, Roaring Woman sent venison stew that tasted odd, but I think it was fresh. She sent a lot."

"Is any left?"

"No, we were so hungry we ate it all."

Whirlwind raised Rising Moon's head to smell her breath, even reaching a finger into her mouth, and then tasting it.

Gifted Tongue recoiled in horror as she recognized what Whirlwind suspected. Rising Moon might have been poisoned.

"Do you think it's poison, grandrelative? Rising Moon told me Roaring Woman hated her. She must want me dead, too."

"We can't know for certain. I don't know why she would

want you dead. You and Rising Moon work so hard you're invaluable. If she poisoned the venison, why aren't you ill? I must consult with an old woman specialist. For now, use these herbs to protect Rising Moon. Boil the roots, mix in the leaves, and feed her the broth. I'll return this evening. I'll assure Tied to Sun that his wife is all right, but she has aborted."

Gifted Tongue felt better after Whirlwind's reassurance. She napped while the roots boiled. When Rising Moon stirred, she fed her the broth. Rising Moon went back to sleep free of fever, while Gifted Tongue dozed. Double Woman appeared in a dream to pounce on pregnant women. Gifted Tongue woke in a cold sweat, certain she had caused Rising Moon's abortion.

.   .   .

Gifted Tongue fed Rising Moon more of the potion, along with squash blossom soup. The blossoms were a treasure so late in the summer. She was indebted to neighbors who had diligently searched for them.

While Rising Moon dozed, her anxiety grew about Double Woman's power. She had failed to take precautions during her co-wife's pregnancy. What a fool she had been, she thought bitterly. But then she remembered that Whirlwind suspected poison. Perhaps Double Woman power had not caused the abortion. Or did it? She worried anxiously. She fretted that Whirlwind might have deceived her about the poison, knowing Double Woman power had caused it.

Her doubts persisted until Whirlwind arrived at dark. She gave him barely time to examine his patient before besieging him with questions.

"How is she, grandrelative? She had no fever all day, but she is so pale. Will she ever recover? Did my Double Woman power strike her?" Before Whirlwind could allay her fears, she resumed her litany of blame. "It can't be poison. I never felt the least bit ill. Anyway, you said it didn't make sense for Roaring Women to poison us. It must be my fault. I forgot all about how I might harm Rising Moon. What can I do?"

Since Rising Moon slept, Whirlwind had time to explain. "You must understand more about Dhegiha religion," he said patiently. "Double Woman is influential but is only a small part of the supernatural. She's one of many immortals. She helps you become part of us. Other aspects of our religion make little sense because the exalted clans have distorted them to exaggerate their importance, like that prayer of the Long Nosed priest. It's a good Dhegiha prayer, except for the last verse," he said with contempt.

"You must understand our origins, and you'll see that Double Woman isn't as powerful as you imagine. Let us begin at the beginning." Whirlwind took Gifted Tongue's hands in his, and they sat down next to Rising Moon's bed.

"Before time existed, Rock floated in a mist. Nothing had form. Being lonely, Rock created Earth from its own blood. It turned into Earth, but Rock allowed a little to flow as rivers to give Earth her necklaces. By losing blood, Rock became solid and steady. We must be steadfast, too, in our relations with everything. Roaring Woman should relate steadily to her co-wives, but she forgets." He smiled ruefully.

"Earth begged Rock to give her a companion. Rock created Sky, a blue dome stretched over Earth. It was dark. Earth could not see Sky. So Rock divided darkness to make night and day. That's when time began."

Whirlwind smiled at Gifted Tongue's rapt attention and

spoke softly. "Earth was happy with Sky. The two were opposites the way man and woman are but complemented each other as husband and wife. Out of opposition came integration. The two were one.

"Earth next experienced cold and hunger. Rock tired of her complaints and designated Sky as decision maker. He told Earth to do without food, but he made Sun to warm her."

When Whirlwind paused, she said, "Is this sun related to our ruler, the Sun?"

"The Muskoki emphasize the sun's life-giving power. They want to associate their human Sun with such power, and claim his priests enhance his ability. The nobles exaggerate how Rock gave Sky the power to make decisions."

Whirlwind touched her cheek as he looked into her eyes. "You're a good student, grandrelative. Are you ready for more?"

Gifted Tongue nodded eagerly, and he continued. "Sun was the fourth god. His heat warmed Earth but burned her. She begged Sky to pity her. Even the gods humbly beg when they want something. Always tell the gods how miserable you are so they will pity you." She smiled that she understood.

"Sky directed Sun to move across the dome and go under Earth to make night cool. Sun divided to become moon as well. Moon was female, and now they chase each other around Earth. They are opposites but the same, like husband and wife." Whirlwind paused to see if she comprehended. Her smile told him she did.

"The four major gods-Rock, Earth, Sky and Sun-Moon-are all aspects of one god. They all originated from Rock." He raised his voice for emphasis. "Likewise, humans are related to the animals, plants, stars, and rivers.

"Sky ranked the gods. Sun is highest because he is above the dome. His color is red. Sky is second highest with blue."

"Is that why the nobles use designs of blue?" she asked.

"A good question. The priests emphasize that the Sun god outranks Sky when they relate our origins. Sun gave Earth the color green and ranked her third. Rock was lowest with yellow, but remember that Rock was the source of everything." His voice rang with conviction as he emphasized, "Steadiness is the universe's foundation."

Gifted Tongue suddenly remembered Rising Moon, and wondered if she had been unsteady in her concern. She studied her co-wife and saw she slept soundly. Whirlwind looked, too, before he said, "The four gods created lesser gods for companions. Sky created Wind. Like himself, Wind was formless. He became a messenger, traveling all over the world. Another companion was Whirlwind who swirls up passions of love and travels endlessly."

He smiled. "As you probably learned, child, I received his name because Whirlwind carried me on my journey of knowledge."

He hesitated, apparently lost in memory, then continued. "Sky prepared a feast to teach the gods generosity. Wind and Sky created the plants and animals with the help of Earth. They created flowers that are the colors of the gods—red, blue, and yellow. The flowers gave seeds and fruits. Amaranth, beans, and squash were first, along with nuts and berries. Sky also created animals to eat. Everyone enjoyed the feast so much that generosity and sharing became virtues."

Whirlwind looked at the blisters on her hands and said, "Your hard work proves not only your generosity but also Earth's. It means Tied to Sun can store food to help others."

He must have seen Gifted Tongue's head nod. He spoke quickly. "Let me tie this explanation to Double Woman."

Reference to Double Woman woke her.

"Wind carried a message to the underground animal people. They were large and had four legs, but down there, they were the first people."

"You mean like gods?"

"Not to worship, but to respect. These people were our equals. They never pretended to be better than others."

He shifted his weight and stretched a leg. "First Man and First Woman had a beautiful daughter."

"The one who became Double Woman?" she said alertly.

"Yes, you remember well. Wind fell in love with her, and they had four children. Children from a god and a mortal are neither divine nor human, but demigods. They became the four directions. Location came to be.

"Because Earth was jealous of Double Woman, she conspired with other demigods to go to the earth's surface. When Double Woman and the others went above ground, they had to grow their own food and hunt. That is why Earth is our mother. She gave us our food."

His brow furrowed, and he said thoughtfully, "My ancestors explained Creation as I have. The Muskoki priests started with the story but added to it to exaggerate their importance. So people disagree on the long ago. Listen, child, to whatever wise people tell you. You must decide what is right and wrong. Don't trust anyone who claims to have the last word."

Despite her exhaustion, she said, "You say Double Woman is human but she lived so long ago she would be dead. How can she still influence people?"

"Recall that she was the daughter of First People. They live forever in spirit. Double Woman gave birth to the four wind spirits so she reaches wherever the winds blow." As if in response to her fear, he put his hand on hers. "Do not fear her. Her presence will help you do good. You intended no evil for Rising Moon so Double Woman did no harm."

Whirlwind's sincerity, more than his words, convinced Gifted Tongue of her innocence. She lay down alongside Rising Moon and slept soundly.

. . .

More than a moon had passed since Rising Moon collapsed in the cornfield. She had recovered slowly but steadily.

Tied to Sun covered himself in ashes although nobles were not required to mourn for the unborn. Gifted Tongue joined Rising Moon in slashing their forearms and offering strips of flesh to show their despair. The pain relieved Gifted Tongue's sorrow, but she could see the sadness in Rising Moon's eyes.

When Tied to Sun visited, he clearly mistook her depression as sympathy for him. "Cheer up, woman. I don't blame you for losing my child. I'll give you another chance." Turning to Gifted Tongue, he added in what seemed an afterthought, "Be patient, servant wife. Your turn will come." He touched Rising Moon lightly on the arm before he left.

For the first time, Gifted Tongue doubted that she should have a child. Her major worry was that Double Woman might harm her as well as Rising Moon, despite what Whirlwind had said. To ease her worry, she worked to repair the roof thatch and replace the loose mud at the sides of their homes. She even welcomed the endless tasks Roaring Woman added.

Rising Moon joined in the toil. Grinding corn relieved them

a little because they talked while they knelt over the metates. Once, after they had ground more than usual because Roaring Woman hosted guests, Rising Moon confided in her. "Our husband is so determined to have a child, his lovemaking becomes frantic."

"I'm not sure I understand, co-wife." Embarrassed, Gifted Tongue said, "Remember I have no experience with sex, aside from what I can't help hearing."

"I forgot. I'd ask Tied to Sun to share your bed, but he wants to use all his semen in my blood."

"You're good to think of me, but I can't miss what I don't know."

"You have a point." Rising Moon almost laughed. Then she grew serious. "Anyway, it's a bad time. Sometimes, Tied to Sun is impotent. He gets furious and blames me. It's best you don't have to be with him."

Their new intimacy seemed to raise Rising Moon's spirits, but Gifted Tongue grew depressed when the work eased and she had time to brood about Double Woman endangering her co-wife's fertility. She wished for more of Whirlwind's reassurance.

As if by magic, he arrived the next morning. She saw he was in a teasing mood, and she kidded him about his gray hair turning black. He joked about her cluttered house and its need for repairs. She realized he sensed her depression.

"It's ironic, grandrelative. Rising Moon has been depressed, and I've worked to cheer her. She's better, but now I'm depressed. I know Double Woman isn't supposed to hurt my co-wife if my intentions are good, but how can I be sure of myself? I could be jealous. If she miscarries, Tied to Sun might turn to me. I could bear his first-born." She held back a tear, but it came when she said, "I've never been able to put such thoughts into words before, but deep down I don't trust myself. I could be evil." She wiped away a flow of tears at the thought.

Whirlwind said sternly, "Let me judge that. I feel no evil emanations from you, nor did I when Rising Moon was pregnant. Remember, Whirlwind is the god of passion. Besides there is a simple explanation," he said gently.

"You recall that I suspected that Roaring Woman poisoned the venison. She used an herb to cause abortion. The Dhegiha seldom utilize it, so I only smelled it twice before. I wasn't sure that I found it in Rising Moon's mouth until I consulted a woman who has potions to cause abortions. She told me that Roaring Woman had bought one." He shook his head in disgust.

"You must now be Rising Moon's guardian," he admonished her. "See that she eats nothing that Roaring Woman gives you." He put his hands on her shoulders and said gravely, "You must make sure Roaring Woman never has another chance."

CHAPTER NINE

Gifted Tongue awoke, for once refreshed, to experience a dry, crisp cool morning. The rare relief equaled a brisk summer day in Kutenai country. A wave of cold had ushered in the Turkey Moon that commemorated the final steps of harvest.

She hoped the change would help Rising Moon, whose depression had returned. The cool weather had rejuvenated Gifted Tongue's humor.

As her mind hummed, she organized the chores. They had to dry the squash, harvest the last beans, find pots to store them, glean the cornfields and bundle ears for storage. She'd have to drop any of these tasks when Tied to Sun or men in Rising Moon's clan brought game to skin and dry.

As she approached Rising Moon's home, her spirits soared when she heard a song seeping from its door. It had been a long time since Rising Moon sang anything.

She stooped at the door, and stepped into the house. "It's a beautiful song, for a beautiful day. I haven't heard it before."

"It's a ditty we sang as girls, about grinding corn, more nonsense syllables than words. Shall I teach you while we work?" Gifted Tongue thought of the squash and beans but suppressed her list of chores in order to share Rising Moon's happiness. Obviously the fresh weather had revived her spirits.

"I'd love to learn it. We can make corn soup, with fresh rabbit to add." Gifted Tongue recalled the venison Roaring Woman sent that she promptly buried. Morsels of meat were rare. Clan brothers of Rising Moon occasionally brought small game, but men were forced to travel farther and farther for deer.

"Gifted Tongue, I've been terrible." Rising Moon rarely used her name, but she clearly meant it as endearing on this occasion. "I couldn't help myself. I wanted to die so I didn't care what happened. Can you understand?"

Gifted Tongue assured her that she understood because she had reached bottom in her own despair.

Rising Moon frowned as she said, "I thought I wanted the baby for Tied to Sun. It's so important he have an heir. But when I lost the child, I didn't care about him. I wanted that baby. I realized how much it was mine. Does that make sense?"

"Of course. Every woman wants a baby." Gifted Tongue guessed it was true, but doubt echoed in her voice. She didn't know if she wanted a child with a father as thoughtless as Tied to Sun. Of course, did it matter what she wanted? Her prospects for motherhood were as remote as Roaring Woman befriending her.

Rising Moon's joy grew along with the mound of corn. Gifted Tongue learned the ditty quickly, and the duet generated warmth. As they finished the last kernels, Gifted Tongue offered to teach a song of her mothers. Rising Moon proved adept, and the two rocked back and forth to a Washo lullaby.

Rising Moon shook her head to break the mood. "The first year I was married, Roaring Woman tried to be kind. Oh, she'd put me in my place, but she sat with me as I worked. Once, she even helped, but I blundered when I corrected her speech."

"You mean her lisp?" Gifted Tongue said.

"Yes. How she can't pronounce an s. It comes out like a th. I had her say 'She sewed sea shells on a soft skin.' That's how one of my mothers corrected my sister's lisp."

"It sounds to me like a good way to practice." Gifted Tongue nodded.

"Roaring Woman tried it. She managed to pronounce the s several times. Then a noblewoman overheard us and mocked her with 'thewed the shells on a thoft thkin.' She yelled out 'thoft thkin' a couple of times so the neighbors heard. Roaring Woman was furious at her, but she took it out on me. When the woman left, she claimed I laughed, too. She hit me so hard she loosened one of my teeth. That's when she began to hate me."

Before Gifted Tongue could commiserate, Tied to Sun threw back the skin draped over the door. His glower revealed he had heard the two talk, but he pretended he hadn't.

"I'm glad to see you enjoy your work. It's a flawless day for it, isn't it? The weather often transforms in the Turkey Moon. It's an auspicious time to finish the harvest. I feel like pursuing the deer." Gifted Tongue wondered if he resorted to big words when he was flustered. His tone made it clear that their talk about Roaring Woman bothered him.

She waited for her senior co-wife to speak. Rising Moon said, "It's good you visit, lordly husband. Perhaps you will share our corn mush. We'll spice it with rabbit."

"Rabbit?" He raised his voice scornfully. "What about

venison? Didn't Roaring Woman send you a haunch not long ago?"

"She did, my lordly husband," Gifted Tongue quickly answered. "I ate more than my share while my co-wife felt poorly. She may not remember." She realized that burying the gifts of meat might require more deception than she had anticipated.

"Well, I can't stay. I'm visiting Dakota Next to Sun to arrange a spring expedition. He'll claim it's too soon to return to the Kutenai, so I'll settle for Aztalan. My partner there should have acquired an abundance of copper, and the Ponca artisans complain of its shortage."

"I'm certain you will prosper at Aztalan, my lordly husband, and you will not have to start so early," Rising Moon murmured. Gifted Tongue guessed her co-wife hoped to become pregnant before her husband left for who knew how many moons.

"I've already had some luck. Do you remember Diving Hawk, a noble who lives near me?" Rising Moon nodded to acknowledge she recalled him as a trader.

"He broke his leg, and it heals slowly. He won't travel this year so he gave me the services of Two Hearts, the orphan captive. Have you met him?"

Again, Rising Moon nodded though apparently she could picture no face with the name.

"I'm sending him here to teach you Menomini," he told Gifted Tongue. "I know some, of course, but I realize how quickly you learn. I don't trust Two Hearts. I feel he doesn't like me. So learn as much Menomini as you can." He added derisively, "It's like other northern languages and you'll become proficient in them, too, they're so simple."

The thought of studying another language caused an inner

ripple. Despite the hard work, she loved the challenge. She would show her husband how useful she could be, and he would learn to love her, she thought. Perhaps then she would welcome his child.

A day later, the door cover flew back in rude introduction to Two Hearts. He watched her with scorn as she quickly dressed.

"I believe you are Gifted Tongue," he said abruptly.

"And you must be Two Hearts," she replied with equal rudeness, speaking his name loudly and slowly.

"Yes, I am he. The man who is twice as brave as anyone else. Has anyone told you that?"

Gifted Tongue hesitated. Surely, he would not reveal the circumstances of his name, although he seemed not to take offense when she used it. His physical appearance marked him as a stranger. His complexion glowed the same rich, chocolate brown as hers, and he stood hardly any taller. She thought her reply might have caused the corner of his eye to twitch. Despite his tic, she thought he might be handsome if he smiled, but his scowl wrinkled his forehead to suggest a permanent frown. Only a dimpled chin drew attention from a face marked by anger.

"My husband told me that you would instruct me in Menomini, not in rudeness. Nor did he say anything about how manly you are, or aren't. Do you doubt your courage so much that you must speak of your bravery?" She surprised herself by her audacity, but she couldn't back down from his challenge to battle.

Two Hearts jerked back as if he expected no mere woman to answer with disdain matching his own. He put his hand to his eye to still his tic and glared at her before he answered.

"You must know I would not tell you anything about the

vision that gave me my name, or are you from such a distant, uncivilized nation that your people never experience visions?"

"It's true I come from far away, and the nobility regard us as savages. But I ate better at home and worked far less. Is that what you mean by uncivilized?" She added in Shoshoni, "If that's what you mean, then I will take savage life anytime."

"What did you say?" Two Hearts gasped.

In Dhegiha she repeated, "I said I came from the far north, beyond the origins of the Missouri River."

"No. Repeat what you mumbled at the end. After you said . . . what you mean by civilization."

Gifted Tongue was amused by his baffled look at her use of Shoshoni. She said in Shoshoni, "I think you're a fool, but you could be a good-looking fool if you'd only smile."

His answer shocked her. "What do you know about fools? And who cares what you think of how I look?"

She continued in her native tongue. "You're not speaking Shoshoni, but I understand you. What are you speaking?"

"I am Paiute," he said in his native language. "But one of my mothers was Shoshoni. I never learned her tongue because we could understand each other if we spoke slowly. I didn't understand all you said, but I got its drift."

She blushed because he had understood what she said about his looks, but after talking more, she realized many of her words were unintelligible to him, so she reverted to Dhegiha.

"I think I could learn Paiute. Will you teach me?"

"Only if you teach me Shoshoni. I swear someday I will return home to surprise my mother, the one who gave birth to me. She was the dearest of my mothers." He smiled at the memory.

"He is handsome," Gifted Tongue thought.

.   .   .

After many days, Gifted Tongue grasped the rudiments of Menomini. She had begun to doubt her special talent since she made headway so slowly, not realizing that Menomini differed completely from Dhegiha as well as Shoshoni.

As she found elements of grammar in Menomini corresponding to Kutenai, she sought to interest Two Hearts in her discovery.

"My elder," she said—using a term they agreed upon because elders instructed the young—"As I learn how Menomini compound their words to make difficult tongue twisters, I'm reminded of Kutenai." She pronounced a Kutenai example.

"It's just a coincidence. The Kutenai live too far away from the Menomini to share anything. Besides, what difference does it make? Menomini will help you learn the northeastern languages. That's enough. I don't need to learn Kutenai because Diving Hawk has no interest in the northwest. Let's get on with our lesson."

Gifted Tongue was disappointed but not surprised that he failed to share her interest in what languages might reveal. It was as if he saw his ability as only practical, and under Dhegiha influence the only use for other languages was to exchange goods.

"Let's review kinship terms. Noque is the word for whom?"

"Father," Gifted Tongue replied.

"And the word for mother?"

"Kio. And brother and sister are nimot and nime if elder sister, nase if younger sister."

"Good. And for daughter and son?"

"Mitan and kis," she said confidently.

"Son's sons and daughter's daughters are noqsese. Did you know some peoples distinguish between the two; that is, they have two different words for grandrelative? I can't imagine why anyone would bother," Two Hearts said, shaking his head.

She welcomed his diversion. He showed little imagination in organizing his lessons, but his persistence ensured her steady progress. Today, a tenacious drill bored her so she smiled when he suggested they tour the city to practice.

In the bustle, few people seemed to notice them despite their different complexion and stature. Gifted Tongue noted that a few men nodded to Two Hearts while others ignored him. One gave him a bag of herbs, handing it to her to carry.

"Let's walk by the stockade," Two Hearts said after nodding to his friend. "The nobles insist that the area be kept clean so they won't smell the commoners. Personally, I don't think it makes much difference, but it's easier walking."

"Where did so many logs come from, elder?" Gifted Tongue never failed to be amazed at the work the stockade demanded. She couldn't imagine what had motivated such insane behavior.

"Would you believe they used more than twenty thousand logs? In Paiute we don't have a word for twenty thousand."

"But surely you didn't count them?" Gifted Tongue gasped.

"I counted the logs in one-tenth of the wall so my estimate is better than a guess."

"But where did the trees come from?"

"I've asked old timers. They say that thick woods grew on the bluffs. The first stockades were not difficult. But new Suns demanded rebuilding. The stockade that was here when I came, has been replaced. Also, our growing numbers demand more homes, and they each take a hundred trees. That's why women travel impossible distances for firewood. When I arrived, finding firewood was easy."

"What happens when all the wood is gone?"

"The city will end," he said simply. "The priests do nothing but draft new layouts of the city and rebuild marker mounds while the Suns scheme to rebuild the temple mounds. They plan years ahead for those events, but never think of tomorrow when it comes to forests and farmland. The city is doomed, and the sooner it collapses the better." He smiled in irony while his eyelid twitched furiously.

"What do you mean, it's doomed?" She read nothing on his face between the smile and the twitch to help with an answer. Instead of a reply, he recalled his introduction to the Center of the World. "I was only eight or nine when raiders struck our camp. They killed all my fathers. They took women and children captive. For a few moons, my older brother stayed with me, but the raiders traded him. Then they gave me to the Dhegiha for copper."

"Didn't your life get better with the Dhegiha?"

"I was lucky," he nodded. "Some captives become virtual slaves, but Beloved Leader adopted me because of my color. He called me Brown Bear. My appearance and my speech made me an oddity in his household, and he'd laugh when I spoke. He treated me kindly, as he did everyone. He appreciated how quickly I learned Dhegiha, but he never wanted me to forget Paiute. He liked the strange sounds and learned a few words," Two Hearts said with a catch in his voice.

"After a while, he loaned me to trade parties to interpret. Since we never traded with Paiute, I never helped, but the nobles wouldn't tell him that. I studied Menomini and related languages so I could be useful. When Beloved Leader died,

Diving Hawk gave his son many chunky stones, the ones with concave holes that are used for games. They were burial presents. That forced the new Sun to give me to Diving Hawk," he said ruefully.

"Diving Hawk regards me as mere property. All the nobles are like that. They think commoners are scum. Our only value is to farm. Or exceptions like us, artisans and interpreters. Otherwise, we're worthless. The Menomini know better. They respect every living thing."

"The Mandan and the Kutenai, too," Gifted Tongue said. "No Shoshoni ever thought himself or herself better than another. It's not the way of human beings."

"Then why did you come here?" he asked skeptically.

"Our food supply failed. My father took me to the Kutenai so that my mothers would have enough food. A kind Kutenai chief almost married me but instead gave me to Tied to Sun. I doubt that he wanted to marry me with all my scars." Gifted Tongue stopped. She couldn't imagine why she had revealed so much to a virtual stranger.

"But Tied to Sun married you. Did you have to marry him?"

"Let's just say it was my destiny." Gifted Tongue tried to put an end to the matter, but Two Hearts persisted.

"People control their destinies." He paused to think and added, "With the aid of their spirit helpers." He dropped the subject at the south edge of the stockade. For a while he said nothing until they approached a small, ridge-top mound.

"Have you been introduced to this mound, young one?"

"Yes, elder. Tied to Sun explained that it served as a marker. He showed me how it lined up with the temple mound."

"Is that all he told you?"

"He said a Sun and his wives were buried here."

"Nothing more?"

"He was on a journey when that Sun died so he didn't see the burial. He seemed to revere him."

"Yes, young one, everyone adored him. Times have certainly changed. Beloved Leader knew how to care for the people," Two Hearts said admiringly.

"No one gave feasts the way he did. He overwhelmed southern peoples with gifts. The southeastern Muskoki sent their priests here to teach and to learn. They brought their knowledge of herbs. The southern peoples west of the Mississippi sent their best artisans. The concentration of knowledge made the city the peak of civilization. If only Beloved Leader had lived."

Gifted Tongue was struck by his lament. Then she thought that perhaps the special favor Two Hearts had experienced under Beloved Leader warped his judgment.

She said with a puzzled brow, "Possibly the next Sun will return the splendor of the city."

"No one will ever match him," Two Hearts said adamantly. "Beloved Leader's works were confirmed by his funeral. I witnessed it first hand," he said proudly. "The father of Beloved Leader did not live long and people showed him little honor. But Beloved Leader's grandfather had established colonies of Dhegiha at Aztalan and Spiro. When he died, they had buried him here, so the mound became sacred. Beloved Leader's burial made it even more sacred." He paused reverently.

"The next Sun ruled only two years. He died young and didn't have any sons. The Long Nosed God Society tried to take over. They insisted that wives of the Sun be sacrificed so they could get rid of wise women who would have advised the new Sun.

"They ordered the mound rebuilt to extend from the north-west to the southeast, in the direction of the Muskoki homeland. The desecration outraged the old time Dhegiha, but they were too disorganized to resist." He shook his head in disgust.

"One noble claimed a vision told him to become the new Sun, but the Suns sought an heir among the Falcon clan. They selected the son of a younger brother of Beloved Leader. If they hadn't acted quickly, the nobles would have taken over." He bent close to whisper, "His name was Beloved by Falcon." Aloud he said, "He was a born leader, and he organized trade parties that extended the city's influence in all directions.

"He died when he was only thirty, about my age now, but he had acquired wives from all over the world. He used their knowledge and skills. They gave him so many children, he restored complete power of the Suns.

"No one can forget his death. Fifty-two of the city's most beautiful women asked to be his wives in the afterlife. The priests strangled them to preserve their beauty," he said in a hushed tone.

"Artisans worked for days on a wardrobe for him. They sewed an exquisite cape with thousands of shell beads in the shape of a falcon. I think the falcon may have been his guardian.

"People from all over the world sent offerings. I never saw so much mica, four or five basketfuls for his spirit artisans. People from everywhere sent their finest quivers packed with arrows." He paused in reflection.

"His son, the present-day Sun, gave a roll of copper to identify him as the Sun of all Suns. No one ever saw so much copper. They used the largest nuggets ever found in the north." Gifted

Tongue tried to divert him from his remembrance, a little frightened by so much talk of the dead. "Is that where we'll go on the spring expedition?"

"By then the Menomini should have acquired enough copper for us. They get it from the Ojibwas who live so far north they can't farm," he said gruffly, determined to finish his story.

"The new Sun started well until he became embroiled in politics. He said the Long Nosed God priests forced his mothers to join their husband in death to deprive him of their aid.

"He ordered four priests killed to accompany Beloved by Falcon. To prevent them from outmaneuvering him in the afterlife, he ordered that their heads and hands be cut off. When one of the southern chiefs heard that, he practiced the same trick to rid himself of rivals." Two Hearts laughed ruefully.

He declared the lesson finished. Gifted Tongue guessed the memories saddened him, and she followed him in silence as they returned home.

Two Hearts signaled a goodbye. "The next time we'll work doubly hard. Do you still have time to gather firewood?"

His question startled her. He had never shown any interest in her life beyond teaching Menomini.

"Yes, elder. Rising Moon and I spend the nights together so we don't burn two fires. We gather enough for several days, but we have to travel far to find it."

Two Hearts disappeared among the huts before she remembered that she held his gift of herbs. Gifted Tongue started after him, but she saw Rising Moon wrestling a large metate so she rushed to help her.

. . .

Days passed before Gifted Tongue remembered to return the herbs. At the first Ponca hut, she asked for Two Hearts. A woman stared questioningly before saying she didn't know, but a boy playing nearby pursed his lips to point at a hut.

Standing before its door, she cleared her throat to announce herself but to no avail. Before a second attempt, she paused to hear who might live in Two Hearts' home, wondering if he had a wife. She heard several men muttering.

A whining voice said, "But who could replace this Sun? Who would be better? No one. I say we flee up the Ohio River to the eastern rim of the world."

"We outnumber the nobles," a gruff voice answered. "We don't need to trade all over the world. Let's take the city. We'd have enough to eat if we didn't feed the exalted clans."

Another voice said cautiously, "We must wait. This Sun is young. When he acquires more wisdom, things may get better. We don't even know if he's sought a vision. Let's be patient."

The second voice said, "Being patient will get us dead. Every year there's less to eat, and more people fall ill."

The cautious voice said, "You always forecast doom. Last year's harvest was one of the best. This one is all right."

"Have you forgotten how things were when we were children? We had plenty to eat. We played in forests that are now cut down, for no better reason than to rebuild the stockade."

Gifted Tongue heard Two Hearts say, "We've each agreed that our life's a mess. The issue is how to change it. Look at us. Most of us are foreigners. We've convinced only a few Dhegiha to change. Flint Knife has lost interest, and his oratory might have convinced others. Now we don't know where he stands."

She stood perplexed. In her confusion, she coughed again,

having stood before the hut longer than was polite. Two Hearts opened the door to scowl at her, his eye twitching wildly.

"What is it, woman?" he said, but from his tone she knew he meant, how much have you heard?

"The packet of herbs your friend gave you when we toured the city. I forgot to give it to you." She looked at her feet, wondering if she should say anything more.

She suspected her flushed face told him she had listened. He grabbed the bag. He dismissed her by turning his back.

She returned home confused, knowing she should tell her husband, but her intuition told her not to. She wondered why the men simply didn't leave if they were so troubled. That's what she would do, she thought but in doubt asked herself how she could return home. She worried that her destiny bound her to the Center of the World.

Tied to Sun suddenly doubled her confusion. She hadn't seen him for days, and suddenly he stood before her glowering.

"Where have you been, woman? When you're not working, I expect you to study with Two Hearts."

"We have studied, my lordly husband," she stammered.

"How can you study while roaming the city with him? People are talking about the two of you cavorting in the wards."

"He only showed me parts of the city while we practiced the language," she said hesitantly.

"I showed you the city," he said pointedly. "What was left to see?" He sneered, "I suppose Two Hearts told you how the Beloved One favored him. Don't let him mislead you. He was nothing but a freak for the Sun's amusement. You'll be no good to me this spring if you're not speaking Menomini as well as Two Hearts." He underlined each word and frowned his warning, then turned on his heel.

His anger resolved one of her doubts. She would never reveal what she had overheard. Still, she didn't understand his anger. For a moment, she considered jealousy. Could his wrath show his love, or was she nothing more than an interpreter? Would she ever know how she stood as his wife? Then she wondered what Two Hearts thought of her. She felt more heat in the blush of her face than she had ever felt before.

CHAPTER TEN

Rising Moon splashed Gifted Tongue at the canal's edge, the icy chill climbing her spine. Although yesterday had warmed, a thin sheet of ice edged the water. Gifted Tongue hoped it was the last freeze because Tied to Sun had told her they would leave soon. The sun had reached the first pole before the equinox marker in the Sun Circle, and he claimed that marked an auspicious time to travel.

Rising Moon told Gifted Tongue that every day added to the departure would help her to become pregnant because when Whirlwind last visited he had brought an herb to aid conception. Gifted Tongue smiled at the thought. In a joyful mood, she pretended to ignore her co-wife until Rising Moon turned her back. Then she threw a jar full of water at her.

"What are you doing? It's time you grew up," Rising Moon said irritably. Her look, as much as her words, stung Gifted Tongue, who worried that the depression had returned.

Rising Moon appeared to realize how much she had

changed, so she forced a laugh and threw water at Gifted Tongue. "Since you're a baby, I'll bathe you," she joked.

The sudden shift of mood mystified Gifted Tongue, but she welcomed it. Before she knew what they were doing, both were ankle deep in water, doused and shivering. They jostled each other on shore, clutching their sides in laughter.

"Will you bathe me, too, little sisters? Heat the water first, though. The ice freezes my old joints." Whirlwind clutched his side, laughing. Gifted Tongue didn't know if he laughed at them in their soaked dresses, or at his own joke.

His presence warmed her even while she trembled from the cold. She had not seen him for a moon. After she chided him for his absence, he told her that patients in the Ponca ward kept him busy. She watched him raptly as he told how he had sucked out a spirit arrow from a frail woman.

He concluded in his most dramatic tones, "My last case was the most difficult one I've ever encountered." Gifted Tongue leaned forward, wholly absorbed. "Do you know that obese Ponca who lives on the edge of the ward? He seldom visits other wards because it's so hard for him to walk."

Rising Moon grinned and reminded Gifted Tongue how her brother had joked that he had made the Ponca pregnant.

Whirlwind tossed back his braids and grinned. "That could be, and he must be carrying twins." Both women covered their mouths as they laughed. "When he doubled in size, he couldn't leave his hut. His sister called me to help. She promised a beaded necklace if I cured him. She's so charming, I couldn't refuse." He paused, and both women bent to catch every word.

"I spent two days singing over him, diagnosing who shot him. It must have been an immortal, but I found what infected him. I spent a whole day and night sucking. My lips are exhausted."

"What was it?" Gifted Tongue couldn't contain herself.

"It was a bear, a real bear inside him. And I sucked it out!" Whirlwind exclaimed.

"What happened then?" Gifted Tongue said excitedly.

"Then the bear swallowed me." Whirlwind guffawed, unable to contain his laughter.

Rising Moon laughed from the depths of her stomach, but Whirlwind drowned her out, while Gifted Tongue squirmed in embarrassment at her question. Still, she couldn't keep from laughing, and she felt even closer to Rising Moon and Whirlwind.

"Now, my grandrelatives, it's time to be serious. I have gifts for you. The bear gave them to me, just before he swallowed me." Whirlwind snickered, but he stiffened, and his eyes became solemn.

"Here is more medicine to help you conceive," he told Rising Moon as he handed her a small packet. "It's difficult to find the wild plant that's the major ingredient. It needs shade to grow, but each year the farmers cut more of the forest. At least it will last you until Tied to Sun departs."

He looked gravely at Gifted Tongue and said, "I know you worry about Double Woman and how she affects your life. Remember, good thoughts protect the ones you love."

He took her hand and looked into her eyes. "Double Woman has another power I haven't explained. She can confuse people around you. When enemies surprise you, use her power. Concentrate on her when you need help. These herbs will focus your thought. Rub a pinch on your forehead or sniff it when you need help."

As he dropped her hand, he said reassuringly, "The northern tribes are at peace so you shouldn't be in danger. But you can never tell when you'll need it." He handed her a small pouch with a strap for her neck. It was decorated with two quilled deer, one a natural brown, the other half-blue, half-yellow.

"Women with Double Woman power are excellent quill-workers. I haven't seen you quill, child. Show me a sample of your work."

"My mothers didn't quill," Gifted Tongue confessed. Here at the Center of the World, she wondered when women found time for art of any kind.

"It could be a dying craft, I'm afraid. I seldom see porcupines anymore. Watch Menomini quillers work. They quill beautiful flowers. The curves require great skill. The Dhegiha use only straight lines and geometric designs. Maybe that's why the priests line up everything in the city in triangles or squares. Next they'll make square sun circles."

All three laughed heartily, but Whirlwind cautioned, "Perhaps we shouldn't joke about the sacred circle. Circles represent the continuity of life and the interrelatedness of everything."

He rose to depart, and looked affectionately at Gifted Tongue. "If a quiller gives you any work for me, make sure it has flowers. I'll use it next winter to forget the cold."

Her heart warmed at Whirlwind's attention, and she forgot her soaked dress. Rising Moon picked up her jar and hummed as the two women headed home.

Tied to Sun awaited them. He checked off chores for them, many already completed. When he asked how much meat they had dried and found less than he expected, he shouted sternly,

"You must be gorging yourselves. What happened to all the venison Roaring Woman sent you?" Rising Moon looked puzzled. Gifted Tongue started to make an excuse, but before she could, he said, "I'll have to call in a debt of pemmican." He added with disgust, "It should suffice, if you don't feast on it."

Gifted Tongue asked about gifts to take. Usually Tied to Sun ignored her questions, but this time he seemed to enjoy discussing the trip's details.

"My brother-in-law wants to make me more subservient. He's limited me to three canoes so that I cannot have litter bearers. I won't be recognized as an official envoy. I almost went to the Sun, but Next to Sun would be furious if I go over his head. So I'll take only superb art in one canoe. Next to Sun will send another load with Dakota art that I'll present in his name. That leaves one canoe for provisions."

He glanced about before continuing, "He claims the two men he's sending with me are skilled hunters. They're really spies to report what I do with the Menomini. Two Hearts had better translate well. I'm counting on you, servant wife, to verify. Has he said why he doesn't like me?"

She replied honestly that she had not learned why he disliked him. She didn't add that he hated all nobility.

A few days later, the party loaded their three canoes near Omaha ward. An equal arm cross, encircled in red, marked Next to Sun's canoe. A blue hand on the bow identified each of Tied to Sun's canoes.

The two large Dakota scowled, as if they resented paddling. Gifted Tongue guessed they were accomplished warriors when she saw all their tattoos after they disrobed.

Weasel kneeled in the stern of the canoe with provisions, with Two Hearts at the bow, frowning as usual. Tied to Sun took the stern of the canoe filled with his gifts, while Gifted Tongue knelt at the bow. Tied to Sun told her that she need not paddle.

"It's been a long winter. The paddling will restore my vigor. Too many endless councils that went nowhere. It's hard to reach a consensus since nobles have many brilliant ideas. You'd be surprised, servant-wife, all that we decide for the city's welfare."

"I'm certain it's hard work, lordly husband, sitting in council so long." Gifted Tongue held her tongue but wondered if they developed calluses on their butts or on their brains.

By midday, Tied to Sun's canoe lagged far behind. The warriors saw that he could not maintain their pace, so they tried to adjust, but regularly they outdistanced him.

"You must have gained some winter weight, my Shoshoni beauty, perhaps you should paddle. It will do you good."

She wondered if her husband did notice her body. It had developed fully, with excellent muscle tone from her hard work. Her calluses protected her hands as she bent into the paddle. She imagined blisters attacking his hands.

She held their canoe to the established pace. "I can see your sweat will help you lose weight," Tied to Sun said. That evening, when they beached their canoes, she found a clear stream, filled a bottle, and took it to her husband. She noticed an open blister on one hand and felt better as she built a fire while he rested on a mat she had carried from the canoe.

Weasel and Two Hearts prepared three windbreaks and started fires before them. The two warriors gathered a little wood, but they expected Gifted Tongue to provide the rest. She cooked and unpacked with a little help from Two Hearts. For the following twenty days, the routine continued until the party reached a village in the Illinois River Valley.

There, several boys called a greeting from the west bank. Tied to Sun said, "The first arrivals of spring always bring excitement. People want to hear about their relatives and city politics. We'll be more than welcome. Of course, being married to me is also important," he laughed, but Gifted Tongue knew that his conceit was genuine.

The party pulled into a small, clear stream that cut its path through the bluffs. A low platform mound, surrounded by a few buildings and a dozen homes, formed the village. Gifted Tongue wondered how fewer than a hundred people had built the mound for a charnel house.

Once beached, a half dozen women rushed to help. Gifted Tongue expected hundreds of questions, but the symbols of nobility restrained curiosity. When she spoke cordially, a few older women replied, and she realized that they treated her as superior. Her explanation that she was a mere servant wife did little to allay the formality.

She fretted in the role, uncomfortable to be regarded as superior, yet she didn't know how to overcome their attitude. Giving in to reality, she let the commoner women carry her baggage to Lesser Sun's home. It easily accommodated her and Tied to Sun while the four others were welcomed by commoners who begged for their company.

The Lesser Sun ordered a feast in four days. Meanwhile, Gifted Tongue found herself in the company of the few noblewomen of the village who were resigned to life in the backwaters. They beseeched her for news of the city. After a day's gossip seemed to satisfy them, Gifted Tongue asked to see their town.

The leader of the group said, "Let's tour the outskirts. The sun will have dried the dew."

A younger woman added regretfully, "There's not much to see. Not long ago we picked berries here, and the hickory nuts and acorns are abundant."

A slim women, who always seemed to smile said, "With the forests so close it's easy to find deer. The Lesser Sun has to insist the commoners farm. If it weren't for our civilization, the woodlands people would be content to hunt and gather. They might convince Dhegiha commoners to go wild."

"That's for certain," the leader stressed. "They're only a step above savages. If we weren't here, they'd never touch a hoe, let alone know about Rock and Sun's divinity," she sneered, her superior attitude reminding Gifted Tongue of Roaring Woman.

"They'd know nothing of doctoring," another claimed. "Before we came they had no knowledge of the Long Nosed God, nothing except superstition."

The women left the fields to show off a large building near the village center. The slim one said with missionary zeal, "Here is our tie to civilization. The Lesser Sun left its construction to Muskoki nobles so it's built in the traditional way to symbolize the four directions." She looked at Gifted Tongue to make sure she was interested. When Gifted Tongue nodded, she said, "It starts with a center square room for the Perpetual Fire. I think people in the city forget the importance of Perpetual Fire." She looked carefully at Gifted Tongue, seeming to fear that she might give offense.

Gifted Tongue assured her. "I've heard that a perpetual fire burns in the temple of the sun, but I know little about it."

The leader passed over the subject. "Priests built another room on each side of the original room so the whole building makes a cross pointing to the four directions." She stopped and blushed, "But you know all this. I must be boring you."

"Not at all," Gifted Tongue said. "I have much to learn."

The reassurance seemed to encourage the leader. "The south room holds the holy relics-you know, the masks and effigy jars, tobacco, the holiest of pipes. The other three rooms are for rituals and meetings."

The women turned from the building to lead her to a low conical mound used for burials. The woman who always smiled, grew serious. "The Lesser Sun's father died a winter ago. You should have seen the mussel shells buried with him. Baskets and baskets full. A beautiful effigy pot, and his pipe. It was a most memorable burial."

The woman with the smile added, "His wife died soon after. She had befriended us. Not like this Sun's wife. The priests prepare her body now. Once the bones are purified, they will add the bundle to her husband's grave."

Gifted Tongue excused herself over the next few days to mend clothes and patch bags. She welcomed the hickory nut and cornmeal mixture as a change of taste and a means to replenish provisions.

On the evening of the fourth day, she envisioned the feast promised by the Lesser Sun. Her curiosity to meet his wife matched her anticipation of roasted venison. Although her new friends thought the Lesser Sun's wife a snob, Gifted Tongue reserved her judgment.

"We should go, servant wife," Tied To Sun said, as he finished combing and braiding his hair. Gifted Tongue touched up his face paint, and added a design to his arms. He frowned at her hair to remind her that she needed to brush it.

"I'll rush, lordly husband," she replied, putting away his shirt with the broken quills she had replaced. She barely stroked her hair before looking for her best dress.

"Will you bestow many gifts, my lordly husband?"

"I have some unusual arrowheads for Lesser Sun, and Next to Sun sent a mantle and mica work. The mica is poor quality, but its artist captured the falcon's spirit. It suffices for the chief of an outpost as insignificant as this one. Have you noticed how few savages he's civilized? I suppose most of them are children of Dhegiha fathers and savage mothers."

Gifted Tongue shook out the tangles in the fringe of her dress, then hurried to catch Tied to Sun as he entered the long, rectangular home of Lesser Sun. She guessed the walls were a black locust foundation for a latticework of branches, plastered with mud. The roof beams were thatched with river reeds to resemble city houses.

Tied to Sun joined the Lesser Sun, his relatives, and the noblemen seated at a central fire. Noblewomen sat against the walls. At one end, four men drummed. Women near them trilled a high-pitched song, much of it unfamiliar to Gifted Tongue who never before heard woodland people sing.

A bent man with tangled hair served as Keeper of the Pipe. He sat next to Lesser Sun. He packed the bowl so carefully that Gifted Tongue guessed the act was ritual. A crafted stem lay next to his thigh. After inspecting the packed tobacco, the Pipe Keeper inserted the stem. He drew an ember from the fire, lit the tobacco, and offered it to Lesser Sun.

Lesser Sun looked insignificant next to Tied to Sun, but his voice commanded attention. "North, I beg guidance, East, show me favor. South, bring me warmth. West, I beg your pity. Father Sun pity me. Mother Earth pity me. I am without wealth. I humbly stand here." He almost whined his humility.

Gifted Tongue bit her lip in a quandary. She wondered if the appeal wasn't addressed to her husband as much as it was to the directions, and she wondered if the poor quality of Tied to Sun's gifts would shake the man's faith.

Lesser Sun passed the pipe around the fire, each noble offering smoke to the six directions. Each promised to be steady in return for wealth. A few invoked Rock's name in their pleas. They all intimated their steady loyalty to the Lesser Sun. When they included the Sun, they looked at Tied to Sun to acknowledge that he would report their fealty.

Gifted Tongue saw that the laments irritated Tied to Sun. He must be worried about the poor quality of his gifts, she thought. He rose slowly, and she wondered if his oratory could make up for his presents. He took a deep breath, gazed at the nobles, then fixed on Lesser Sun. "I have gifts for everyone from the Center of the World." The customary refrain was greeted by hous. He opened the parfleche bags with a flourish. "Behold these flint points." His voice rose, as if his shouting would conceal the workmanship. "This flint came from the farthest reaches of Dhegiha aegis. The city's most expert flint knappers worked them. Contemplate these notches. The hands that made these points are the most experienced in the world," he said solemnly. As he looked around the lodge, all eyes riveted on him. Perhaps his rhetoric would suffice, Gifted Tongue thought.

He gave flint points to each of Lesser Sun's relatives. When he opened a second bag filled with chert points, his spirit seemed to slip. She wondered if their inferiority swamped his inspiration. However, he found a kin term for each noble, and as he presented the chert, he regained his momentum.

Lesser Sun hid his eagerness to find what Next to Sun had sent by suggesting that they finish feasting. His wife took advantage of the break to sit next to Gifted Tongue.

"I see you admire my husband's new ear spools. They are the finest I've ever seen, too. The wood work is elegant, but the copper foil covering them is exceptional. You'd think they were completely made of copper, wouldn't you?"

Gifted Tongue hadn't noticed them, being accustomed to the grandeur of the city, but she tried to react properly by saying, "They are magnificent. And such fine cougar teeth. His necklace is made of cougar teeth, isn't it?"

Gifted Tongue wondered if she responded satisfactorily since the woman persisted in praise of the ear spools. She didn't realize the woman meant to prepare her own presentation, thinking Gifted Tongue to be highly placed.

Once the roast venison and duck were consumed, Lesser Sun's wife whispered in his ear. He nodded approval. She arose, looked down her nose at the other woman, then beamed at Gifted Tongue. In a commanding voice, she said, "Wife of Tied to Sun, I welcome you. Your party brings many gifts. In return, I give you these ear spools. My husband wore them until the diplomat from Quapaw outpost gave him the new ear spools he wears now." She held the jewelry high above her head to display it. She made certain everyone watched, then said, "Take these ear spools to remind you of our hospitality. We may be a backwater hamlet now, but my husband will make it a town to be remembered."

The weight of the stone spools surprised Gifted Tongue. She wondered how anyone could wear them. They required huge openings in the earlobes. Then less frivolous thoughts struck. Seldom were women singled out for presents so early. The gift would force Tied to Sun to compete with Quapaw Next to Sun. She wondered if he would be able to, or if he would blame her for admiring the ear spools. She concealed her anxiety as she proclaimed their beauty. She assumed that she was to give them to Tied to Sun since she never observed women wearing ear spools. Another thought struck her, that the ear spools would be a wonderful gift for Whirlwind, so she kept them.

She knew Tied to Sun must be irritated, but he hid it well. Perhaps he could guess that she was too naive to appreciate the Dhegiha jewelry. Whatever his reasoning, he rose in dramatic show, made sure every eye was on him, and proclaimed the glory of the Dhegiha empire. Gifted Tongue never heard him speak so well as he gave Lesser Sun a well-worked mica piece. He praised each facet of it to emphasize the beauty of diffused light where it was translucent and reflected light where it was opaque.

Once or twice Gifted Tongue thought his speech sounded insulting, as if he regarded his audience as savages. But his gestures conveyed sincerity, and she guessed that he might believe every word himself.

When the time came to present Lesser Sun with the mantle that Next to Sun had sent, Tied to Sun matched gift with words. He praised the beauty of its design, tracing out each turn of a zigzag line. Gifted Tongue gasped when he reached into a bag meant for Aztalan, especially when he brought forth the effigy pot he had described as intended for an up-and-coming trader who controlled a significant copper source. She guessed that he meant to prove Dakota Outpost surpassed the Quapaw. From his smirk, she assumed he must think so. Lesser Sun praised his generosity to such length that she noticed several heads nod drowsily. His wife startled her when she touched her arm to whisper, "You'll be sure to spread the word, won't you, how loyal my husband is to the Sun and his Next to Suns."

． ． ．

A moon later, plus several long portages, the Dhegiha party reached Aztalan in late afternoon. The resemblance of the town to the Center of the World amazed Gifted Tongue. A long, rectangular stockade surrounded four mounds at each corner, one with a temple atop it and another with a charnel house. A river ran along the east side of the rectangle.

As the sun moved toward its western home, the town's people thronged about the newcomers for news from the south. Dhegiha noblewomen circled Gifted Tongue to pepper her with questions about relatives she did not know. Still, they hung on her every word, composing their own version of what happened that winter.

She noted a periphery of people, the men dressed in frayed breechcloths, the women in tattered dresses. Their hair hung in disarray. They stared curiously but with no enthusiasm. She thought they must be the Menomini savages the Winnebago pioneers came to proselytize. She had yet to learn from Tied to Sun if the Winnebago were once a city ward, or if they had taken a new name after coming north.

The gossip continued as the crowd dispersed, men and women sharing tidbits of news they had garnered. Gifted Tongue saw Two Hearts leave with two Dhegiha commoners, and wondered how far away he would be from her. Nor did she know where she would be.

A gentle hand touched her shoulder. "You are welcome in my lodge, friend. You can find it, if you tell people you are with Gourd Woman," a slim, middle-aged woman said softly. She ushered her to a house near the chief's large lodge. Gourd Woman explained that Distant Sun was absent because he traveled to the Center of the World to receive yearly orders. She added in a guarded way, apparently wondering if Gifted Tongue would approve, "Tonight begins four days of gambling festivities among the Menomini. They are still savages in some ways. They would gamble every night if it weren't for our influence."

She nodded with disdain, "They didn't even know how to farm before we came. They don't see why they should when they can gather all the wild rice they need. And you should see the numbers of ducks and fish they take. The deer and elk are plentiful, too, since the forests remain."

Her brow furrowed, apparently puzzled by what she said, but then she dismissed the thought. "Regardless, tonight they begin gambling. Four nights straight in the plaza. Even we Winnebago participate, so we can limit the time they waste. Distant Sun has aligned the gambling with the spring equinox so we can wean them from their games to our sun ritual."

Gifted Tongue grinned inwardly recalling the wonderful times she had experienced among the Shoshoni gambling with abandon. People discussed the wins and losses for days.

Tied to Sun appeared at the door, followed by Weasel who carried two large bags of goods that he sat inside. Tied to Sun nodded at Gourd Woman and began to sort his goods. He said, "We arrived just in time. I didn't know if you still celebrated in the old ways or not."

Gourd Woman said defensively, "We haven't quite weaned them away from all their savage tricks."

"I wouldn't worry about it. They'll be more enthused for the sun cycle after the excitement of the moccasins." He smiled and left with Weasel.

Although her husband had not invited Gifted Tongue,

Gourd Woman did. When they reached the plaza, they stood in an outside circle watching the excitement. As commoners took note of them, they made room so the two women joined an inside circle that sat around the gamblers. The rhythm of chants and drums seized Gifted Tongue.

Two Menomini teams of four players entered the large seated circle to face each other in two lines. They sat before the wife of Distant Sun, who took his honored place. The drums on the periphery stopped, replaced by a handheld drum beaten by a player. A teammate held a crystal quartz, waving it before his opponents, singing to confuse them. His hand darted under four moccasins before him: twice under one, three times under another. His opponent guessed where he hid the quartz.

Gifted Tongue saw the game required more skill than she remembered. The number of participants swelled the excitement. Gourd Woman tried to appear neutral but clearly favored the left-hand line, cheering when they won.

Tied to Sun squatted at Gourd Woman's side to praise the right-hand line although they lost five times straight. "Watch how deceptive their leader is. Did you ever see such confusing motions? Listen to his team sing," he said excitedly. "They must have a powerful shaman backing them."

"Both sides will have a shaman's backing, I'd guess." Gourd Woman said politely, "The left-hand team has been winning." "Yes, you're right," Tied to Sun said. "But watch those hand movements." He could not contain his fervor for the losing line.

The right-hand leader took his turn. He flashed the crystal nimbly, then concealed it in his hand before it darted under each of the four moccasins. No one could guess where he left it.

After moments of obvious indecision in the left-hand line, Gifted Tongue heard shouts. "Don't take all night to make a fool of yourself, friend. Guess. Which one?" A dozen taunts added confusion.

His opponent chose an empty moccasin. The man next to him chose. He too lost. Cheers went up from the winner's fans. Tied to Sun grinned broadly and said, "This will be easy pickings." He disappeared into the crowd to place his bets.

The excitement of the crowd could not keep Gifted Tongue awake. She had paddled the whole day and endured arduous portages before that. She failed to see which line won more often, though she noted a tone of victory in her host's voice. Back at the lodge, she dropped onto a bison robe wondering if Tied to Sun would join her. He had held himself aloof on the journey north. They had wrapped themselves in their own robes in the cold spring nights. Now their hosts had prepared a single, warm bed for them. She wondered how she could explain his absence if he slept elsewhere.

Her tired body demanded sleep before she could think of an excuse. She seemed to sleep only minutes before Tied to Sun shook her. Her thoughts came in a jumble. Did she have to prepare a morning meal? Pack the canoe? Another day to paddle? "We have wasted the trip, servant wife. Wasted it. Only my brother-in-law will profit from it. A whole summer gone."

"I don't understand, lordly husband. We arrived safely. As soon as the gambling is over, you'll give your gifts."

"Don't you understand?" he shouted in distress. "I lost all my gifts last night. Those stupid Menomini made me lose everything. I have nothing left."

CHAPTER ELEVEN

Tied to Sun mourned his losses all day. Gifted Tongue had never seen him so despondent. She tried to console him, but Gourd Woman's grown son arrived and ruined her effort.

"You lose magnificently, nobleman. The Menomini can't stop talking about you." The lean, pockmarked Black Bear said with a smirk, "How faithful you were to those losers, even when everyone else deserted them. I don't understand why they lost. A powerful shaman backed them." Then he chuckled, "But I guess the other team's shaman had more power."

He couldn't stop teasing, "Seems like the Menomini figured it out early. Even the Winnebago. You sure are persistent."

Gifted Tongue read "foolish" in "persistent" and guessed Tied to Sun did, too. She could see him churn with anger as he imagined the town reviewing his losses and his persistence.

When Black Bear left, Gifted Tongue urged a swim in the river fronting the town's edge. When he showed little interest, she suggested Two Hearts needed exercise. Perhaps, he could find him and the two swim together. Tied to Sun grunted that

Running Turkey hosted Two Hearts and left, his head down and shoulders bent.

She imagined Running Turkey to be a woman but hoped it was a man. She said forcefully to herself that it didn't concern her. What mattered was that Tied To Sun forget his losses.

After she straightened the bedding, she sought Gourd Woman who sat near the fire, mixing corn and acorn meal. Her cheeks glowed, and Gifted Tongue guessed she had bathed in the river.

Gourd Woman smiled apologetically. "I hope you don't mind the nuts. We have enough corn, but I've grown to like the taste of hickory and acorn. My husband teases me that I threw away my name, 'Gourd Woman' because I raise so few."

"I know what you mean about the nuts." Gifted Tongue said, "Corn fills the belly, but it doesn't have the taste of hickory."

"Here's a little fish from yesterday. We catch them even in winter since the river comes from springs. That's why the founders built here, that and the marshes full of food. The Menomini harvest canoe-loads of wild rice, so they're called 'wild rice people.'" She shook her head and added, "Maybe it's too abundant. The Menomini hate to farm. If it weren't for Winnebago, I mean the Dhegiha commoners, they'd never plant the fields." She paused in thought. "Maybe I shouldn't say Dhegiha. Most pioneers came from Chiwere outpost, west of the Mississippi."

She looked pensive and said, "We shouldn't settle our commoners permanently in an outpost. The second or third generations think of themselves as Winnebago instead of Chiwere or Dhegiha. I don't even know where the word, Winnebago, came from. I guess when Chiwere men marry Menomini women, the children blend their ways and become a new people."

She quickly added, "Of course, Distant Sun remains loyal to the Center of the World. He has important titles for someone as young as he is. I wish the Sun recognized us nobles as well."

Gifted Tongue hoped to avoid Aztalan intrigue, yet she could hardly turn her back on her host's frustration.

"Tied to Sun speaks often of your service. If you did not furnish raw resources, how would the city artisans manage? Dakota Next to Sun is so appreciative he sent many gifts." She bit her tongue. She must not meddle in her husband's affairs.

"You are kind. The spring visit means much to us. Everyone talks about your news from the Center of the World. The gifts remind us that we remain part of civilization."

Gifted Tongue hoped to avoid any talk of gifts, so when Tied to Sun appeared at the door, she rushed to his side. He took her arm to lead her away from the lodge and whispered brusquely, "I found the shaman who backed the winners last night and gave him the copper falcon." He smirked and said in his pretentious way, "Tonight he backs me. I'll win everything."

"But, lordly husband, you lost everything last night."

"All that I brought." He emphasized the I, and Gifted Tongue noted a hint of hesitancy in his exclamation. "The falcon was a gift from Next to Sun. I'll have to use another of his gifts to get in the game."

He frightened Gifted Tongue. She asked breathlessly, "Isn't it dangerous to use Next to Sun's gifts as your own?"

"My brother-in-law might be angry, but the next three nights are individual matches," he said with fervor. "Every man for himself. Or woman," he added. "The last time I visited, a Dhegiha noblewoman jumped in. Of course, she lost."

Gifted Tongue quivered. Given the little she knew of Dhegiha politics, gambling with Next to Sun's fortune struck lier as folly. She wondered what would happen if her husband lost again. She sensed he was beside himself with anxiety, but before she could do anything to calm him, he left.

She worried the rest of the day what might happen if he gambled away everything. When she spotted Two Hearts at dusk, she rushed to him and said, "Tied to Sun lost all his gifts last night. He told me the summer is ruined."

"I know. The Menomini can't stop laughing at his foolishness. The Winnebago have been more discrete, but commoners never sympathize with nobility."

"I'm scared, elder. He gave Next to Sun's copper falcon to a shaman who claims to have backed the winners. To get in the game, he'll use more of Next to Sun's gifts. Can he do that?"

"If he wants to commit treason," Two Hearts said scornfully. "Next to Sun will banish him if he finds out, even if he is his brother-in-law. The fool takes a terrible chance." He frowned as he shook his head.

"You must not call my husband a fool. But let's not quarrel. What can I do to stop him?"

"You're only a woman. You can't do anything. If your husband wants to gamble with his life, that's his concern," he said with disgust. Then in a different tone, he added, "He's hardly your husband anyway."

Gifted Tongue blushed. She wondered how Two Hearts knew she had not consummated her marriage, and how many other people knew. Her discomfort must have struck him, because when he spoke, his tone was gentle, with a hint of guilt.

"You are truly married. I went too far. Although being a servant wife is hardly being married. You should feel no regret for whatever happens to him."

"He can be kind, even if thoughtless."

"I know, child. For a noble he's almost decent, but he never forgets his superiority. He always manages some pompous word or act after he's done something likable."

Gifted Tongue grew increasingly uncomfortable at how intimate their talk had become. He evidently thought she resented his attempt to help so he made an excuse and left.

She almost called him back but sucked in her lip instead. She returned to Gourd Woman who greeted her with jokes about joining the gamblers.

The two arrived at the gaming lodge early and found seats behind Tied to Sun. Gifted Tongue saw him exchange a piece of mica engraved with a cross for a large number of tally sticks. The gambling began with big winners individually betting. Although she knew only the rudiments of the game, she recognized how skillfully each player deceived the other.

Early players began losing their places. Gifted Tongue watched her husband, his eagerness obvious. From his expression, she doubted that anxiety over his losses motivated him as much as compulsion. Most men threw themselves into the game, but she had seen a few consumed by it. She wondered if their guardian spirits abandoned them on such occasion.

Her fear doubled when Tied to Sun took the crystal. A young man opposed him, equally eager. Her husband gestured wildly with his hands, caught his opponent's eyes, and hid the mark. His smirk at winning betrayed feelings of superiority more than skill. In a few more turns, he won the young man's stakes.

The next opponent bet higher, as if to inspire Tied to Sun to even greater taunts and wilder gestures. The effort paid off, and Tied to Sun outdid himself in mocking and flourishing his hands. His stack of tally sticks reached a respectable height before his opponent won a turn. Gifted Tongue assumed the opponent had experienced much gambling, but his initial, clumsy efforts made her question her judgment. Then Tied to Sun began to lose. He resorted to ridicule rather than concentrating on his opponent's hands. As his pile of tallies shrank, his opponent's sarcasm mounted, throwing Tied to Sun into confusion.

Gifted Tongue watched with dismay. She didn't know what to do and decided that Two Hearts was right. A woman could do nothing except sit hopelessly. She couldn't imagine how Next to Sun would react. If not exile, she thought, then what?

When Tied to Sun lost his last tally, her insides thrashed. Never had she seen such despair in a person's face. His shoulders slumped. He staggered, more than walked, from the plaza toward a stockade gate.

She feared suicide, an act she had never heard of until Whirlwind had described it in a vocabulary lesson on Dhegiha. He had smiled when he said the custom supposedly proved that nobles were more responsible than commoners who weren't expected to kill themselves. It was a duty for nobles when they failed in their obligations to the Sun.

She wondered if she should try to dissuade him or seek Two Hearts to help. She knew that his response would be that a woman shouldn't interfere. Would he do anything? She doubted that Tied to Sun's death would make her miserable. The thought barely surfaced in her mind, but it raised doubts about her future even if he didn't kill himself.

Gourd Woman said little that evening. Gifted Tongue knew that she had witnessed Tied to Sun's losses and wondered if she believed he might kill himself. She couldn't think that, Gifted Tongue told herself, since she didn't know her husband had used Next to Sun's gifts. Or could she guess? She suspected that Gourd Woman had compared the value of two canoes filled with gifts against her husband's extravagant bets. Her host's behavior perplexed her. Gourd Woman acted as if nothing had happened. Perhaps she hadn't guessed the truth about her husband's losses. Gifted tongue sighed silently in confusion. If only Whirlwind were here to help.

Whatever Gourd Woman's thoughts were, she acted the part of host. "Let's tour our town in daylight," she said with a smile. At the river's edge, she pointed with her chin. "Across the river, people long ago built mounds in the shape of animals. One's a bear, another a lizard. The engineering is beyond the mentality of the Menomini. We call whoever built those mounds, the Mysterious Mound Builders."

Gifted Tongue thought the term equally appropriate for the Dhegiha, from her viewpoint.

"We do know the history of our town. It's nothing compared to your city, but the last two Distant Suns greatly improved it. The plaza was too cramped for significant ceremony before they rebuilt the stockade. It could never impress the Menomini."

"It impresses me now," Gifted Tongue nodded, trying to show enthusiasm and forget her husband's predicament.

"Our present home stands where the western edge of the stockade used to be. See the gravel knoll in the southwest corner? The early settlers used it for their temple mound. The old stockade barely circled it. The pioneers built on it until they could erect a proper mound. They did a good job on the priest's temple. That must have impressed the Menomini."

Gifted Tongue gritted her teeth. Her host must know that she failed to concentrate because she was troubled by her husband's absence. Focusing on the town, she spotted a natural knoll, not a pyramid as she first thought. For once, the Dhegiha resorted to practicality.

"The engineers didn't follow city standards in expanding. Perhaps no engineer priests came to plan the new walls. Whoever took charge built the original temple mound by the river. Most pioneers lived at its base. They threw their mussel shells on the bank. One of these days, we'll get them cleaned up."

When the two women reached the base of the temple mound, Gourd Woman stood in awe of the large building atop it. She boasted of the town's ancestors who had duplicated the grandeur of temples at the Center of the World.

Gifted Tongue hoped to flatter her. "Your builders did a splendid job, and you keep it well thatched. It's awe-inspiring," she exclaimed.

Gourd Woman said, "To expand the stockade, Distant Sun's father persuaded people to build a charnel house mound in the northwest corner. He laid a large base as the first stage for it. The priests used it briefly before he died. His son built a second stage with a burial home atop it, four paces by two paces. Nine retainers joined Distant Sun in death. He followed the custom of burning down the house with a flame from the Perpetual Fire. He buried a relative's bone bundle in a third stage when the mound reached its present height."

Gifted Tongue would never understand the Dhegiha obsession with death. As she and her host walked toward the southwest corner, she thought of all the arduous labor that it required, at least from commoners. From the center of the plaza, the temple mound resembled the pyramid of the sun in the city.

"The temple mound is largely due to the present Distant Sun. Such ambition," Gourd Woman said, her eyes shining with devotion. "He thought the old mound opposite the knoll lay too close to the river. He determined to take advantage of the terrain and have his own temple. After his father died, he persuaded the priests to construct a second stage in memory of his father."

Gifted Tongue wondered at the ease with which the nobility took credit for building when the dirt moved on the backs of commoners.

"After a while, the priests argued that temple mounds weren't memorials, so the second stage remained incomplete." Gourd Woman smiled proudly. "But Little Sun turned the tables and persuaded the commoners to add a third stage to take advantage of the terrain. So from here, the height of the mound rivals the largest of the Center of the World, no?"

Gifted Tongue agreed, silently noting that one didn't have to be an engineer to see that the mound rose from a natural hillside. But when viewed from the plaza, she had to admit that the effect inspired reverence.

"The people must love him to work so hard." Gifted Tongue hoped she hid her skepticism.

"He started off well, an able politician and administrator. He gave the grandest feasts and displayed imposing valuables, but he did better at displaying than giving away. Later that hurt his reputation, but now he's learned to give."

Gifted Tongue regretted she would have no chance to meet him because he would spend the summer at the Center of the World to cement relations with other Suns.

"I'll never know where he got his gifts to manage as he did. After undertaking the mound building, he revived the first Distant Sun's idea of expanding the stockade. He kept the river as an eastern boundary, but made the northern and southern walls four times longer. That forced us to build a new western wall more than five hundred paces long. You wouldn't believe the trees they felled. The Menomini helped at first, but after breaking many axes they quit. The Winnebago had to finish."

"Clearing the forest must have opened up much farmland," Gifted Tongue said.

"It did. You'd think the new land would persuade the Menomini to cultivate, but they found more excuses to hunt. In fact, their elders complained bitterly about damage to the forest when it became hard to find firewood for the winter."

Gifted Tongue silently empathized with the Menomini complaints, but she said sympathetically, "I guess they don't know what's good for them."

Apparently, Gourd Woman failed to detect any sarcasm and nodded emphatically. "They fail to appreciate us. Why, I doubt that such a stockade exists anywhere in civilization, except for the Center of the World. The work impressed my son so much that he counted the logs they used. There were four thousand."

Gifted Tongue didn't care about numbers. She did notice that the distances between bastions equaled those at the Center of the World although the esthetics of the Aztalan stockade were more impressive. Squared bastions jutted from the walls in regular fashion at precise distances of about twenty-five paces. She also noted a curving wall behind entrances to the stockade. From a distance, an observer saw a solid wall broken only by the bastions so the barrier presented a solid face its entire length. Gourd Woman broke her contemplation. "Your husband will find his way back, I'm sure."

The mention of Tied to Sun unnerved Gifted Tongue. She had forgotten him.

. . .

When the third night of gambling began, Gifted Tongue stayed home anxiously awaiting Tied to Sun. Her heart fluttered when the door flap opened. Instead of her husband, Two Hearts came in. "Has your lordly husband returned?" he asked with sympathy.

"No, elder. I fear he has killed himself. What is the word for it?"

"Suicide. But Tied to Sun is neither brave enough nor foolish enough to commit suicide."

"I'm not sure I understand you. I feel he is dead."

"It may only mean you wish he were dead," he said, his eye twitching. "If he has killed himself, then he's more of a fool than I thought."

"Why should I wish him dead? He's my husband. And my guardian spirits directed me to his city."

"Guardian spirits can mislead a person. Keep an open mind. You might be better off without him, just as the world would be better off without nobles and Suns."

"How can you say that? You've been treated well by your noble protectors and the Sun who adopted you."

"I was lucky as a child. Now I don't need them, but one of them may need me," he said mysteriously. After a pause, he bragged, "I've watched the Menomini winners. I'll make losers of them tonight. When I win back Next to Sun's gifts, we'll see how your husband shows his appreciation."

Two Hearts' boast raised Gifted Tongue's hopes. Perhaps

her instructor could outwit the gamblers, she hoped. She wondered how much skill it would take to win back Tied to Sun's losses. She also pondered what he meant that she might wish Tied to Sun dead and suddenly realized that his death would not distress her. She put aside the thought as drumbeats drew her and Two Hearts toward the plaza.

Two Hearts carried a cloth mantle to exchange for tallies. Only a simple print zigzag decorated it, but its fine weaving caught the eye. He told Gifted Tongue that Diving Hawk had entrusted the mantle to him, allowing him to give it to a noble of his choice.

Instead of saving it for a gift, he bartered with a Menomini for tally sticks. "You see the woof in this cloth? Observe how uniform the milkweed fiber is. Do you see the basswood warp? The woof almost hides it, but you can see its strength. The spinner took care that its fiber is all the same size." His voice compelled attention, while he flourished the cloth.

From his scowl, Gifted Tongue guessed Two Hearts settled for fewer tallies than he wished. She hurried to keep up with him as he rushed to the plaza. At the circle, two young men ahead of him lost to an older expert. Two Hearts whispered to her that he had observed the hunchbacked gambler the night before and was onto his deceptive tricks.

The Menomini opponent lost his opening move, and Two Hearts' pile of tallies grew. His eye quit twitching as his confidence soared along with Gifted Tongue's hope. She smiled in admiration. When the Menomini stretched, Two Hearts said to her, "He follows a pattern. I can tell his hiding place from a glint in the eye. I'll win back Tied to Sun's fortune in no time."

Gifted Tongue relaxed but worried still at how easy Two Hearts made it sound. Years of experience must have made the

Menomini a better player than he seemed. The gambler confirmed her suspicion when he consistently hid the crystal where Two Hearts never guessed. She tugged at his elbow, but he pushed her hand aside. The gesture dashed her hopes. She knew the hunchback had trapped Two Hearts in the thrill of winning.

Two Hearts sat dumbfounded when he found his tallies gone. Gifted Tongue was on the verge of tears, in agony for him. Suddenly, she wondered why her heart went out to him when her husband's career had been ruined.

She fled the plaza, knowing she could not console Two Hearts. His dark expression walled off any comfort. When she reached Gourd Woman's house, she thought of Tied to Sun. If he were dead, she wondered if she could return to the Kutenai and Eloquent One.

She didn't wait long to search for an answer. The excitement had drained her energy, and sleep overcame her as soon as she lay down. It seemed only moments later she awoke to a summer-like day. Her eyes opened to see her husband creep toward her, blood dripping from both sleeves of his shirt. Dirt and ashes covered his face.

"I spent a full day and night begging Rock's pity. My guardian conveyed my message. No vision came, but how could Rock help but pity me? I offered a hundred pieces of flesh to prove my misery," he said with pride. "He'll find a way, you'll see."

Gifted Tongue felt helpless. Her husband gave her no chance to comfort him. Picking up a fresh shirt, he went to the river to bathe. Afterward, he sought a shaman to treat his cuts.

She sat depressed, then decided to overcome it by walking to the village outskirts. At its edge, she saw a middle-aged woman, smiling contentedly as she quilled a moccasin. She sorted quills by size, glancing at Gifted Tongue, inviting her to speak.

"It's a beautiful design," Gifted Tongue said, fingering a finished moccasin.

"Do you work quills, honored guest?" The woman looked up.

"No, I'm from a western tribe. My mothers didn't teach me."

"You are welcome to watch. I've almost finished the moccasin. I'm quilling a dress for my brother to give to his new wife's parents. See how I bend the quill so the right color shows. Then I insert the points into the sinew thread."

Gifted Tongue admired the dexterity, matched by moons of effort. Moreover, the graceful curves surrounding bouquets of flowers demanded an imagination she deemed beyond herself. She yearned for a quilled dress like it for Whirlwind.

Thoughts of him reminded her of Double Woman. She frowned slightly as she remembered his admonition that concentration could confuse any opponent. Surely, Menomini gamblers opposed her. They had taken her husband's possessions and threatened his life. She would test her power.

.   .   .

Gifted Tongue spent the afternoon in a maple forest watching a commoner tap trees for the spring sap. She hoped for a sign to validate the use of her power. As the sun set, she returned to Aztalan, upset at lack of any guidance. At the forest edge, an owl swooped toward her. Her startled cry did not deter it from pouncing on a field mouse scurrying to evade her feet. Surely this was the sign she hoped for.

Back at Gourd Woman's, she sniffed a pinch of Whirlwind's powder and headed for the plaza. She experienced elation, with her mind focused in a new dimension. She felt invincible.

The drums drew spectators and the big winners along with a handful of women who dared try their skill. On the periphery, she bartered the ear spools for tallies. With them in hand, she joined others waiting for a chance. Individual matches began, and the air filled with taunts and chants. Several women faced opponents, their eyes fixed on the other's hands.

Soon Gifted Tongue's turn arrived. A brash young Menomini faced her, scoffing at playing a woman. He laughed with disdain at her initial, clumsy efforts, easily guessing her hiding places. She sucked her lips as her tallies diminished. When her opponent stretched his legs, she took more medicine. Focusing on nothing but Double Woman and helping others, her hands flew so rapidly that they blended with the moccasins.

Pass after pass, the young man sat at a loss. His tallies shifted to Gifted Tongue's pile. An older woman next opposed her. She apparently guessed Gifted Tongue an easy mark, but the young woman's sleight of hand never faltered.

While awaiting the next gambler, Gifted Tongue sniffed more medicine. A large man with loose hair, boasting of his skill, asked if she wanted to give him her tallies. She smiled demurely and said, "You are welcome to them, if you earn them."

He guffawed in scorn but appeared a bit confused at her taunt. He tried an insult, then shifted to flourishes that did little to conceal his hiding place. When Gifted Tongue won her turn, her fingers flew under each moccasin to leave her opponent befuddled. The crowd buzzed with news of her victories.

A Menomini elder elected to take his chances with her. He

figured a powerful shaman backed her, but he reckoned he had spent far more years gambling than she had lived.

She bowed her head respectfully and said, "Welcome grandrelative. You honor me. I trust you pity me."

He raised an eyebrow in surprise at her fluency in Menomini.

"From what I hear you need no pity. I hope you haven't learned to gamble as well as you have learned our language."

"You are kind. I'm a beginner, and my tongue ties itself in knots with many of your words."

He laughed and said, "Then listen closely to the words of my song and pay less attention to the moccasins." She saw his smile was warm but wary.

With that, he made his first move. Gifted Tongue guessed correctly, and in the next four moves deceived her opponent. Her victories made her overconfident. She imagined a mountain of tallies. After all, she thought, she had not only Double Woman power but also her mother's talent as a gambler.

When she lost her turn, her opponent deceived her in a long run. When she won back her turn, her brow sweated, and her hands trembled. She felt panic in her chest. She seldom fooled the old man, and his darting hands bedazzled her. Soon she realized that even the tallies for her ear spools were nearly gone. It was time to quit, but the old man's taunts held her in place.

When he rose to excuse himself, she heard two owls call to each other. She wondered if they came to warn her or advise her. A warning was too late, but what advice could they offer? She asked herself what Whirlwind would do.

He had warned her to use Double Woman powers only for the good of others she remembered. She had hoped to win wealth for herself. What a terrible mistake, she thought bitterly.

Before her opponent returned, she sniffed a bit of the potion and rubbed the last on her temples, beseeching her owls to intercede with Double Woman.

The elder returned and nodded that he was ready. Gifted Tongue began. She sang Washo songs as prelude and followed with Shoshoni and Kutenai chants. As soon as she began, she knew the elder never had a chance. The strange words and melodies clouded his eyes. The distracting sounds blurred the girl's hands as they flew under the moccasins.

The man's victims of the previous nights delighted in Gifted Tongue's victory and cheered her on. She felt Double Woman watch over her to provide dexterity, and she never hesitated. Thinking only of Double Woman and others, her concentration never ceased until all the tally sticks were hers.

CHAPTER TWELVE

"So, sister, how was your journey to Aztalan? On cold nights, did you share your blanket with Two Hearts? I don't suppose Tied to Sun kept you warm."

Gifted Tongue flushed at Whirlwind's banter. After months of separation, his teasing surprised her. And confused her. He shouldn't joke with her about sex if he was her brother, but she had often called him sister when she teased him.

She tossed her head as if his question wasn't worth an answer and said, "I have no desire to share his blanket." Then, she decided to jest. "Perhaps he's invited you, sister, since he returned. Did he share a blanket or complain about the nobles? Do you know he gambled away Diving Hawk's gift to win back losses of Tied to Sun?"

Whirlwind's eyebrow shot up in surprise. "Really? But he loses no love for Tied to Sun." He added, only half joking, "He must have been trying to impress you."

"Why would he want to impress me?" Gifted Tongue retorted.

"I've seen the way he looks at you. He's interested in more than teaching you Menomini."

"Don't be ridiculous. He'd never make advances to the wife of a noble."

"Are you really a wife, my sister?" Whirlwind said gently.

"I'm married." Gifted Tongue answered defensively, but with enough emphasis to dismiss further discussion. It was well she stopped because Two Hearts appeared out of nowhere with a goose that signaled the approach of winter. As he handed it to her, he said with a sneer, "This is for the family, woman. I'll bring a deer if I'm lucky, but I suppose you feast on venison most days."

"Elder, we seldom have venison. The goose is a treat." Gifted Tongue struggled to be polite. She didn't want to fight, but he excited anger. She wondered how he could be so indifferent after she had won back his losses.

"With your powers, you must have anything you want," he said with a scowl. "Too bad you weren't here to heal my master's leg. Then you wouldn't be watching out for me." His words rang with sarcasm. Before she could reply, he stalked off.

"Whatever has gotten into him?" Gifted Tongue gave Whirlwind a perplexed look. "Why is he so irritable? He seemed halfway human on our way to Aztalan."

"Perhaps you haven't heard, sister. Diving Hawk"—he whispered the name—"died from an infection when a Long Nosed God priest broke the skin to set his leg. His brothers sought Water Monster doctors, but they called them too late. It means more trouble between the two societies. The Water Monster doctors have pride. No telling what they might do to show up the Long Nosed God doctors."

Gifted Tongue nodded bewilderment at the complexity of the city's politics. Whirlwind returned to Two Hearts. He said gently, "I don't understand why he acts as if you thought your-self his superior. Did you put on airs with him?"

"What do you think, grandrelative? Why would I?" By call-ing Whirlwind grandrelative, Gifted Tongue switched to a seri-ous tone. "After Tied to Sun and Two Hearts gambled away their gifts for Aztalan, I pawned ear spools a woman gave me and won back what they lost, including a present for you." Gifted Tongue couldn't wait to see his face at the sight of the quillwork.

When she brought the dress from the Menomini quiller, his features danced with appreciation. No words were needed to feel his delight.

"I can smell the flowers. The porcupines gave their best. You're a superb gift-giver as well as a gambler," he smiled cor-dially.

"Not I, grandrelative. Double Woman and the potion you gave me did it all. They confused the Menomini. Their best gam-blers never had a chance except once, when I started thinking of myself instead of others. I almost lost everything."

"Look at it, sister," Whirlwind exclaimed, "Besides the smell of flowers the leaves tremble in the breeze. It's the best work I've ever seen. Can I try it on?"

Whirlwind did not wait for an answer but swooped into Gifted Tongue's house, returning in an instant to show off his new dress. When he swayed, the flowers quivered, and the fra-grance of spring blossoms wafted in the air.

"You look exquisite," Gifted Tongue said admiringly. "A spring flower yourself."

"Yes, it's a dress to make men forget my gray hair," Whirlwind joked. "I'll have to be careful. Some noblewomen might kill me to get this dress. It's good I don't dance within the stockade. Too many women there would envy me."

In a serious tone, he said, "What did you do to Two Hearts to make him so irritable?"

"No more teasing, grandrelative. I'm not in the mood."

"I didn't mean to tease, child. I'm curious as to why he's acting the way he is."

"As I said, he lost a beautiful mantle Diving Hawk gave him to exchange. He used it to gamble in order to win back Tied to Sun's losses. When he lost, I used Double Woman power to get everything back, along with this dress."

"You saved the day," Whirlwind exclaimed.

"Then why does Two Hearts hate me?"

"I don't think it's hate. Perhaps a Trickster story will explain how he feels."

Whirlwind sat down cross-legged for his story. Gifted Tongue recalled Trickster tales from her childhood that made a moral point, but she didn't see how one could explain Two Hearts' rejection of her. She sat before him entranced.

"Once, Trickster found no one to beg food from, so he trapped ducks. Because he was too lazy to build a trap, he invited them to dance. He used six of his eight legs to beat a rhythm that the ducks had never heard."

"But coyote has only four legs," Gifted Tongue protested. "How can you say he has eight?"

"Trickster has many forms. People in the west think he's a coyote. In the north, he's a rabbit. Among the Dhegiha, he's a spider with a stinger like a wasp." Whirlwind darted two fingers and gave Gifted Tongue a pinch. "The ducks lined up. Spider told them to wait for the rhythm. Their bodies shook with his beat. He told them to shut their eyes. When the line came close, he grabbed the first and wrung its neck." He gestured wildly as he wrung four imaginary necks. "He worked so hard to gather firewood and to pluck the ducks that by the time he roasted them, he was sleepy. He worried a fox might smell the roasting ducks and steal them, so he ordered his stinger to stand guard. His stinger watched, but it got sleepy, too." Whirlwind closed his eyes and dropped his head.

Then he whispered, "Fox smelled the ducks. He crept up to find Spider and stinger fast asleep. He snatched the ducks and enjoyed a feast fit for the Sun." Whirlwind smiled at the thought.

"The next morning when Spider awoke, he missed the ducks and saw stinger fast asleep. He was so furious, he grabbed an ember and burned his stinger black. In his anger he didn't feel the pain until too late. He raced for the river, but the water did no good. Trickster suffered for days."

Gifted Tongue chuckled at the imagery. The story reminded her of Trickster's foolishness, she thought, but she sucked her lip as she wondered what moral his adventure might teach her.

"Don't you see?" Whirlwind said, "Two Hearts acts like Trickster. When you won back the gifts, you saved Tied to Sun's life and Two Hearts' honor, maybe even his life. Who knows what Diving Hawk would do to a servant who squandered his wealth?

"Tied to Sun reacted logically," Whirlwind said matter-of-factly. "He was grateful that you pulled his roast ducks from the hungry Menomini. But Two Hearts is too proud to appreciate a woman saving his ducks. So what does he do? He can't burn you, but he makes life miserable for you. Also for himself, I'll bet. Be patient. After a while he'll realize he's burning his stinger and hurting himself."

Gifted Tongue contemplated the explanation. Why did she care if Two Hearts liked her? she wondered. She did welcome the goose. She and Rising Moon seldom ate meat since they had learned of the danger from Roaring Woman. A haunch of deer would be a treat. Maybe it was just as well that Two Hearts begrudged her winnings, she thought. Let his shame feed them.

.　　.　　.

"Did you see the side of deer that Two Hearts left?" Rising Moon said. "How many times has he brought us meat this winter? Do you think he's as generous with Diving Hawk's wives?"

Gifted Tongue cursed her heart. Why should mention of the venison cause her face to flush and her heart to race? she asked herself. And why had she been absent when he delivered the gift? She had crafted a pair of moccasins for him. Now she wondered when she could give them to him.

The two women set aside choice parcels of the meat for the winter solstice celebration. The rest they cut into thin, narrow strips to smoke. Smoking was easier in winter since they used the fire that warmed their home. Gifted Tongue loved the mingling aroma of smoking hickory and drying venison. These days she often had to substitute sycamore for the scarce hickory.

"I'll never understand that man, co-wife. He taught me much Menomini, and we got along on the trip. He grumbled about the nobles, but he tried to recover our husband's losses. But when Double Woman helped me win back what he lost, he resented me." Rising Moon spread the last of the meat over the fire and wrinkled her brow. When she rubbed her back and stretched, Gifted Tongue suggested a walk.

Near the edge of their ward, Rising Moon said, "Some men are forever a mystery. We have to accept them as they are." She shrugged. "Let's go to Osage ward. The gossips claim they're competing with the nobility for the Sun's recognition."

"How can they?" News of Dhegiha politics distracted her thoughts of Two Hearts.

"We talk as if commoner clans were always a level below the nobles, but my father told me about commoner clans that twice claimed noble status. In one case, the Sun recognized commoners as nobility, at least for awhile. Another time, he exiled a clan for its attempt. The Sun declared them heretics."

Gifted Tongue stopped walking to ask, "I've never heard the word heretic. What does it mean?"

"It's a person who denies his religion is the true faith. A noble or a Sun heretic is executed, commoners are exiled. The Sun decreed exile worse than execution." Rising Moon smiled and said, "I wonder if the exiles agree? One band fled up the Ohio River to the eastern mountains. Rumors claim that they prosper there in a life of equality."

The two continued to walk. Rising Moon stopped talking as they reached Osage ward. An ill-defined dance ground served as its plaza, dominated by a conical mound. East of it, workers had cleared the prairie grass, and ward elders were completing a ritual to beg Mother Earth's permission to use the clay.

A thin layer of fresh soil served as the base for a platform mound. The conical mound and new platform mound would duplicate the twin mounds within the stockade.

Rising Moon gritted her teeth in fright. "The Osage Water Monster doctors tread on dangerous ground. They plan a charnel house to rival the nobles. I wonder which Osage sub-clans will claim exalted status."

Gifted Tongue stood puzzled. "Can they do that simply because the Long Nosed God priests failed to cure Diving Hawk? His relatives must be in danger for asking the Water Monster doctors to help."

"A good question," Rising Moon said apprehensively. "One incident doesn't spark rebellion. Of course, it won't be called a rebellion if their claims stick. The Osage have plotted a long time to outdo other societies of Water Monster priests in order to claim nobility. They must figure that the time is ripe to use Diving Hawk's death as an excuse.

"When will the challenge come?"

"I doubt the Osage can work while we celebrate the winter solstice. Then the ground will freeze. The showdown may wait until spring."

"Perhaps I'll be gone. Won't our husband travel the Missouri this spring?" Gifted Tongue said hopefully. "If he visits the Kutenai, we'll leave early. I'd love to see my adopted relatives, and maybe hear about my Shoshoni family."

"You're right. He leaves early when he travels to the northwest. He talks about fighting the ice all the way to Mandan country. It will be a long summer for me without you."

"Oh, sister, how thoughtless of me. You'll be here alone to work the fields and to guard against whatever Roaring Woman tries." Gifted Tongue felt torn between the need to help her co-wife and desperation to see her homeland.

"I've worked the fields alone many summers. My clan sisters pitch in when I need them. Don't fret. The work gets done." Rising Moon obviously didn't mean to stir guilt, she had simply stated facts. Nevertheless, Gifted Tongue's conscience reacted as she recalled the hard days spent cajoling the corn and beans.

.   .   .

The two women had no time to worry during the next few days as they prepared feasts that Tied to Sun and Roaring

Woman would host. Once they waded in icy water to spear catfish and gather cattail roots. The feast depended on cornmeal so the two sweated in the cold to grind ear after ear. When they finished, they took samples of their work to Roaring Woman.

The joy of the season seemed to have infected even her. She welcomed them warmly. While she tasted the various soups and corn balls they had prepared, the two co-wives waited anxiously for her approval. Despite the anxiety, their mouths watered as Roaring Woman slurped the delicacies. Although they had sampled more than usual, their stomachs never experienced the bursting bellies the nobles forced upon themselves.

Roaring Woman took her time to sample everything thoroughly before she praised the results. Gifted Tongue noted that she chose words that lacked any s sound so that some of her vocabulary was as unusual as Tied to Sun's. Gifted Tongue concentrated so hard on listening that Rising Moon had to touch her arm to show that Roaring Woman had dismissed them.

The day after the solstice, when the nobles attacked piles of venison, bear, roast turkey and goose, along with dozens of stews and soups, Gifted Tongue said to Rising Moon in disgust, "It's terribly wrong for the nobles to eat so much that they become sick, while commoners have so little that they sicken at the slightest cold. How long will the Dhegiha tolerate it?"

"Talk with Two Hearts. I've heard he's asked the same thing for years. But what can be done?" She shrugged.

"I don't know," Gifted Tongue shuddered. "I just want to leave. I can't wait to get back to the Kutenai. Life is so much more pleasant among the peoples the Dhegiha call savages."

"It's hard to believe," Rising Moon said perplexed. "You

paint such a different picture than our husband. He's always so glad to return to city comforts."

"I suppose it has to do with how you are reared. We get comfortable with what we learn early and take it as natural." "Do you think there's anything natural about Roaring Woman's lisp? I don't think her parents lisped."

Gifted Tongue had no idea but grinned as she mimicked her other co-wife. Th rolled off her tongue to substitute for s as she said, "Roaring Woman sews sea shells on a soft skin."

"Oh, co-wife," Rising Moon giggled, "You have not only her lisp but her voice. You sound exactly like her. I mean, you sound exactly like her." Rising Moon tried to imitate the lisp, but she hesitated before the s in sound, and she failed to change the s sound in exactly.

Gifted Tongue continued with her game, replacing all the s's with th's. "Do I sound so simple? We must be careful. Suppose she does not sleep silently but is sneaking up on us?"

The warning came too late. Roaring Woman had come with a pot of leftover stew and stood at the door. She bellowed, "You ungrateful dogs. Will you mock the Sun next? I never want to hear your crude mimicry again, slave wife."

Ordinarily, she would have sent for one of them to fetch the food, but the holiday mood had led her to visit. Now the two had ruined her good humor. She flung the pot into the fire. A flying ember burnt her ankle.

"Curse you. You'll get it when I tell Tied to Sun." Her face was mottled red and pink, and her eyes flashed anger. "Even that tongue of yours won't save you this time, slave wife." The way she turned and limped away made it clear she would never forget her humiliation.

Gifted Tongue was too stunned to speak, but finally she

stammered, "What did she mean when she called me slave wife? The only time I heard the word slave it meant people whom the Dhegiha took prisoner."

Rising Moon shook back tears of fright at what Roaring Woman might do. "She should never call you a slave. The Dhegiha never practiced slavery until the Muskoki priests came. Slaves are no good for farming because guarding them is so much trouble. But they are sacrificed. One can't kill a servant because servants have rights."

"So you think Tied to Sun might sacrifice me?" Gifted Tongue said incredulously.

"Never. He does some foolish things, because he's so pompous, but he likes you. Besides you're too valuable as an interpreter."

Gifted Tongue's spirit sank at the thought that only her ability to interpret made her a valued member of the household.

.   .   .

A few moons later, Rising Moon and Gifted Tongue recalled the solstice feasts with bitterness as they calculated their scarce inventory of corn, a little amaranth, depleted beans, and disappearing squash.

"We'll have enough succotash for a moon, another of corn mush. We won't starve, but we may eat any meat Roaring Woman sends." Rising Moon tried to joke to cheer Gifted Tongue. She had been quiet since Roaring Woman surprised them, and Rising Moon regretted speaking the name. She added quickly that she had glimpsed Whirlwind wearing his quilled dress.

Whirlwind's name made Gifted Tongue forget Roaring Woman for a moment. An image of him made her jump when he suddenly appeared. His lean, muscular body filled the door. Instead of a dress, he wore leggings and a fur cape which both men and women used in freezing weather. A pouch hung at his waist, and he reached into it.

"I thought of you, grandrelative, when one of my patients gave me these."

Gifted Tongue looked at the two turtles he held. She wondered what kind of joke he planned. "Did they remind you of how slowly I learn your stories?"

"You know that's not so," he said dryly.

"I guess it's because they're snapping turtles. You remembered how I snap at you over your bad jokes."

"Well, they are snapping turtles. The patient was looking for an obsidian piece her husband threw into a slough in a fit of anger. The turtles surprised her. I thought you could add them to a soup, one you might share with me."

"It's been a while since we've eaten meat of any kind, sister. I'll prepare our best soup. Is it because we cook so well that you thought of us?" Gifted Tongue smiled.

Whirlwind laughed. "You do cook well, almost as good as I do. But the turtles reminded me of Two Hearts. Since he means so much to you, I thought I should share something about him."

Rising Moon raised a puzzled eyebrow since Gifted Tongue seldom mentioned him and had told her nothing of her feelings.

"Of course, he never related his vision to me so I'm not sure why he is called Two Hearts. Since Diving Hawk always claimed he was loyal and especially after he tried to help Tied to Sun recover his losses, rumor says his heart lies in two places so he can't be trusted. He talks against the nobility but helps them. Before such gossip hurts you, here is what I first heard." Whirlwind sat cross-legged and cleared his throat.

"I'm glad you'll tell me, grandrelative." The eagerness in Gifted Tongue's reply caused Rising Moon to stare at her.

"Before Two Hearts sought his vision, he hunted turtles. He ate their hearts to gain their endurance. It's an ancient custom. If he found a really large turtle, he might have discovered a double heart. Not just large, but almost two hearts. That's how he got his name, I'd bet."

Rising Moon nodded in agreement. The explanation fitted Dhegiha custom. Gifted Tongue also felt certain that Whirlwind must be right.

He rose and stretched to say, "Well, sisters, I don't want you to rush the soup. I'll be back tomorrow. Will you be ready then?" Their grins answered him. "Perhaps Two Hearts will join us, so make enough for four." With that he disappeared.

"Why should Two Hearts join us?" Rising Moon asked.

Gifted Tongue sat silently in hopeful expectation. In a moment, she shook her head and said, "We haven't seen Whirlwind in ages; suddenly he shows up. Why not Two Hearts?"

Rising Moon gave her a quizzical look, and Gifted Tongue guessed she saw her smile. Then she recalled Two Hearts' anger on his last visit. She said emphatically, "But who cares?"

At the day's end, as Gifted Tongue covered the household embers, Two Hearts coughed at the door, struggling with one end of a pole from which most of a bear dangled. A friend tussled with the other end.

"I bring meat for our household. I suppose it will go to waste in such a wealthy family, but you can share with friends. Most of its fat is gone, but there's enough to sweeten the corn."

Rising Moon could only shake her head in amazement at the mountain of meat. Gifted Tongue stood speechless. She couldn't understand why Two Hearts would bring such a gift, nor why he had said our household.

After a few polite formalities with Rising Moon, he asked Gifted Tongue if she still practiced Menomini. He seemed about to leave before she remembered to invite him for turtle soup the next day, adding that he could visit with Whirlwind.

He took so long to decide that Gifted Tongue grew angry. When he accepted, a rush of joy overwhelmed the anger, and she regretted she said nothing more before he left.

At first light, Gifted Tongue sorted herbs for the turtle soup. Rising Moon awoke, and the two discussed their favorite recipes. Gifted Tongue added firewood, and Rising Moon rinsed their largest pot.

"It's cold enough, isn't it, that the bear can wait until evening?" Gifted Tongue said. She knew it was but asking Rising Moon acknowledged her seniority.

"Yes, we can wait. But I expect Tied to Sun tonight. It's been a month, so he should be at full seed. Whirlwind left his fertility medicine yesterday when he handed you the turtles. Do you think he knew Tied to Sun planned to visit me?" Rising Moon's voice rang with respect.

"His powers are great, but it might be coincidence. Yet it is strange how he shows up when we need him most. I do hope you become pregnant, co-wife. Only a moon or two remain before we leave for Kutenai country."

Rising Moon said, "If I knew I was pregnant before you left, then Tied to Sun could use his seed to make you pregnant. Whirlwind's medicine may help us both."

The thought of pregnancy that once elated Gifted Tongue now gave her pause. Anticipation of Two Hearts' visit confused her feelings even more.

Two Hearts arrived early, sat next to Rising Moon and made small talk, while avoiding Gifted Tongue. She left in search of firewood until curiosity got the better of her, and she returned with a small armload.

She sat opposite him and said, "Elder, I forgot the Menomini word for bear. Your present made me realize my ignorance."

Two Hearts searched his vocabulary, but before he answered Gifted Tongue said, "Neither Rising Moon nor I understand what you meant when you said the gift is for our household."

"No one told you?" Two Hearts said in surprise. "I thought Whirlwind would tell you, if not Tied to Sun."

"Tell us what?" Gifted Tongue said, leaning closer to him.

"Did you not notice that Tied to Sun feasted Diving Hawk's brothers during the solstice?"

"We were so busy grinding corn we didn't keep track of the guests," Rising Moon said. She was too embarrassed to confess that Roaring Woman never told them whom she invited.

"You fed them so well they had no alternative when Tied to Sun praised my services. They had to give me to him. Besides, his brothers don't trade so they didn't need me. I hope bringing the bear to you instead of Roaring Woman won't make trouble. I'll pretend I didn't know the custom." He laughed shrewdly and said, "Maybe she won't find out until we've eaten it."

The three smiled at their conspiracy, and Gifted Tongue flushed at the thought of Two Hearts joining their household. She fantasized about the time they would have together on the trip to the mountains.

"While we eat bear fat, I can teach you Kutenai," she said, unable to contain her excitement. "You can call me elder. We'll have a moon or more to practice while we travel." Happiness hummed in her words.

"We won't go to Kutenai country while I'm part of the household," Two Hearts said flatly. "Even Tied to Sun must know I'd run away if I got that close to where I was born."

CHAPTER THIRTEEN

"Another gray day with more snow, co-wife. Won't it ever stop?" Dismay in Gifted Tongue's voice spoke louder than words.

"At least we can lie here a while longer," Rising Moon said as she reached to shove unburnt firewood toward embers of the evening fire. "Enjoy the warmth of this bearskin. It's the first winter I've had such luxury."

"Perhaps your clan brothers can track." Gifted Tongue imagined fresh meat to shake her gloom. She focused on Strawberry Month when they'd have the first fruit.

Rising Moon said, "Tied to Sun plans to hunt with Two Hearts so they may bring us meat also."

Gifted Tongue wished to share the optimism, but she was more realistic. "Yes, except Tied To Sun takes it all to Roaring Woman, unless Two Hearts can hide a little. Should we tell him how she tried to poison you?"

"Have you forgotten what happened when she discovered that he brought the bear to us? Poor Two Hearts," Rising Moon said sympathetically. "The way Tied to Sun forced him to do woman's work. We can't let that happen again."

Gifted Tongue failed to share her co-wife's concern when she recalled his scowl and how slowly he had ground corn. Her conscience tweaked her, though, when she remembered teasing at the lumps in his meal. The look he had given leaped to mind. She decided she could go a while longer with the stringy dried bear though her mouth watered at the thought of fresh venison.

"I guess you're right. We shouldn't tell. Have you seen him? I haven't, since he brought the bear."

"Neither have I," Rising Moon said. "Tied to Sun seldom mentions him since his punishment. In fact, he says little, despite frequent visits. He's desperate for an heir, but after we make love he rarely stays." Rising Moon looked down and said demurely. "He claims that he's busy preparing for the equinox."

"I can understand concern for the solstices when the sun is at its extremes, but why bother when it's halfway in between? The Shoshoni and Kutenai know nothing of equinoxes, and it's never made a difference," Gifted Tongue said.

"Don't let Tied to Sun hear such skepticism," Rising Moon glanced around. "But I've wondered the same thing. The equinox celebration isn't nearly as enjoyable. We don't dance or feast since there's not enough food. Tied to Sun once told me the midway sun foretells the position of certain stars, but I didn't understand. In fact, I don't think he understood." Rising Moon grinned. "Yet, he never doubts that he knows everything."

Her smile stirred Gifted Tongue to roll out from under the bearskin. Wincing at the overcast sky and swirling snowflakes, she added a few pieces of sumac to the small flame and set last night's pot of mush near it.

Rising Moon joined her, the two poking at embers to watch

sparks jump while they waited. "Does the snow make you feel so good?" Gifted Tongue asked. "I've never seen you happier. Are you so sure hunters will bring us meat?"

"No," Rising Moon laughed. "It's that I'm pregnant."

"No wonder you're so happy. I'm so glad." Gifted Tongue felt a tear of delight. "How long have you known?"

"I missed two moons. I feel a change in my breasts."

"I'm so glad for you!"

"Be happy for yourself. Once I have a child, it will be your turn. You'll soon be pregnant, too. Our children will be about the same age. Imagine all those brothers and sisters."

Gifted Tongue shared Rising Moon's joy at the prospect of their children being siblings. She could imagine them at play. Yet, she regretted they must share the same father.

The arrival of Tied to Sun added to her discomfort. Weasel escorted him, carrying a large pot of cold stew. A nose-teasing aroma of venison wafted through the air. Deer would be a welcome alternative to bear, Gifted Tongue thought longingly, but then realized Roaring Woman had cooked the stew. She probably anticipated Rising Moon's pregnancy, and the poison might affect her own fertility. The idea of eating it to prevent pregnancy crossed her mind.

"Welcome husband," Rising Moon said. "You bring cheer on a cheerless day."

"Hou, my wives. It's good to see you so robust. Have you any special news of your health?" he asked, looking at Rising Moon and obviously inquiring if she were pregnant.

"I'm feeling very well." Rising Moon answered in what was not exactly the whole truth.

Tied to Sun ended his inquiry with a noncommittal, "That's good." He had a way with words but not with feelings.

"Roaring Woman sends venison stew. She intended it only for you," he said, looking at Rising Moon.

Turning to Gifted Tongue, he asked, "Did you make Roaring Woman angry? She said explicitly that you were not to share it. I won't tolerate discord among my wives. Roaring Woman is my premier wife. So do as she says, and we'll have the perfect family, once heirs are born." At the mention of heirs, he again stared at Rising Moon, who lowered her eyes and said nothing.

"Stir the fire, you, and warm the stew," he told Weasel.

Gifted Tongue commented on their lack of firewood, saying she had to borrow from neighbors. Weasel glowered his displeasure at missing a meal from the pot he had lugged so far, but Tied to Sun seemed to welcome the opportunity to leave. No doubt the warmth of his noble council house called, Gifted Tongue thought bitterly.

As an afterthought, he turned to her, "Oh, yes, servant wife. When we finish the equinox ceremonies, you may prepare for a trade expedition to Spiro. You'll get a break from this cold."

"Do you mean we won't trade with the Kutenai?" she asked with a note of desperation. Despite Two Hearts' premonition, Gifted Tongue had hoped she might somehow return home.

"No. Dakota Next to Sun says it's too soon to return, and he's sent no envoy to the Caddo people for several summers. It's time we presented them with wealth. They undoubtedly have gifts for me. They make the finest embossed copper plates imaginable." His eyes gleamed with the image, then he said coldly, "The Caddo language differs from ours. The people aren't savages so their tongue is complex, and I have trouble with it. Two Hearts speaks a little so learn what he knows, but we'll have to use signs. Practice those with him, too."

"What about next summer, my lordly husband. Will we

visit the Kutenai then?" Gifted Tongue said as sweetly as she could.

Anger knitted Tied to Sun's eyebrows, and Gifted Tongue knew she shouldn't have questioned him. She expected a reprimand, but apparently he recalled her value as interpreter and told her what she wanted to hear.

"Almost surely we'll go next summer, servant wife. You can visit then. Remember, we are your people now."

Gifted Tongue breathed joy, but her skeptical side held it in check. She suspected he lied. Surely, he knew Two Hearts might flee to his home, and, she thought, perhaps I would, too.

. . .

When the Dhegiha finished the spring equinox ceremony, Tied to Sun ordered his staff to prepare for the Caddo expedition. He visited Rising Moon often, and once he stayed all night. In the morning, he conferred with Gifted Tongue.

"I hope your lessons go well, my gifted interpreter." His partial use of her name stirred her. Perhaps she could accept this tall, handsome man as the father of her children, she thought, if he just weren't so arrogant.

"I'm slow-witted with Caddo," she said humbly. "Its words confuse me." She exaggerated in order to protect Two Hearts who had spent only two afternoons of inept instruction with her. She had not decided if he knew little, which he claimed, or if he wished to avoid her.

To protect him, she changed the subject. "Maybe you can help me understand their culture. When Two Hearts described their religion, he said they borrowed many of our ideas while retaining their own. I'm not certain what he meant."

"Their religion centers on the stars. They fail to appreciate the importance of the sun. So their royal chief is not divine as ours is. He's more interested in exchange so I hope he will shower me with gifts. I gave him a spectacular stone figurine in our last exchange," Tied to Sun boasted.

"What about our own Sun, noble husband? Do you ever deliver gifts from him?" Gifted Tongue saw her diversion worked well. Her husband had forgotten Two Hearts as he swaggered about, describing his exploits in exchange.

"Most of the Suns mastered exchange, but the present one leaves the administration to his Next to Suns. He's all caught up by priestly knowledge. He listens to anyone who claims to know anything," he said derisively. "Right now it's the upstart Water Monster Society who claim to be favored by Morning Star. If he swallows that line, we may sacrifice someone at the rising of a star or some other ridiculous sign. The Caddo gave him that idea so we need to learn as much about their customs as we can."

He put his hands on Gifted Tongue's shoulders and said, "Take an interest in their religion, but for now, confer with Weasel. He's in charge of logistics. A few lesser nobles will join us. Those upstarts must not upstage me," he said warily.

Gifted Tongue had barely acknowledged his commands before he hurried off. The thought of other nobles accompanying them perplexed her. She wondered if Dakota Next to Sun had learned that her husband had gambled away his gifts because Rising Moon warned her that the Sun used informers to filter out fact from rumor. She worried, too, about Weasel's loyalty.

Weasel instructed her to pack all she had, and then consult Roaring Woman about what she intended to send. Gifted

Tongue braced herself for the dreaded encounter, practicing a subservient voice and demure look.

Either her attitude or the warmth of an early spring day put Roaring Woman in a decent mood. She had gathered quilled bags and filled them with pemmican and included token amounts of choice cornmeal in decorated cooking pots. She ordered Gifted Tongue to trade the bags and emptied pots for sculpted Caddo ware. Despite her good mood, Roaring Woman bawled a parting shot, "Of course, I don't expect much profit from an exchange conducted by a slave wife, and a savage one at that."

Gifted Tongue shrank within herself. She knew she could never find a home in the Center of the World.

. . .

Tied to Sun ordered Two Hearts and Gifted Tongue to share a canoe. In three days, Two Hearts exhausted his knowledge of Caddo and became vexed with Gifted Tongue's questions. "Look, I was only there for a summer, and I didn't have anyone to instruct me," he scowled. "Besides, there are untamed Caddo to the west who still live on bison and raiding. They're the people who killed my family and kidnapped me. I'm only interested in a way to get around them and head home."

Gifted Tongue sucked in her breath at the thought that he might leave and said, "Wouldn't that be impossible?"

"Not if I made the right friends. But I guess I'm just dreaming," he said, his eye twitching more than usual.

She changed the subject, but no matter what she said, he seldom responded. It seemed he had built a wall around himself. She remembered Whirlwind's explanation and decided talk of him might interest Two Hearts. She said thoughtfully, "If you don't want to talk about Caddo, tell me more about Dhegiha. I've heard a little about the Water Monster Society. Do you think that Whirlwind has learned their cures?"

Two Hearts looked interested. He said in a fatherly way, "Whirlwind has nothing to learn from those priests with their silly mumbo-jumbo. Their dances and costumes impress the commoners, but they're useless. It's really all politics." His eye twitched at the thought. "Priests in the Osage Water Monster Society are advertising their cures to the nobles and do well at it since Diving Hawk's death. But so what? Will they treat commoners equally when it comes to curing? No, the fools simply want to be nobles. They'd get nowhere if Beloved Leader lived, but now only a revolution will solve anything."

"Won't revolution give you a chance to escape?" Gifted Tongue asked, finding it hard to breathe at the thought.

He said nothing, but the vigor of his tics revealed that she had touched a vital chord. They paddled the rest of the morning in silence.

Gifted Tongue's thoughts turned to Rising Moon. She considered telling Tied to Sun of his likely heir. An opportunity arose when they turned up the Arkansas River. Tied to Sun ordered Two Hearts to another canoe while he paddled behind Gifted Tongue to test her Caddoan. His questions demanded thoughtful answers, and she sweated at the work required, but it wasn't long before he ceased his test. Sweat poured from him as he fought the current.

Gifted Tongue paddled with all her strength while he complained of his sore back and her lack of effort. Soon, he ordered a servant to take his place while he rested in the middle of the canoe and asked questions in Caddo. He surprised her with a knowledge exceeding Two Hearts', but she recognized his limits.

The next day, they faced a practical test of their Caddoan when they reached an outlying town. Tied to Sun directed an advance party to announce their arrival and gave orders to prepare his litter. He told Gifted Tongue he usually bypassed such a village, but he wanted to put the lesser nobles in their place. Their titles did not allow them to use a litter nor a herald.

As the villagers gathered to greet the new arrivals, Gifted Tongue laughed inwardly when one of the lesser nobles spoke almost fluent Caddo. Most Caddo gathered around him while Tied To Sun presented his projectile points to a handful of his trade partners. He made no new contacts nor did he impress village elders with his oratory. He complained of his luck that night when he joined Gifted Tongue in bed.

She wondered if he had learned that Rising Moon was pregnant and intended to consummate their marriage. He ended her doubts with a harsh snore from a body exhausted by paddling and frustration.

.   .   .

The party paddled steadily the next few days with Tied to Sun settling in to boast that he could keep up with the others while he instructed Gifted Tongue. One night he announced they would arrive at Spiro the next day, and he wanted everyone to help make a grand entrance.

Before they arrived, they were met by a fleet of canoes. Tied to Sun recognized the commander of a large war canoe in the lead. "It's a friend of mine, Victory Call," he boasted to Gifted Tongue.

The man yelled a greeting that startled Gifted Tongue because the Dhegiha considered it bad manners to shout. Tied to Sun explained in a condescending tone, "It's all right, it's their custom." He returned an equally loud greeting. "I guess nothing's the matter," he said anxiously to Gifted Tongue, "yet I've never before been met by a war party."

Victory Call reassured Tied to Sun as soon as his canoe drew close. "Scouts were slow to inform us of your arrival, or we would have greeted you in proper style. The Respected One sent me to escort you because renegades make trouble." He signed as he spoke so Gifted Tongue understood. How much her husband understood of Caddo she could not determine, but he nodded his head continually as if he hung on each word.

He said in his inflated way, "Our party will accompany you to wipe out these rebels. I and these lesser nobles stand ready to help in any way we can."

"Respected Leader said you would volunteer, but I doubt it's necessary. The troublemakers live in their savage ways to the west. We've urged them to farm, but they only want to raid and hunt bison. It's unlikely they'll bother any of our friends, but one never knows about savages."

The next day, a son of Victory Call asked Gifted Tongue to instruct him in Dhegiha. The boy, known only as son of Victory Call, proved to be an apt student. His eyes seemed to burn as he studied Gifted Tongue, and she gave him her full attention. Often, she shifted to Caddo to learn more of it, and in two days, she had learned more from teaching than she had from Two Hearts. By combining signs with speech, she could discuss most subjects.

When she asked about kinship, the boy told her his grandfather was a prominent priest among the outlying Caddo known as Pawnee.

"But aren't they the people your father protects us against?" she asked.

"There's the troublesome Jumano and a renegade band of Pawnee, but my grandfather's group is friendly. They're like the Teihas in the south. Both Teihas and Pawnee mean friends, and they have a reputation for hospitality."

The son of Victory Call described his father's importance in the complex politics of Spiro. He led Gifted Tongue to expect a city like the Center of the World. When they rounded a bend, and she glimpsed the town, its small size surprised her. It rested on a low terrace with only a single mound to dominate a plaza.

As her new friend led her to his home, she noticed numerous low, conical mounds that she assumed to be for burials. When she inquired, she discovered former Respected Ones were interred in them. Although a temple now stood at the top of the large mound, she learned that the Caddo built their charnel houses and temples at surface level. Most mounds served the dead.

On close inspection, she saw that the largest mound consisted of several mounds. An original, medium-sized mound had been joined to three small ones, with the connection making a long, narrow mound sloping upward from south to north. A second mound, three hundred paces west, rose at the center of the town. She thought it must be a burial mound because a charnel house and temple stood beside it at ground level. The only other mounds were six low, conical burial mounds.

Caddo houses were scattered at random. A few large ones served Respected One and his attendants, but except for size, they were undistinguished. The son of Victory Call led her to a large one, showing by signs to wait there while he went to find one of his mothers.

Tied to Sun arrived at the boy's departure and nodded approval that she had been invited to Victory Call's household. He looked haggard, and she said, "Can I help, lordly husband?"

"My problems are beyond what any woman can do," he said as he hung his head.

She was about to remind him of what she had done at Aztalan, but, on second thought, she held back.

"While we paddled, Victory Call told me that Quapaw Next to Sun sent splendid presents last summer. My figurines can't begin to compare, but the Respected One will expect me to outdo Quapaw Next to Sun." His head sunk even lower as he said, "I'll only bring shame to myself." Gifted Tongue stepped to his side to hold him, but he shrugged her off and walked away.

She sat dejected, alone in the house. It looked Dhegiha with a touch of Mandan. A square of four posts supported a thatched roof with mud daubed walls. It could hold as many people as a Mandan earth lodge, but the thatching was in the Dhegiha style. Before she could study further, several women greeted her loudly and asked what she would like to eat. They welcomed her as warmly as the Mandan had. She smiled, relieved that the town lacked the impersonality of the Center of the World.

.   .   .

Gifted Tongue soon discovered that women headed the household. Two extended families, one on the north side, the other on the south, divided chores. Try as she might, she discovered no one person in charge. The women stacked firewood, ground corn, and rearranged beds apparently as they liked. The next day, when she helped in the fields, she found they farmed the same way.

That evening, they praised her work and friendly attitude before Sitting Hawk. The women claimed that he headed the household, but he gave no orders, and the women joked with him as they did with grandchildren. His hair, streaked with gray but still mostly black, made Gifted Tongue think he might be Victory Call's father. She could hardly believe it when Victory Call's son told her the elder was his great-grandfather.

Several nights after she joined in joking with the women, Sitting Hawk called her to his side. He rubbed his finger joints as if easing pain, then placed a hand on her shoulder. "You learn our language quickly, and my granddaughters tell me you work hard. We don't enjoy many visitors like you," he said with affection.

"Sit here beside me, and I will tell you about us." They sat a few paces from the fire. "First, you should understand how Heaven created earth and life."

His shift to a serious tone drew the children to his feet. "In the beginning Heaven reigned over a misty universe. He concentrated on the four directions, creating Evening Star in the west with Moon as her helper, Morning Star in the east with Sun as his helper, followed by South Star and North Star. He put four other stars in between, Black in the northeast, Yellow in the northwest, White in the southwest, and Red in the southeast. These four stars hold up heaven. Then they created People and gave them Sacred Bundles."

"But where did Earth come from?" a toddler asked.

Sitting Hawk lifted his arms in a circle and said in a booming voice, "A thunderstorm created Earth as a body of water. After that, Heaven told Evening Star to order her gods to sing. A thick cloud gathered," he said dramatically. "Heaven dropped a crystal into it and ordered the four directions to strike the waters with a war club."

"Are the war clubs in the sacred bundles today?" an older child asked, her tone suggesting she knew the answer.

"Yes, the priests of the in-between directions have them. Heaven sent another storm to create the wild plants." His hands fluttered to indicate a downpour. "Another storm dropped bean and squash seeds to Earth." He smiled when he saw younger children yawning, and he spoke quickly. "Next, the in-between stars directed Morning Star to mate with Evening Star, but she resisted. She ordered wolf, wildcat, mountain lion and bear to protect her. But Morning Star enlisted Sun's help, and the two broke through her defense. After mating, she bore a girl who descended to Earth on a whirlwind.

"Then Moon and Sun mated, and she gave birth to a boy. The four directions instructed the boy and girl to have children. They taught the girl how to speak, build a lodge, and plant seeds. They showed the boy how to trade and hunt."

Sitting Hawk hesitated while a mother gathered up children who had fallen asleep. Then he turned to Gifted Tongue and said, "I hope you'll understand us better now." He yawned, rose and headed for his bed.

Victory Call's son said, "Great-grandfather usually takes four nights to explain our origins, but he gave you a good idea of our beliefs."

"I learned a lot, and he spoke so I could understand."

"Good. It's late, and I know you worked hard. My sister, Clear Day, has just returned. She speaks a little Dhegiha and uses signs. She'd like to share her sleeping mat with you."

Gifted Tongue guessed her host to be her age although she was taller with braids almost to her waist. She seemed bashful and hesitated to speak, but signed a welcome and told Gifted Tongue they would begin planting rituals in the morning.

At first light, Clear Day woke Gifted Tongue with a bowl of corn mush. She explained that an old woman, Grieves the Enemy, had experienced a vision in the winter that called upon her to direct the Ground Breaking Ceremony. She would come to their lodge because Sitting Hawk kept the sacred bundle for farming and had prepared it for her.

The women of the lodge sent the boys to gather willow sprouts. They left when they heard Grieves the Enemy approach. Bending low and dancing into the house, she swirled toward the sacred bundle, calling four times, "The bundle needs light." When she reached its resting place, she wheeled rapidly around it, picked it up and lifted it high four times. She filled the air with awe.

Grieves the Enemy carried the bundle to a tripod outside, while the women of the lodge picked up all mats and swept the house clean. When the boys returned with their willow, the women laid a fresh covering all over the lodge. Clear Day signed to Gifted Tongue that everything had been renewed.

In the afternoon, four priests arrived, entered the lodge, and asked for Grieves the Enemy. When she came, Clear Day led her to the place of honor in the west. Two guests sat at the north, another two at the south. The women of the lodge and their guests sat behind them. The men of the lodge stood outside the entrance.

The four priests sang while Grieves the Enemy led the women in dance. Gifted Tongue joined them, the steps like those she had learned as a child. Different arm movements puzzled her until she realized the women imitated hoeing. As the beat increased, the gestures changed into dramatic flourishes that induced a hypnotic frenzy.

Toward sunset, the drums slowed, and the dancers returned

from the extraordinary world to the ordinary one. Gifted Tongue was exhausted and hungry. Her nose caught the aroma of stew which the older women had cooked.

She sat next to Clear Day while they ate. "I've never seen anything like it. I never thought hoeing could be so dramatic," she said with a grin. "Is the ceremony over?"

"The public part is, but our lodge has more to do." Clear Day's face grew serious. "Grieves the Enemy will close the bundle while the priests pray over it. Then we return it to its place of honor."

"I feel much better after eating. Can I help close it?"

Clear Day looked frightened. "The ceremony is dangerous to everyone except our family. The son of Victory Call will take you to where your husband stays until we finish."

Clear Day touched Gifted Tongue's shoulders. She seemed less bashful. "Come back tomorrow. We can talk further."

Victory Call's son hurried to take Gifted Tongue to her husband. Once he pointed out the lodge, he left with a friendly nod. As she approached, she saw Tied to Sun violently gesture at Two Hearts. She heard no words, but had no doubt from their faces and Two Hearts' wild twitch that the two were angry. She coughed loudly and decided to act as if she knew nothing of their argument, but they argued so vehemently that they failed to notice her.

"I know my place, noble lord. It's my duty to advise you. I would never think of ordering you or refusing an order. But I insist on advising. We have too little to gain from such an adventure and too much to lose."

"Can't you see that it's my only chance. I can't match the gifts that Quapaw Next to Sun sent last fall. I'll be shamed with so little to present. I must get Victory Call's support. How can I do that if I don't join him on the bison drive? Think what he'll owe me if we help him subdue the renegades."

"We know nothing of Caddo warfare. The frontier Pawnee use tactics we've never seen."

"Where is your heart, Two Hearts?" Tied to Sun said, insulting his servant not only by use of his name but by implying cowardice. The tactic almost ended the argument, but Two Hearts tried one last ploy.

"At least leave Gifted Tongue here. She'll be in extra danger. You know the Pawnee use foreign women in their Morning Star Ceremony."

"Nonsense. Victory Call will protect us, and she's gained his friendship through his son. She's been indispensable. Too bad you haven't served as well. Now desist, servant." The venom in the hiss of "servant" finished the argument.

Gifted Tongue stood frozen in distress, unsure if her husband considered her expendable or indispensable. Two Hearts' concern mystified her. Nor did she have any idea why renegade Pawnee might want foreign women for their ceremony. Chills shot down her spine.

CHAPTER FOURTEEN

Despite the calluses Gifted Tongue developed paddling up the Arkansas, the corn planting that followed raised blisters.

Clear Day noticed and said kindly, "The elders will finish, my friend. Today, we pack for a trip west to hunt bison."

"Do we go by canoe?" Gifted Tongue asked, looking at her hands one more time.

"No. We'll head for the plains to drive bison over a cliff. There'll be enough meat for the town as well as our brothers on the frontier."

Gifted Tongue watched Clear Day pack a bundle of robes, then helped pack another with bone bowls. She wondered why the bundles were so small until Clear Day explained that dogs would carry them on a travois. Smaller packs went on the dogs' backs.

The next day when the women strapped on the loads, the dogs growled at Gifted Tongue whenever she approached. Clear Day gave her bones to feed a pregnant hound, and by noon when they headed west, Gifted Tongue had a four-legged friend.

Two Hearts surprised her at the first rise and spoke as if he wanted to talk. "These Caddo amaze me when they venture out. Nobody takes charge, but they start at the same time, then they appear to wander aimlessly."

Gifted Tongue said in as pleasant a voice as she could, "I've noticed the same thing in their homes. Six or eight families share our lodge. No one ever gives orders, yet everything falls into place."

"Look how they fall into place here," Two Hearts said, glancing into Gifted Tongue's eyes. "See the young men on the far edge. Scouts beyond them are out of sight. The warriors make up that ragged line on the horizon while flanking parties guard the sides. They search for bison, but at the same time they guard against renegades."

From the good-humored calls and joking among women and the play of children nearby, Gifted Tongue found it hard to believe that two hundred or so Caddo risked their lives.

The novelty of the trek made the next ten days pass quickly, especially since Two Hearts visited in the mornings and seemed eager to talk. Afternoons, Clear Day included her in a group of women whose constant joking made learning Caddo enjoyable. Victory Call's son occasionally joined her for Dhegiha lessons, but the excitement of the hunt attracted the boy more than language lessons.

Eventually, Tied to Sun visited to ask how she was, before talking of himself. "The hunt affords excellent opportunity for me to impress Victory Call. He is even more influential with Respected One than I thought. We get along well," he bragged. "I've convinced him I'm influential with Dakota Next to Sun."

Gifted Tongue said to herself, "If you just don't overwhelm him with your haughty talk."

"I am concerned about this bison drive, however. Victory Call asked twice if I knew how to call the beasts. I've never bothered with superstition. Did you ever hear Whirlwind discuss it? He knows everything. I thought I could pretend to work a charm or mutter a prayer and hope for the best."

"I'm afraid I heard nothing, my noble husband."

"What about Mandan? They hunt bison. Or the Kutenai?"

"I've heard them discuss bison hunts but not their magic. Scatterscorn told me about a relative who called the bison but nothing specific."

"Well, see if you can learn something. Yet, I don't want to get in front of a herd to call it, no matter what magic I know," Tied to Sun said cynically, revealing his contempt for Caddo beliefs. Gifted Tongue let it pass. She wondered what he thought of Shoshoni if he disdained the Caddo whom he regarded as superior to most people.

She had no time to ponder long because two youths appeared on the horizon, one waving a bison tail tied to his spear. When they caught the main party's attention, the other young man hurled his spear to his right.

"They located the herd," Tied to Sun said excitedly. "I must find Victory Call. Be careful, wife. You'll have to help drive. With luck, I won't be called for any calling magic."

Better a poor joke than rude sarcasm, Gifted Tongue thought, as she watched her husband run toward the warriors.

As the mass of Caddo reoriented to advance with new energy, Two Hearts joined her. "I know you'll be in the midst of the drive. You won't face danger there. But afterward, warriors will call from all sides to help butcher. Stay with Clear Day."

"I can butcher a bison without guidance, elder," she said with an edge.

"I'm sure you can cut to the quick. I'm not worried about how well you butcher, but if renegades patrol, they'll kidnap lone women."

"I'll remember. But why your sudden concern? For moons, you've acted as if I didn't exist." She spoke half-teasingly.

Two Hearts said, "It's my duty to protect your welfare. Nothing more."

The words "nothing more" stung, but she found comfort in his tone that appeared to conceal other feelings.

Why can't men ever say what they mean? Gifted Tongue thought. Moments later, Clear Day approached, repeating Two Hearts' warning.

Once they reached the rise, Gifted Tongue gasped at the mass of bison in the distance. The herd stretched endlessly.

"Be careful," Clear Day warned. "We must not frighten them. Sometimes nothing scares them, other times they stampede at a sneeze. Victory Call assigned a police detail to supervise. They'll whip anyone who interferes."

"I don't see how we dent that mass of flesh, let alone move it," Gifted Tongue said.

"Women never cause trouble. It's young men who charge early for the glory of a first kill. But we must be careful. When you hear the calling, remain perfectly still. Look over there," she pointed with her chin. "Sitting Hawk signals. We'll move parallel to the herd up that slope that ends in a cliff. We'll drive the bison over its edge."

The two joined other young women who jogged ahead of the older women. Near the cliff, Gifted Tongue found herself in a line of young women and boys on the far side of the slope.

The elders formed a line several hundred paces opposite.

"Take this skin," Clear Day said. "When the bison come, wave it and yell as loudly as you can. Wait until I start."

The instructions seemed simple enough, but Gifted Tongue wondered why the bison would run toward the cliff.

The gray-streaked Sitting Hawk strode to his place between the two lines. Gifted Tongue failed to recognize him at first because his stride matched that of a young warrior. She realized he was a man at home in the center of danger.

A high-pitched keening startled her. "Almighty, pity us." Clear Day signed to Gifted Tongue that Sitting Hawk sought Wakan's guidance. She continued to interpret. "Our brothers and sisters, we beseech you. You are everything to us. We are everything to you," his voice rang. Clear Day signed that Sitting Hawk implored the bison with an archaic oratory.

The high-pitched prayer amplified into a cadence that transformed into song. The chant drew Gifted Tongue into a near-trance. She saw images of misty bison swarming up the hillside, drawn by the prayer-song.

A roaring thunder shook the earth to bring her to reality. Her eyes focused on Sitting Hawk who cried to his bison brothers to come. His voice rose to a commanding pitch, and the bison herd started toward him. The stampede raised a deafening roar. When Gifted Tongue saw the brown and black swarm about to devour Sitting Hawk, she darted toward him. Clear Day grabbed her and shouted, "Wakan protects him! The bison won't harm him."

The other women waved their robes and screamed. Gifted Tongue yelled, and waved her robe with abandon. Her sweat soaked up the dust that floated everywhere. Through the dense cloud, she glimpsed the leading edge of the herd at the cliff's rim. The young bulls in front circled back, but they couldn't resist the surging power behind. The bison in front seemed to pull the ones behind as much as those in back pushed forward.

At a few points, bison broke through the sides or retreated to the rear. Boys and young men pursued them, hurling spears with their spear throwers. Here and there a man tried his luck with bow and arrow, but only at close range.

The flank of older women retreated when the bison charged off the ledge so the rear of the herd circled in their direction. A few bison stumbled and fell, breaking legs, but most of the herd stampeded to the safety of the plains. Sitting Hawk called an end to the hunt. Only a dust cloud lingered to mark the demise of a hundred bison.

Gifted Tongue, exhausted by the exhilaration, failed to notice Clear Day's nudge but responded to her yell. "It's time to work. We'll mix blood with the sweat and dust, and you'll use muscles you never knew you had. We'll gorge ourselves on fresh liver, but save space for tonight's roast tongue."

A few parties of older women left to butcher the isolated animals that had breached the lines. Young men accompanied them, but wounded animals tempted pursuit. Out of nowhere, Two Hearts appeared. "Be sure to stay with your friend while you butcher."

"I suppose you'll help us?" Gifted Tongue replied, intending to open the old wound of Two Hearts being forced to do women's work. She regretted her jibe as soon as she uttered it.

"As a matter of fact I will butcher, just as Pawnee men help their women. I'll work with friends on the isolated animals. Take care of yourself," he said with genuine concern.

"And you take care of yourself," Gifted Tongue said as he left. She hoped her sincerity canceled her earlier sarcasm.

After joining Clear Day, she forgot Two Hearts and everything else. Young men, using flint spear blades, cut long slices in the tough, thick hide while women separated flesh from skin with obsidian knives. They toiled, resting only to stuff themselves on liver, dripping with blood. Gifted Tongue had experienced its taste once before and liked it, but she did not relish it as the Pawnee seemed to. Soon, she found herself soaked in blood. Her hair was encrusted and her moccasins slippery from it. The combined sweat and blood left a smell she would gladly forget.

Clear Day demonstrated how to sever the larger joints. "Two can cut through with ease if one person breaks the joints while the other slices. Yes, that's it. I know it's backbreaking, but it beats the drying," she panted. "Stripping the meat is tedious, along with gathering bison dropping. The chips burn well, but give no smoke so we need to add wood."

"Remember that the meat is vital, sisters," a nearby woman added, nudging into the conversation. She startled Gifted Tongue with her clipped speech and nasal voice. "It's up to each of us to hunt our brother bison to feed ourselves."

"You're right, and I hope to do my share." Gifted Tongue assumed the woman berated her clumsy efforts, but Clear Day turned her back and signed to her, "She's a gossip and is about to slander someone else, not you."

As if on cue, the woman continued, "My husband, Old Bull, helped stampede the bison. He faced grave danger, but someone has to. All the men joined him except Noted Fox. He fell and complained that he twisted his ankle. What would happen if everyone sprained their ankles? Who would feed us? We need men as brave as my husband."

Clear Day lifted a haunch onto Gifted Tongue's shoulders

and heaved a heavier one to her own back. She said to Old Bull's wife, "We must go now to help our grandmothers pack."

Once out of hearing, she explained, "Don't think too harshly of her. She does her husband's bidding. The man is a vicious slanderer. I feel sorry for poor Noted Fox. Maybe, with so much work on our hands, the gossip will end before it harms him."

In the close-knit butchering, Gifted Tongue soon heard rumors of Noted Fox's cowardice. When the slander reached his brothers, they informed him. Their words disturbed him so much that he left as soon as his family finished butchering.

•   •   •

Gifted Tongue's muscles ached from the slaughter well after the Pawnee returned to their main camp on the plains, and the young women only gathered firewood and stripped meat. Older women scraped the skins to let younger women talk with friends while they finished the drying.

Clear Day used the time to teach Gifted Tongue more of Pawnee custom. "I have heard that the Dhegiha sometimes sacrifice women to accompany their Respected Ones."

"I haven't seen it, but I heard about it. They call their Respected One the Sun, and his wives and servants may join him in death," Gifted Tongue spoke hesitantly. She still found such a practice hard to accept.

"What do you think of the custom, my friend?"

Clear Day's question suggested she wanted to pursue a topic seldom discussed with outsiders. Gifted Tongue hesitated to speak, giving her answer careful thought. "The peoples who reared me never sacrificed humans, but we honored the holy with the first catch of the season, like the first salmon caught. I guess people must each make up their own mind. I can't judge others."

Clear Day looked around, and then said cautiously, "Soon, we'll give Morning Star a girl in return for his daughter who was our First Mother. Did Sitting Hawk tell you how Morning Star and Evening Star became parents of our ancestors?"

Gifted Tongue nodded. "Yes, he explained Caddo origins."

Clear Day drew near and said in a low voice, "The ceremony began last fall when a warrior dreamed of Morning Star. He went to the Morning Star priest who explained the vision. He instructed the warrior to beg Morning Star for guidance. The two purified the contents of the priest's medicine bundle. The warrior wore its contents when he went to capture a young woman to sacrifice."

"Was it like a war party?" Gifted Tongue said in a hushed voice.

"Not exactly. He searched for a daughter for Morning Star among the Jumano, although we don't like taking a captive from friends, even if it does honor them."

"Taking a captive gives honor?" Gifted Tongue said incredulously.

Clear Day shook her head and said kindly, "It's not being captive that is the honor. It's sending the girl to Morning Star so she'll live in heaven forever."

"I see," Gifted Tongue said, trying to hide her skepticism.

"The girl has lived with us six moons, eating the best food and wearing the finest clothing. She's learned Caddo well."

"Does she know she's going to be sacrificed?"

"The priest explained that she was to become a daughter to Morning Star."

Gifted Tongue noted that the answer evaded her question.

"The adoption should be soon," Clear Day said dramatically. "The keeper of the Wolf Bundle cares for the girl. Did Sitting Hawk tell you that the ancestors murdered Wolf because he stole their children? That's why all living things die, but Wolf found everlasting life as the southeast star."

"I haven't heard of Wolf Star. Is he associated with death?"

"Yes, so it's the Wolf Star priest who prepares the girl."

In a few days, Clear Day awoke Gifted Tongue early.

"Come friend, today Morning Star adopts a new daughter."

The two women rushed to the lodge of the Morning Star priest to see the Wolf priest lead the young girl inside.

"The two will be purified in incense." As Clear Day spoke, Gifted Tongue smelled burning sweet grass. Then the wife of Wolf Priest arrived, carrying his sacred shield. She beckoned to Clear Day to enter the lodge. Although crowded to the back, Gifted Tongue saw the Morning Star priest unpack a dress for the girl while the Wolf priest anointed her with red ocher.

Clear Day said, "The wife feeds the girl while he dresses the warrior in a belt of otter skin. Otter is first to break the ice at winter's end and takes the first breath of the year. The priest then gives the warrior a war club." Clear Day paused to catch her breath. "Soon we'll hear him run through the village to beg his relatives to bring food and mats. All the old mats have been discarded, so the lodge will be renewed. They put out the fire and build a new one with a different wood for each direction. Willow represents the direction of the death star. But it's the first tree to leaf in spring, so it symbolizes life as well."

"It's interesting how your symbols can stand for opposites, especially life and death," Gifted Tongue said with a raised eyebrow. "It's the same among Dhegiha."

"The top rung of the sacrificial scaffold is made of willow and fastened with thongs of otter skin," Clear Day added.

An elder rose to lead the Wolf priest and girl to the southeast corner. Other priests sat according to their affiliation with the four directions. Once everyone was seated, the Evening Star priest chanted a ritual song, answered by the Morning Star priest. Wolf priest led the girl to an altar at the west end, anointed her right side with more red ocher, and painted her left side black, to represent night and Evening Star.

The warrior with the vision pointed a burning log at the girl. Gifted Tongue swallowed hard, wondering if he would burn her. She felt her scarred cheek twinge. But the man only circled the flame in the air. He repeated the gesture with other logs, concluding with the southwest one. Gifted Tongue noted that he ended with the death log. She wondered if the captive knew.

"They'll sing a while. Let's go see the scaffold," Clear Day said, touching Gifted Tongue's shoulder to lead her away.

As the two walked several hundred paces from the lodge, Gifted Tongue said, "Did the Pawnee ever sacrifice a Dhegiha?"

"My father told me that the Dhegiha gave us captives twice," Clear Day said. "Once, the girl came from far away. The other was Dhegiha. Her parents sought the honor." Before Gifted Tongue could ask more, Clear Day pointed with her chin and said, "Can you see the scaffold? The moon is so dim. Over there's a ravine where all the men and boys hide until Morning Star comes."

"You mean the Morning Star priest will bring the girl here?"

"Well, he will bring her," Clear Day smiled, "but I meant the star in the sky. When Morning Star rises above the horizon, he will receive the girl as his daughter."

"I see," Gifted Tongue said, although she was puzzled.

Clear Day said, "About now, the priests sing of the meteor that became Morning Star. The song is of our grandfather, but he is also father and brother to us. They finish with more singing and with offerings of tobacco."

Several times, Clear Day pointed to the horizon where Morning Star would rise. Gifted Tongue shivered as the night ended, reacting less to the cold than to thoughts of the captive. A creeping light interrupted her mood. She guessed it was the eerie light of dawn, but then recognized Morning Star's glimmer.

Clear Day stiffened to attention. "See how he gives first light? He's the star of stars." She spoke with reverence. In the silence that followed, Gifted Tongue trembled. She wondered if the sun enraptured Tied to Sun.

Boys and men filed into the ravine to break the night's stillness, though their stealth suggested but a handful. A procession of women, the Wolf priest, and directional priests followed, leading the captive.

At dawn, the Wolf priest appeared. His sacred shirt of painted buckskin caught Gifted Tongue's attention. His commanding presence made her feel that he could do no wrong. He led his trusting victim by the hand to the scaffold. Before this exotic altar, the priests sang of the heaven's power, the power of bear, mountain lion, wildcat, and wolf.

To conclude, he said, "Now daughter, you will meet your new father. Take your first steps toward Heaven on this scaffold."

Once she reached the top, the priest tied her spread arms to the willow pole, highest of the rungs, and her spread legs to the lowest rung so her limbs pointed to four directions.

"We suspend you here, daughter, to await your new father. See him? That bright star rising on the horizon comes for you."

The Wolf priest descended amidst a crescendo of song praising Morning Star. When it ended, the Northwest Bundle priest shot an arrow into the victim's breast. The twang of the bow string signaled the men and boys to charge the scaffold as if it were an enemy camp. Each one shot an arrow into Morning Star's daughter. Each sang a war song to signify bravery.

The celebration of death and birth in sacrifice ended quickly. The crowd dispersed to feast while priests carried the body to the plains to offer the flesh to Mother Earth.

Gifted Tongue found herself feasting on consecrated bison before fully realizing the young girl's death. When she did, she gagged and her insides rebelled from being so close to death.

Her sudden revulsion drove her to seek solitude, but when she left the lodge, Two Hearts joined her. She brightened at his company, realizing it was not solitude but separation from foreign custom that she needed.

"So do you envy the new daughter of Morning Star? You know you are still young enough that he could adopt you, too."

Gifted Tongue didn't need such jests, but she agreed with Two Hearts' aversion to human sacrifice. It felt good to be with someone who shared her feelings.

"I suppose you would be the first to fill my body with arrows," Gifted Tongue said.

"I don't want to joke about it, my Shoshoni friend. I tried feasting with lodge mates, but the meat sickened me."

"The same thing happened to me, Paiute friend." Gifted Tongue was consoled to find that she wasn't the only one repulsed by the death, and she liked his use of "Shoshoni frlend" which solved their problem of what to call each other.

"Be careful while we're out here on the plains. The Jumano will seek revenge, and renegades would relish your capture. I'm not sure how much Victory Call might help since your sacrifice would honor you."

"Don't worry so. I'll stay close to camp although at times I need solitude. I appreciate your concern, my Paiute friend." The two managed to brush against each other in parting, both feigning the touch was accidental.

.   .   .

Gifted Tongue had lost track of how many days they stripped bison flesh to dry before they headed back to Spiro. No one seemed eager to return to farm fields after the elation of hunting and feasting.

As they lashed the travois and packs of meat to the dogs' backs, Clear Day shook her head sadly and said, "The summer hunt is too short. Of course, we must return to the fields to help our grandmothers. But perhaps you'll be spared, if your husband decides to leave."

Gifted Tongue hesitated to answer. Although the drift down the Arkansas would be easy, fighting the Mississippi threatened sweat and blisters. Any farm work she evaded at Spiro awaited her at the Center of the World. She wondered why anyone would ever choose farming over hunting. She could only guess that crops supported more people, but she couldn't imagine any advantage to a larger population.

An approaching party of warriors ended her speculation. Even from a distance, she recognized three of the four as foreign because of their hairstyles.

"Noted Fox returns with three Jumano. It's good they arrive after the sacrifice. I doubt they appreciate how we honored their sister," Clear Day said, drawing a deep breath.

"Could they cause trouble?" Gifted Tongue asked.

"Noted Fox gave his sister to a Jumano friend to marry so these men must be his brothers-in-law. They won't cause trouble while they're with him."

"Isn't it strange that no women accompany them? Look at the packs they carry. I never saw Dhegiha men carry so much."

"It is unusual," Clear Day said, straining to see better. "It's strange, too, that they go to the lodge of Old Bull after he slandered Noted Fox."

The mystery deepened as Noted Fox summoned Old Bull. The slanderer skulked to face Noted Fox and his relatives.

Noted Fox stood fully erect and said in a booming voice, "You ordered your wife to tell others that I was too scared to stampede the bison, and that I thought more of my life than of feeding the people." He glared and nearly shouted, "So sit, my friend while I show you what I think of your words."

As Old Bull dropped to sit cross-legged before his lodge, Noted Fox nodded to the Jumano to bring their gifts. The first one, with a fierce frown, laid a war club at Old Bull's feet.

"The Jumano took this club from us years ago. Now I honor you with its return." Noted Fox chanted a give-away song that drew a large audience, including Tied to Sun and Two Hearts. Old Bull's face twisted at the torture he anticipated.

"Now I give you the finest flint points the Jumano ever made. They're better than any you ever had." He sang more give-away songs as the second Jumano laid a bundle of points beside the war club.

"Now I present you with a jaguar skin," Noted Fox said in

a condescending voice. "Have you ever seen a finer skin? Have you even seen a jaguar?" he said sarcastically. "I guess not." The third Jumano waved the skin to display its beauty before he placed it before Old Bull.

In his shame, Old Bull said nothing. Gifted Tongue knew he could not refuse the gifts. From the look on his face, she knew he could never forget what he had done, and she watched Noted Fox depart in triumph.

Tied to Sun rushed to the Jumano. Gifted Tongue followed, watching him converse in signs. She had to guess at a few gestures, but she understood that the jaguar skin fascinated him. He appeared desperate to learn its source.

The next day, Tied to Sun and Two Hearts came at dawn to the lodge where Gifted Tongue had started to dress. Tied to Sun told her that she must be ready to go in moments because he had learned that Noted Fox and his brothers-in-law were about to leave. She finished dressing quickly, gathered up a bag of food, and went to the door to hear Two Hearts argue against joining the Jumano. Tied to Sun would not listen to him.

He said excitedly, "I have never seen jaguar skins. Can you imagine the Sun's delight with one? We must move quickly before one of those upstart nobles back at Spiro hears of them. I have talked Noted Fox into letting us go with him so the Jumano can show us the river that leads to their home. I want you two to learn as much Jumano as you can. Find out what they know of copper or whatever else we can exchange for those skins."

The sun was hardly up when the three set out with the Jumano and Noted Fox at a trot. The pace exhausted Gifted Tongue by noon, and she had to rest. Tied to Sun berated her, but he sat and seemed to welcome the break. Before sundown, the party reached a river where everyone drank. Two Hearts helped

Gifted Tongue gather wood and start a fire. After eating, the Jumano signed that the river ran to their home, four days away.

Gifted Tongue slept fitfully. Two Hearts' early stirring awoke her. She felt his anxiety. He asked the Jumano in signs what had happened to Noted Fox. The older Jumano signed that his son came late in the night to tell him his wife was ill. He had left, and they planned to leave after finishing the fresh bison.

Gifted Tongue welcomed the chance to return to Spiro and Clear Day's lodge. The older Jumano made her uneasy by the way he looked at her sleeping husband, and then fixed her with a stare that sent shivers along her arms. She knew Two Hearts fretted because Tied to Sun slept. She shook her husband, who scowled at her, but apparently the thought of jaguars aroused him. He signed to the Jumano about a future exchange, but they showed little interest.

While Gifted Tongue prepared the last of their food, she missed many signs between the Jumano and Tied to Sun. She did sense Two Hearts' concern from the ceaseless twitching of his eyelid.

After watching the signs, she realized that the Jumano promised many jaguar skins in exchange for her. Tied to Sun joked at the idea, signing that she was a worthless wife, and he could not give her away because he never exchanged wives with commoners. She sensed the Jumano failed to understand, but she guessed they intended to seize her in revenge.

When Tied to Sun turned to her and joked about her scars, the oldest Jumano attacked. Two Hearts yelled a warning. The elder swung his war club in a sideways blow at Tied to Sun's head, but he ducked. His right hand drew an obsidian knife. He slashed it along the Jumano's thigh, cutting the right leg's hamstring, to render it useless. He smirked as he recalled his adolescent drills in combat, but his instructor had failed to warn him that a man might stand on one leg. As he gloated, the Jumano delivered a blow to his head. The two dropped together.

Two Hearts' cunning gave him a moment's advantage over the Jumano who failed to foresee his brother's attack. He jabbed his flint knife into the man's chest and ripped upward. The stone snapped, but not before the point touched his heart.

Two Hearts withdrew the useless handle to face the third Jumano who held a long blade spear point. His grin at an unarmed opponent appeared as deadly as his weapon. The two men stepped in a mortal circle, the Jumano relishing the prospect of slashing and jabbing an opponent without a weapon.

Gifted Tongue lamented the Double Woman medicine that she had left in camp, but she jumped to the war club dropped by the elder Jumano. The move distracted Two Hearts' enemy. When he turned toward her, she threw the club to Two Hearts. The handle hit his palm, and he stood better armed than the Jumano.

The man charged recklessly, and Two Hearts took full advantage of his rashness. He feinted a blow to the head. The Jumano lashed out at the space where he thought Two Hearts' arm would be. Instead, Two Hearts' club crushed the man's knee. The next moment, his club crashed into the skull, splattering blood in a sickening, cracking sound.

Two Hearts dropped the club, disgusted that Tied to Sun's ambition had steered them into such danger. Gifted Tongue dashed to his side, voicing her gratitude with wide eyes. She wanted to tell him how she felt, but the words caught in her throat. His smile told her his heart felt the same as hers. In Shoshoni, she whispered, "I love you, you handsome brute."

He replied in Paiute, "I love you, too, Gifted Tongue." His unfamiliar words needed no translation since he took her in his arms. Their short embrace meant everything to Gifted Tongue, but then he pushed her back. In Dhegiha, he murmured, "Love can't be for us. The nobles will cut off your nose if they think that you were unfaithful to Tied to Sun. I won't endanger you."

"And your fate could be worse, my Paiute love. You're right, we must forget each other."

"I'll never forget you. But I won't put you in danger."

"Nor I you," she whispered.

A moan from Tied to Sun startled them. Gifted Tongue ran to him, amazed he had survived. The ugly gash left by the Jumano's club caused a geyser of blood. Ragged edges of bone marked an open wound that she had no idea how to treat. She saw parts of the skull that squeezed the brain. As Two Hearts splashed water on his face, Tied to Sun's eyes fluttered open, but they failed to focus, and he began to gibber like a child.

CHAPTER FIFTEEN

A cold fall rain prodded Gifted Tongue and Rising Moon from the fields where they gleaned for squash. While Rising Moon stopped to invite a neighbor for a meal, Gifted Tongue savored her solitude to recall the journey from Spiro. She suppressed her thoughts of the grueling days spent fighting the current of the Mississippi to dwell on the drift down the Arkansas. She reveled in the two evenings when she and Two Hearts accidentally met to spend the night joking and teasing in Shoshoni and Paiute.

Both tried to avoid each other on the trip back, but she wondered if her destiny hadn't directed her to Two Hearts those two nights. She would relive them forever, one marked by a full moon with light clouds shading it, the other highlighted by a horizontal sliver of crescent with a star riding in its bowl.

Rising Moon interrupted the reverie. "Look who is here co-wife, our grandrelative. Our sister wants to gossip." The use of two different kinship terms for Whirlwind allowed him to choose either to chat or raise serious matters.

He grinned good naturedly. "What gifts did you bring me,

sister? The Caddo can't match the floral designs of the Aztalan dress you gave me, but they work wonders with bison horn."

"Here's one of those wonders for you, sister," Gifted Tongue said with a laugh, rummaging in a deerskin bag for a horn soup spoon. "You'll never get a splinter in your tongue with this. See how the artist worked the shades of color into the length of the spoon. At the tip is the smallest bison you've ever seen. The tiny horns and tail are perfect."

"You are a dutiful grandrelative," Whirlwind said in order to shift to a serious level. "Always thoughtful. I know you nurse your husband. I heard a Pawnee almost killed him."

"A Jumano did it. Our husband's nearly dead. The Jumano struck him so hard you can see a hole in his skull. Bone splinters came through the scalp. I don't know how he survived."

"So, did Caddo priests help him? Or a shaman?"

"A Wolf Star priest insisted on a trepanation operation," Gifted Tongue said anxiously. "I never heard of it. He wanted to cut another hole in the skull to relieve the pressure. The other Dhegiha didn't know what to do until Two Hearts urged them to bring his lord here. He wanted you to cure him, but the nobles insisted that the Long Nosed God priests were skilled trepanners. We've been able to delay them, in the hope you would get back soon. Where have you been?"

"On one of my trips," he said mysteriously. Gifted Tongue didn't know if he meant a vision journey or an ordinary one, but felt she shouldn't ask. Instead she said, "You can cure him, can't you?"

"It's hard to know. I'm not sure about trepanation. I've seen people die from the operation, but others survive to a ripe old age. It leaves only the scalp to cover a hole that's as wide as an open mouth."

"Can't you help him with your plants?" Rising Moon said, imploring him with her eyes.

"I have herbs for headaches. Do they bother him much?"

"He doesn't seem to suffer, but we don't know how he feels. Or if he thinks," Gifted Tongue added.

"Boil these roots with his food. See if they help," Whirlwind said without much hope in his voice. "You must also consider another possibility, but you don't have to decide now." Gifted Tongue glanced at Rising Moon for a clue, but her co-wife looked equally perplexed during Whirlwind's long pause.

"The Sun is deathly ill though it's been kept a secret," he said solemnly. "His cough is so bad that his sisters consulted me when the Long Nosed God priests failed to heal him. The cough tells me that he won't survive the winter."

From the look on Rising Moon's face, Gifted Tongue realized that the consequences of his death must be awful. She bit her lip in distress and asked, "How will his death affect us?"

"When the Sun dies, retainers must accompany him to the afterlife. The wards will select women for the trip, and noble wives will volunteer. Noblemen may volunteer also."

Gifted Tongue sensed the awesome possibility Whirlwind silently suggested. "You mean that we may volunteer Tied to Sun? He can't make such a decision."

"Wives never decide for their husbands," Whirlwind said with a twinkle in his eye. "But sometimes we wives interpret their minds for them. He may not verbalize what he thinks, but reflect on it. Tied to Sun is loyal and obedient. Would he not die for the Sun? He'd be guaranteed a place in the afterlife."

Gifted Tongue scoffed at the idea that Tied to Sun would die out of loyalty, but it wouldn't hurt to stress whatever obedience her husband felt toward the Sun. Whirlwind had a point.

Before he left, he added a further complication. "Of course, it's Roaring Woman's decision because she's a noble. She'd like the honor of her husband joining the Sun. On the other hand, she won't like to make it obvious that she wants to be a widow. I don't know what she'll do. She may leave the choice up to you."

"I suppose you won't help us decide," Rising Moon said.

"It's not up to me," he replied. "But, I'll keep you informed of what I learn. Meanwhile, prepare the roots. They may help his memory. The Sun should live another moon, so take your time to discuss your husband's sacrifice, and find out what Roaring Woman thinks, if you can."

A few days later, when neighbors visited, Gifted Tongue realized that the Sun's impending death eclipsed all other gossip. At first, people talked of heirs or about the afterlife, but always the conversation turned to who might be sacrificed. She learned that the selection of commoner women presented a major problem since none would volunteer. Instead, clan elders decided, choosing someone with few relatives.

One night around their fire, Gifted Tongue turned to Rising Moon and said anxiously, "If Tied to Sun joins the Sun, couldn't I be sacrificed? I'd have no relatives."

"Oh, sister, I thought you knew," Rising Moon reached for her co-wife's hands. "I'm sorry I let you worry. Servant wives are never sacrificed. They're unworthy." Gifted Tongue sighed in relief but felt hurt at being deemed worthless.

Then she realized that she had forgotten Rising Moon. "What about you? Aren't commoner wives sacrificed?"

"Yes, it's one of few honors we enjoy, although I can do without it," Rising Moon smiled. "I needn't worry because I'm pregnant. No one will threaten Tied to Sun's child, except Roaring Woman."

"Do the victims know in advance that they'll be killed?" Gifted Tongue said as she recalled the Caddo sacrifice.

"Best you don't speak of them as 'victims' to others," Rising Moon said in a hushed voice. "They have a moon or so to enjoy their honor."

Gifted Tongue detected sarcasm in her use of honor.

"After the Sun dies, the Long Nosed God priests determine a date of burial based on the calendar. The sun must pass over a certain number of posts."

"Are the vic-, are the honored ones well fed and clothed?"

"Oh yes, they enjoy the best. The women are treated as brides of the Sun because they'll be his wives in the afterlife. They're strangled to preserve their beauty. The honored men are his closest retainers." After a moment's pause and a wry smile, Rising Moon said. "Too bad we have no chance for such honor."

Gifted Tongue laughed dryly. "While we bemoan our poor luck, let's stew some roots for our husband. We can add squash and fish in the morning. I wonder if the roots have much taste."

In the morning, they added the squash and fish, and salted the stew to cover the bitterness of the medicine. Once they decided the stew was edible, they took the pot inside the stockade gate where Roaring Woman had ordered a hut built for her husband, claiming he needed privacy. The location meant that Rising Moon and Gifted Tongue had to care for him.

The next day, when they returned with corn mush, Tied to Sun looked better. He seldom moaned, and once he uttered a word among his nonsense sounds. Gifted Tongue thought he even recognized her for a moment.

After a few more days, the co-wives used up the roots. Only once, after his glimmer of recognition did Tied to Sun say anything more, "I must think more of Roaring Woman," he muttered. Gifted Tongue shook her head in dismay at the words. She saw a tear in her co-wife's eye.

Rising Moon insisted they go to Whirlwind for more roots. Gifted Tongue led the way, and the two found him near his home. "Our husband is stronger," Rising Moon said. "But, we have used up all your roots." Gifted Tongue told him about the one sentence that Tied to Sun had uttered.

Whirlwind frowned and said, "I don't know why you want to help him, but I've got a few roots here." He entered his house, and returned moments later. "I'm dumbfounded that he can speak. I'm surprised he's still alive."

.   .   .

Tied to Sun lived on after the Sun took his last breath late one night. Priests announced his passing at sunrise the next day. They crowded the top of the pyramid of the sun to perform an intricate dance of mourning while drummers and a chorus heralded the Sun's death.

Rising Moon explained mourning custom to Gifted Tongue. "Runners set out in the four directions with the news. Of course, rumors have reached everywhere, so envoys from as far away as Spiro and Aztalan are already on their way. Their leaders will send quivers full of their finest arrows, and the artisans here will give their finest work to be buried with him."

"You haven't mentioned the honored ones who accompany him," Gifted Tongue said.

"I don't want to discuss it," Rising Moon said with a deep breath. "But, until he's buried, that's all anyone will talk about."

"Will any of your clan sisters be sacrificed?"

"There's one poor girl whose parents died before they bore

other children. The grandmother who raised her has died. The girl is lazy too, so she may be convinced to volunteer."

"How many volunteers are likely?"

"Since people volunteer, there's not supposed to be a quota, but I'd guess four commoners and four nobles will be sacrificed. One commoner from each ward, two nobles from the city and one each from Quapaw and Dakota outposts."

Gifted Tongue began to appreciate the morbid curiosity that she'd heard from neighbors, but she decided to change the subject. Roaring Woman did it for her, surprising them with a rare visit.

"I've just come from visiting our husband, and I brought you venison to flavor his soup." Gifted Tongue hid a smile as she listened to the lisp. "I'd cook more for him, but we nobles have so much work to do planning the Sun's funeral." She looked down her nose to say, "You'd never believe the time it takes."

Gifted Tongue knew that whatever work the nobles planned, commoners would do it. She wondered if Roaring Woman had more work in mind for them beyond care of Tied to Sun. But, her only concern at the moment seemed to center on him.

"I think always of our husband's health," Roaring Woman said piously. "I could help him better if I knew the circumstances about his wound. You were there, weren't you, Gifted Tongue?" Even when Roaring Woman wanted a favor, she wouldn't refrain from an insult by speaking her co-wife's name.

"Yes, he insisted that Two Hearts and I go with him to learn the way to Jumano country."

"But, I mean, exactly how was he wounded?"

"There were three Jumano. One threatened us. Tied to Sun

tried to humor him before the man raised his club. Tied to Sun slashed him with his knife, but the man clubbed him before he fell. Two Hearts attacked the other two. He killed one immediately. He had to fight the other one much longer. He's very brave."

Roaring Woman raised a puzzled eyebrow at Gifted Tongue's admiration for Two Hearts before she pursued what interested her most. "What I don't understand is why Two Feather and Night Hawk didn't protect our husband. What were they doing?"

For a moment, Gifted Tongue failed to grasp who Roaring Woman meant. Then she recalled the two minor Dhegiha nobles who accompanied the Spiro expedition.

"Tied to Sun didn't tell them we left because he wanted to keep the Jumano route a secret. Two Hearts protested. He knew we shouldn't go alone, but Tied to Sun wouldn't listen."

Rising Moon frowned in wonder at Gifted Tongue's regard for Two Hearts. Roaring Woman hesitated, appearing to make a mental note of Gifted Tongue's praise. She asked a few more questions about Two Feather and Night Hawk, then complained again of all her pressing duties, and left.

Gifted Tongue tilted her head and said, "Why does she think the whereabouts of those two nobles might have anything to do with Tied to Sun's health?"

Rising Moon smiled and said, "You don't yet appreciate the intrigue of the nobility. You may think they're all united, but they're always at each others' throats. I guess Roaring Woman wants to blame Two Feather and Night Hawk for our husband's wound, if not now, then in the future."

"Do you think I helped her?"

"No, but who knows how she might twist your words,"

Rising Moon said as she shook her head. "I wouldn't put an out-right lie past her. Do you think we dare use the venison she brought?"

Gifted Tongue gritted her teeth in disgust. "No, but we can give it to that old widow a few houses down the path."

The next few days passed uneventfully, except for growing concern about who might be sacrificed. While the two co-wives cared for Tied to Sun, they discussed the decisions of the three ward chiefs who had selected brides for the Sun.

One morning while rumors flew, a runner approached the hut where Gifted Tongue and Rising Moon fed Tied to Sun. Rising Moon whispered, "He wears the insignia of a messenger for Dakota Next to Sun." The slim, young runner stopped before them, breathless for a moment. "Dakota Next to Sun comes to visit his brother-in-law, Tied to Sun. Be ready." He left before Rising Moon could say a word.

She told Gifted Tongue that the Next to Sun had never before visited their husband and warned her not to speak until spoken to and to lower her eyes in his presence. Moments later, they recognized Dakota Next to Sun, dressed in a red mantle with a sun design. His leggings and apron were of the finest white cotton trimmed in red. A burly, square-jawed guard accompanied him, dressed in buckskin leggings and a furred cape.

"Good day, sisters-in-law," Dakota Next to Sun said in a friendly, but hurried way. "I meant to visit your husband earlier when I heard of his terrible wound, but the Sun's death has kept me busy. Give my apologies to Roaring Woman for not announcing my visit so she could be here, but I didn't have time." Rising Moon promised to deliver the apology.

"You must be Tied to Sun's commoner wife," Dakota Next

to Sun said with a smile to Rising Moon. Turning to Gifted Tongue, he said, "And you must be his servant wife." Gifted Tongue glanced up, startled by his recognition of her presence. His next words surprised her even more. "I have heard about you and your magical tongue. You learn languages overnight, do you?"

"Oh, no, my lord." She demurred, keeping her eyes on his feet. "Learning any language is hard. But Tied to Sun wanted me to learn other tongues, so I do my best."

In a grand gesture, Dakota Next to Sun said, "I hear the Jumano almost made you a widow. In that case, many nobles would want you. Perhaps I would set out to trade, if I had as useful a servant wife as you."

Gifted Tongue stood speechless, her eyes riveted on the ground. Rising Moon saw Dakota Next to Sun grimace at her co-wife's scars. He appeared as repulsed by her looks as he would be by an expedition's hardships.

To change the subject, Rising Moon said, "You'll see how terrible his wound is, my lord, even though the scalp now covers a little of the hole. He only jabbers, except one time he spoke a whole sentence."

"I'll be curious to see if he recognizes me," the Next to Sun said, entering the hut while the two women knelt at the door.

Tied to Sun turned his head to his lord but with no glimmer of recognition. When Dakota Next to Sun spoke to him of Spiro, Tied to Sun answered in gibberish. When his lord pressed him about discovering a unique skin, Gifted Tongue realized that the Next to Sun had heard of the jaguar hide. Apparently he had come only to find out more about new wealth. Her stomach churned in revulsion at the Dhegiha obsession.

She saw that the Dakota Next to Sun tried to conceal his disappointment. He nodded to the two and said, "I know Roaring Woman must be concerned and that she takes good care of her husband. Tell her I regret his wounds in my service."

The day after he left, a retainer to the Sun arrived, a short man, with a wisp of a beard. While he bent over Tied to Sun, Rising Moon whispered to Gifted Tongue that she couldn't believe the timing of the two visits was a coincidence.

The retainer asked Tied to Sun about his health before he asked about jaguars. When none of his attempts got a response, he rose and turned to ask Rising Moon what herbs she gave. When she told him, he shrugged his shoulders and started to leave.

The three of them stood over Tied to Sun's bed. Whether Whirlwind's medicinal roots or talk of the Sun's death sparked his memory, Tied to Sun rose to his elbows and spoke clearly. "Roaring Woman," he stammered. "I dedicate my wife to the Sun to be his bride." He so ardently announced his wish that the retainer swore to fulfill it.

The man waited for Tied to Sun to speak again, but nothing followed except gibberish. As the retainer left, he told Rising Moon that he would go directly to the funeral council and report Tied to Sun's words.

Overnight, news of Tied to Sun's consecration of his wife spread everywhere, though it took two days to reach Roaring Woman. No one wished to face her when she learned of her honor.

·   ·   ·

Gifted Tongue could never know that Roaring Woman's cunning matched her dancing skills. When the relative who felt duty-bound to relate that Tied to Sun had dedicated her as a bride, she replied, "What an honor." When the relative told others what she had said, endless speculation followed. However, no one guessed her thinking. She left the city for an isolated bluff to calculate how she could escape the marriage. When she returned the next day, she wore a satisfied smile that others took as acceptance of her honor.

She hastened to the father of Two Feather, a Long Nosed God priest, with a story to imply that Two Feather could have prevented the attack on Tied to Sun. She had a plan to protect Two Feather. "Tied To Sun will never talk again," she said shrewdly. "You have nothing to fear from him. But, his servant wife witnessed how your son failed to help. That woman will ruin your son," she said.

"However, you can protect him because no one remembers her marriage to my husband. The ceremony excluded her, and the priest who blessed them has died. You can swear that you performed it."

"How will that protect my son?" the priest said.

"Swear it was a commoner marriage. Then Gifted Tongue can be sacrificed. I'll bribe the retainer who heard my husband mumble about sacrifice. He'll say Tied to Sun didn't mean that I should be killed. He called my name, only to say I should carry out his wish. When he said, 'I dedicate my wife to the Sun,' he meant Gifted Tongue."

The priest rubbed his cheek and said nothing. Roaring Woman made a final offer. "Look. If everything goes right, I can persuade the girl to be sacrificed without a marriage. I only need you in case her co-wife protests too much."

The priest nodded his agreement and grinned. Roaring Woman then asked if she could send his apprentice to Omaha ward with a message for Two Hearts. The boy had a witless look about him. When Roaring Woman had him alone, she stressed the need for secrecy. She made him repeat how he was to tell Two Hearts to bring the trepanner, Sweet Grass Rope, from Quapaw post.

She explained over and over that she didn't know if the man belonged to the Water Monster or Long Nosed God society, so Two Hearts must search among both groups. She smiled at the name she had made up. Two Hearts would spend a moon searching.

Roaring Woman took a breath and hurried to Tied to Sun's hut. When she found him alone, she went to Rising Moon's home. Gifted Tongue stirred a pot of soup while Rising Moon sliced squash. She told Rising Moon that Tied to Sun needed her.

. . .

When Rising Moon left, Roaring Woman spoke to Gifted Tongue as if she were an equal. "I don't know what we should do about Two Hearts. We can't trust him, the way he hates the nobility." Gifted Tongue said nothing, but her eyes showed concern. Roaring Woman studied them.

She said, "I understand how Two Hearts could fall in love with that young wife of Diving Hawk. She probably led him on. She's free to marry now that Diving Hawk's mourning is past, but you'd think they'd have waited until after the Sun's funeral."

"Do you mean that Two Hearts is married?" The dismay in Gifted Tongue's question confirmed Roaring Woman's hunch, and the girl's next words delighted her. "It should be I, not you, who is sacrificed."

"I can arrange it. I'll inform the priest in charge." Roaring Woman grinned inwardly, amused at how well her scheme proceeded. She praised Gifted Tongue as a dutiful wife, related the wonders of the afterlife, and explained how the girl could be remarried to Tied to the Sun as a common wife. She even argued that it was her place to be sacrificed. The ruse made Gifted Tongue more determined than ever.

Gifted Tongue was in such anguish at losing Two Hearts that she failed to see the delighted look of Roaring Woman. When Rising Moon returned, Roaring Woman told her that Gifted Tongue had volunteered to be sacrificed. Rising Moon protested that servant wives were unfit for such honor. Roaring Woman swore that Tied to Sun had told her earlier he intended to take Gifted Tongue as a commoner wife. He had gone so far as to arrange for Two Feather's father to marry them. She explained the practice was rare, but assured Rising Moon that custom allowed it.

•   •   •

When Roaring Woman left, Rising Moon hugged Gifted Tongue, urging her to change her mind. She sobbed, "I must do what our noble wife commands, even though I know it's wrong. I don't know what else to do." Gifted Tongue held her tightly, so dazed at the news of Two Hearts' marriage that she felt nothing but despair. As Gifted Tongue sank into depression, Rising Moon grew equally despondent. The two sat by the fire with downcast eyes. Whirlwind suddenly appeared and placed a hand on each one's shoulder. Rising Moon brightened at his touch. "Grandrelative," she cried, "you must help Gifted Tongue. When Roaring Woman told her that Two Hearts married Diving Hawk's widow, she became terribly discouraged. She's hardly spoken except to tell Roaring Woman she would take her place of honor."

"She can't do that," he said with alarm. "Gifted Tongue is a servant wife."

"Roaring Woman has arranged for a Long Nosed God priest to hold a commoner marriage for her," Rising Moon said with a dismal look.

"Wait a moment. What did you say about Two Hearts? He isn't married. He's gone to Quapaw post; Roaring Woman sent him to search for a doctor."

"Tell Gifted Tongue that," Rising Moon said urgently. "You'll bring her to her senses."

"It'll be better if Two Hearts tells her. I'll send a Water Monster friend. He'll gladly make trouble for a Long Nose. His society at Quapaw will find Two Hearts in no time."

Whirlwind called to a nearby house and summoned a young man to his side. He explained that he needed Two Hearts as quickly as possible. His friend dashed off. Gently Whirlwind and Rising Moon roused Gifted Tongue from her grief. "Co-wife, Two Hearts isn't married," Rising Moon said emphatically. "Roaring Woman lied to us. Look who is here, our grandrelative. He knew that Two Hearts left because Roaring Woman sent him away."

Whirlwind's news lifted Gifted Tongue's spirit only for a moment. She and Two Hearts still couldn't see each other while Tied to Sun lived, and he seemed to be regaining his health with Whirlwind's help. Helplessness overwhelmed her.

"You are kind to me," she said, choking back her tears. "But everything will be better if I'm sacrificed. Two Hearts can find another love, and Roaring Woman will help you raise Tied to Sun's child as a noble."

"Nonsense," Whirlwind said sternly. "You and Two Hearts have a future. Don't give up."

Gifted Tongue did not respond. She stared blankly at him. She wanted to sleep. He turned to Rising Moon. "I brought more Double Woman herb. She might need it to confront whatever schemes Roaring Woman hatched. Maybe it will change her mind. Mix it with whatever you feed her."

The next day, Gifted Tongue hardly opened her eyes as she prepared for her wedding to the Sun. Rising Moon lit cedar incense for her while persuading her to chew Double Woman herb. Rising Moon listed endless reasons why she should refuse the honor of a commoner marriage, but Gifted Tongue listened to none of them.

When Roaring Woman arrived to direct final arrangements, she sent Rising Moon away. At sunset, Roaring Woman led Gifted Tongue to the pyramid of the sun.

They ascended at the rear, at the end of a line of brides and their escorts. A slow, steady drumbeat pulsed in the air. Cedar incense swelled the air on top of the pyramid to drift downward. Gifted Tongue looked for Tied to Sun and the priest who would marry them. At last, she might be the center of attention at her marriage, she thought.

When Roaring Woman pressed her to hurry, Gifted Tongue asked for the priest. Roaring Woman told her that he wasn't needed. Gifted Tongue balked. Surely, she thought, she couldn't be married without him. A nagging doubt crept into her mind.

"Come, servant wife, uh, now commoner wife. As commoner wife you will glorify Tied to Sun's household. Don't hold back. We are already last in line. Look how eagerly the others go forward. Shame on your reluctance."

"But surely a priest must be here to marry us," Gifted Tongue muttered in confusion.

"Our husband is too ill to be here. The priest is with him. Where's your consideration for him, wench? Come along." Everything had worked so well for Roaring Woman that she lost her patience at this last minute hesitation. Yet, she had prepared for it.

"Here is powerful medicine," she admonished. "It'll let you enjoy your marriage. It makes you forget all worries and be happy beyond belief. You don't need to swallow it. Just breathe deeply."

Roaring Woman yanked Gifted Tongue's arm. She had a black powder in her hand and lifted it toward Gifted Tongue's nose. She squeezed the girl's arm so hard that the pain rallied Gifted Tongue's instinct to live. With grim determination, she shoved Roaring Woman's palm to her own nose, then blew the powder into her face. Roaring Woman screamed her wrath and sneezed. The drug's effects were instantaneous.

She loosened her grip and giggled, then continued to climb. Gifted Tongue thought to flee, but hesitated as a plot formed in her mind. Now, Roaring Woman made things easy.

"The evening is getting so warm," Roaring Woman giggled again. "It's nice to be warm before winter. I'm so glad you're here with me to enjoy it. Have I told you how much I like you, serv-, uh, commoner wife? Are you warm, too?"

"Let me take your parfleche bag," Gifted Tongue said in a disarming way. "Its weight makes you warm." Roaring Woman handed over the bag with its quill designs that denoted nobility.

"And, my lady, your heavy mantle makes you sweat. Let's trade mantles." Gifted Tongue felt the protection of the bright blue designs as she slipped into it while Roaring Woman donned the plain, thread-bare mantle of a commoner.

"We must be nearly there, dear," Roaring Woman remarked as the effects of the powder made her graceful feet skip. The gait seemed to take ten years from her age.

A moment later, the two reached a gate in the stockade surrounding the temple of the sun. Gifted Tongue observed that the brides' escorts stood on the right. She twirled Roaring Woman, as if skipping with her, to place the woman to her left. The procession disappeared into the compound. Gifted Tongue hurried to catch up, half dragging Roaring Woman.

The change of position was rewarded at the entrance to the temple stockade. From behind the wall, a warrior stepped to Roaring Woman's back, and clamped her arms to her sides. A priest in front of her slipped a coiled rope over her head. When he pulled it tight, Gifted Tongue recognized the sound of cracking vertebrae. The woman didn't even gasp. As she dropped to the ground, two other priests carried her away. For a moment, Gifted Tongue stood paralyzed until she glimpsed an older woman head for a gate opposite. Her feet took over.

Once outside, Gifted Tongue searched for the nearest canoe dock. Despite the rapidly growing darkness, she spied one not far to the north, but then realized she'd be quickly overtaken. She had to plan some other escape.

At the foot of the mound, she saw two priests and a warrior stop the women ahead of her. Gifted Tongue remebered overhearing a neighbor talk about a reluctant honoree and her chaperon at the last funeral. They had changed their minds while ascending the mound, and fled to the eastern mountains. Their escape had caused endless embarrassment for the priests who conducted the ceremony.

Gifted Tongue realized she must make the priests think she was Roaring Woman. She inhaled a pinch of Double Woman herb and her mind quickly focused. The sliver of moon gave little light and Roaring Woman's mantle would protect her. If only she could add weight, she thought. Her mind was riveted on the problem—then she rapidly folded and refolded Roaring Woman's parfleche bag and stuffed it into her skirt strap. She trusted that in the dark, her increased girth looked natural.

She strode boldly to the warrior and priests, hoping that they seldom saw Roaring Woman. Whirlwind's protection hovered over her, she thought, because none of them seemed to know Roaring Woman except by reputation. "Servants of the Sun, I salute you," Gifted Tongue said boldly, using all the words she could think of with an s in order to imitate Roaring Woman's lisp. She added a challenge as she said, "Will you accompany him later? I sent off a commoner wife with him to serve as his interpreter."

The priests seemed reluctant to question Roaring Woman in any way, and they waved Gifted Tongue on. She longed to sniff more Double Woman power but decided against it since the guards might be watching. She thought again of a canoe, but knew that if she headed for a dock it would arouse suspicion. Roaring Woman would have returned home. As much as she wanted to bolt for the river, her mind forced her feet toward the stockade.

She decided wisely. Two Hearts and Whirlwind stood before Tied to Sun's hut. She heard Two Hearts say between panting breaths, "I'll kill that woman for sacrificing Gifted Tongue. I should kill myself for not getting here earlier. These blasted short legs of mine are worthless."

Gifted Tongue allowed herself a backward glance. No one

watched. She dashed toward Two Hearts. At the sound of her running, he looked to see Roaring Woman's mantle. A gaze of pure hatred from him froze Gifted Tongue. But, when Two Hearts recognized her, he leaped forward.

Whirlwind grinned with delight at the sight of the two in each other's arms. Rising Moon, who had been tending Tied to Sun, looked at the two and gasped in dismay. "You don't know what revenge the nobility will take on you," she said fearfully.

Then she said in shock, "How can you be alive? What happened?"

When the lovers pulled apart, Gifted Tongue led Two Hearts to Rising Moon. She hastily explained her deception, and when she told Rising Moon how her mimicry of Roaring Woman's lisp saved her life, both women smiled and hugged each other.

Whirlwind took over. "You two must leave tonight," he said to Gifted Tongue and Two Hearts, holding their hands. "When the priests prepare the sacrificed bodies, they'll discover Roaring Woman. They may hide their mistake, so they'll want you dead. You can't travel these sloughs tonight." He nodded at Two Hearts. "This one is exhausted by his run from Quapaw."

"I can go on. Let's steal a canoe and flee."

"We can avoid stealing a canoe by waiting a day," Whirlwind said calmly. "A theft will alert the priests. I have a patient who will give me one."

No one could argue with Whirlwind's logic. "Tomorrow, I'll have a light, serviceable canoe for you. Tonight, you can hide in a slough I know, where the undergrowth is so thick you'll never be found. Then, you can start your downriver run."

"Upriver," Gifted Tongue said with determination. She was so decisive that Whirlwind hesitated to argue. But he had solid reasons for his choice of downriver.

"The warriors will expect you to go up the Missouri to reach your homeland. That's why I suggested downriver."

"I know, grandrelative. But I'm familiar with the upriver route, and I have friends at Mandan. They'll hide me."

Whirlwind frowned and said, "Everyone will expect you to go north." He paused and then said thoughtfully, "But, my diversion should work equally well downstream. If we're lucky, the priests may guess that you went downriver because it would be unexpected." He took Gifted Tongue by the hand and said softly, "You have a moment to say farewell to Rising Moon before I hide you."

In a rare, long embrace, Gifted Tongue held her co-wife and wished Rising Moon could go with them. She hated to leave her. Gifted Tongue could feel Rising Moon's love in how tightly she clung. Unable to hold back her tears, Rising Moon sobbed, "Don't worry, sister, Tied to Sun's child protects me. I'll remember you always. Go with Two Hearts. He's your destiny."

CHAPTER SIXTEEN

Gifted Tongue and Two Hearts spread grass for a bed under the thick brush that Whirlwind had used to hide them. They were too excited to sleep. He looked into her eyes and said, "I was a fool to allow Roaring Woman to trick me. She must have guessed I wouldn't let you be sacrificed."

"It wasn't your fault," Gifted Tongue said, gazing longingly at him. "When she told me you had married a widow of Diving Hawk, I wanted to die."

"Don't ever think that." Two Hearts shuddered. "We have too much to live for."

He took her in his arms. She had never felt such joy. They spent the night holding each other, dozing off, wakening to recall some precious moment they had shared.

The next morning they heard a rustle in the brush and Whirlwind's familiar voice. He crawled into their lean-to and whispered, "The Suns play politics. Dakota Next to Sun pretended outrage at his former wife's sacrifice. What hypocrisy," he laughed scornfully. "Unloading Roaring Woman on Tied to Sun was his cleverest stunt. Now he claims Tied to Sun betrayed him. He ordered his warriors to kill your husband. I can only guess, but the Next to Sun may want to claim you as a servant wife. Traders would pay dearly for you."

Two Hearts swallowed hard to hold his anger. Gifted Tongue asked in fear, "What about Rising Moon?"

"The child she carries protects her," Whirlwind said. "A noble will marry her. She'll be happy without Roaring Woman."

"I'm so glad to leave all this intrigue," Two Hearts said. "Do you have a canoe for us?"

"It's ready, but there's a problem. Weasel rushed to serve Dakota Next to Sun. He claimed that he knows the Missouri better than anyone, and he'll find you. I think it best that you flee down the Mississippi."

"Weasel may know the river better, but he made no friends along the way. More important, my destiny lies to the west." The determination in Gifted Tongue's voice seemed to reassure Whirlwind. He did not try to sway her.

"All right, I can see you've decided. I have a birch bark canoe ready. Weasel will need a day or two to get organized, and he's likely to use heavy dugouts. That'll help you. Let's go."

Whirlwind led them from their hiding place to a small creek where he had concealed a canoe. He whispered to them to expect a friend of his. When Two Hearts saw the man, he reached for his knife. "It's the father of Two Feather. What's he doing here?"

"He'll pretend to be you to revenge his son's honor. I've stained his face so he's as dark as you, and kneeling in a canoe, he'll look as short."

"I won't leave Gifted Tongue," Two Hearts nearly shouted.

"No need to," Whirlwind whispered harshly. "Even in starlight, you ought to see that my beautiful gray hair is now black." He stood erect and twirled in a tattered dress. "I'll add Roaring Woman's mantle at daybreak, so when people see us paddling downriver, they'll report they saw you."

Gifted Tongue took Whirlwind's hand and said, "You risk your life for us. I'll never forget you, nor the power you gave me with Double Woman."

"Her herb doesn't grow in the north," Whirlwind said. "But I've stowed a pouch of it with other supplies. You won't need the potion much longer. You're gaining Double Woman strength. Remember, use it only for the good of others." Whirlwind gave a solemn farewell.

Gifted Tongue moved to the bow of the canoe as Two Hearts knelt in back. Whirlwind lifted the stern with ease and launched it. He said softly but distinctly, "Follow this stream to a canal that branches left. Take the next one that veers to the right. It leads to the river. The fishing is poor so no one will be about until the Mississippi. Then one of you hide in the bottom while the other paddles. My friend and I will reach the Mississippi by a fishing stream before we head south. Some gossip is sure to report you headed downriver. We can't pass for you in daylight so you'll only have a few days' head start."

Before Gifted Tongue began to paddle, she chewed a pinch of Double Woman herb, relishing the bitter taste that focused her concentration. She never missed a turn in the network of canals. They slipped into the Mississippi in full darkness.

Two Hearts sighed in relief and said, "I can't believe how easily we got here. You seemed to know the exact way to come."

"Whirlwind gave good directions. I'll lie down now, while you paddle across the river."

In a while Two Hearts said, "We've reached the Missouri. Rest some more, my Shoshoni friend."

"It's your turn to rest." Gifted Tongue smiled at how quickly he took her place as she moved to the stern.

.   .   .

For more than a moon, the two fugitives paddled all night and took turns during the day. When they found a hiding place along the shore, they nibbled at the pemmican Whirlwind had given them. A few times they fell into exhausted sleep.

After one long night and much of a day of paddling, they pulled to shore to eat the last of their food. "I'll have to hunt," Two Hearts said. "We can hide the canoe, and you watch the river. We'll let Weasel pass us. It's an old trick so he'll expect it, but it might work."

She heard little hope in his voice and felt too tired to answer. In desperation, she opened the pouch at her neck for a bit of Double Woman potion. The bitterness sharpened her mind. She recalled the long float downriver and how Whirlwind joked at one point that the river turned north to return to its home.

She said excitedly, "We'll be coming to a big bend in the river. We could portage it and gain a day or two."

"That's not much time," Two Hearts said, his eye twitching.

She swallowed a little bit of the herb, which was almost gone, and thought only of saving Two Hearts. Suddenly, she knew what to do. "We can lay a false trail across the bend," she said boldly. "We'll let Weasel gain time while we wait. You can hunt. We'll add more time by canoeing around the bend."

"It just may work," Two Hearts said, his face brightening. "How will you recognize the portage?"

"The bluffs opposite it are high and gray, and we passed a

long, narrow island." She bit her lip. "I'm afraid that's not much help."

Two Hearts said, "We'll look for the island together. I know you'll recognize the bluffs." She detected a note of apprehension.They passed one island that struck her as familiar, but the bluffs beyond were low and yellow. The next day, they came upon another island that proved to be long and narrow. She took a small pinch of her medicine. The bluffs along the shoreline changed from pale yellow to gray. Before long they rose to an unusual height. Gifted Tongue studied the opposite shore. A well-worn trail led into the river, and she recognized it as the portage.

She suggested they beach the canoe above the portage but leave a slight trace, as if they had attempted to hide their tracks. They walked cautiously to the trail, but, farther along, they left the barest of tracks to indicate they carried a canoe. Then they leapt to a tree branch, climbed to the tree's other side and dropped down to make their way back through the thick brush. They returned to the river well above the trail and waded to their canoe.

The excitement of their deception gave them renewed energy to paddle. By the end of the day, they reached the point where the river turned west. "Look at that rise. It would be a good lookout point," she said.

Two Hearts answered, "I see a stream to the left of the peak. We can hide the canoe there."

The two paddled well up the stream before they had to beach. The brush was sparse but the shore rocky. They found a clump of tall, thick grass where they hid the canoe.

"You climb the bluff to watch while I hunt. Whirlwind left us a good bow but not many arrows," Two Hearts said, with his eye twitching more than usual.

Gifted Tongue found a clump of grass to hide behind and fought sleep as she laid on her stomach. She watched until dusk. Just as she started to worry about Two Hearts, he appeared carrying three rabbits he had already roasted. The two attacked the fresh meat, then lay down to watch. They could see little in the starlight, and their full stomachs lulled them to sleep. Gifted Tongue woke with the light of the morning star and fretted that Weasel might have passed. She also worried that he might have missed the portage if he had traveled at night.

When Two Hearts awoke, he expressed the same fear, and chided himself for having slept. She took his hand, urging him to be patient. He said he would, but his eye twitched rapidly. While they waited, they made up reasons why Weasel could not have passed. When the sun reached overhead, she saw canoes along both riverbanks. Bow men peered intently at the shorelines.

Two Hearts whispered to her. "If it were just those two, they would have overtaken us by now. Look downriver. You can see a dugout. There'll be more of them. Standard tactics for a search. An advance party in light canoes. The main body in dugouts. Weasel's taking no chances."

They heard a cry from the canoe that patrolled the west bank when it reached the portage. Obviously, the scout had found their tracks. The men patrolling the east bank hesitated, not far from the fugitive's hiding place. A scout who had run up the portage trail returned to shout he had discovered fresh tracks. The canoe near them turned to cross the river. Two Hearts spotted Weasel in the lead dugout. When he beached at the trail, he shouted orders for everyone to portage.

"In two days, they'll be well ahead," Two Hearts said. "Maybe I can find an antelope." He shot two gophers, but the rest of his hunt yielded only rabbits. Gifted Tongue roasted them and judged they would suffice until they reached the Mandan.

Upon reentering the river, Two Hearts discovered a hole in the canoe near the keel. He pinched off pitch from near the gunwale, chewed it to soften it, and rubbed it into the crack.

"I'm not sure this will work. Let's try it," he said fretfully. His worry about the patch made him careless about where he was walking. Gifted Tongue heard the rattle and called a warning, but he stepped too quickly. He stifled a yell, but she knew he had been bitten. She saw the snake slither into a hole.

She grabbed the quiver that Two Hearts had put into the canoe and pulled out an arrow, She slashed his ankle with a point to drain the poison.

"It was a small snake. It can't be serious," Two Hearts said, trying to sound convincing, but the twitch of his eye told her he worried.

They could do little except paddle steadily. They did not want to overtake the search party. Gifted Tongue had faith that Scatterscorn would have snakebite medicine if they could reach the Mandan village in time. Two Hearts tired often while she used every muscle she had.

. . .

One cold morning, she glimpsed several vertical spirals of smoke. Then her eye caught a waving movement from the shore.

"It's Scatterscorn," she told Two Hearts. "It's as if she expected us. She's signing us to come to shore."

"How could she expect us?" Two Hearts said, then raised an eyebrow in realization. "I'll bet Weasel warned the Mandan nobles we might be behind them. Won't they take us captive?"

"The Mandan don't have nobles, but a few chiefs may be friendly to the Dhegiha. We can't trust everyone, but my friends will take care of us."

Moments later, Scatterscorn stepped into the water to reach for Gifted Tongue's outstretched hands, and the two women beamed at each other.

"It's so good to see you," Scatterscorn said in Kutenai.

"You, too, sister," Gifted Tongue replied.

"I haven't used Kutenai since you left. I hope you can understand me."

"I'll have as much trouble speaking it."

"We have so much to tell. But more important, a Dhegiha search party left a lookout here. They wouldn't tell anyone except Black Wolf why, so I came down here to find out for myself, far enough downriver that the lookout can't see us."

Gifted Tongue smiled as she recalled how much her friend talked. She translated for Two Hearts as he beached the canoe. When he hobbled from it, he grimaced, and Scatterscorn rushed to him. She signed that she would carry his end of the canoe, and she helped haul it up a small draw to thick brush.

"Can we portage behind the village?" Gifted Tongue said anxiously.

"You won't need to. The lookout has a friend he spends the night with. While he's with her, he'll never see you."

Scatterscorn had stared at Two Hearts several times in wonder. Gifted Tongue smiled to herself a moment before relieving her friend's curiosity. "This is my Paiute friend, who lived among the Dhegiha. We had to flee the city when I was to be sacrificed. It's a long story, I'll tell you later."

Scatterscorn held her tongue, but as she watched Two

Hearts struggle, she said to him, "I can't help notice you're limping. What's wrong?"

"A snake bit me. I'm not sure I got rid of the poison. The ankle throbs."

"My mother-in-law, Otter, has a poultice for snakebite. It's the best. What do they use at the Center of the World?" Before Two Hearts could answer, she said, "By the way, is it true that Dakota Next to Sun will become the Sun now that the Honored One is dead? That's what Weasel claimed."

Two Hearts said with a disgusted look, "The Sun died before he named an heir. Even if he had, the Next to Suns would vie to be the next Sun. One of these days, their intrigue will topple the city, and the people will scatter to the four directions."

Scatterscorn looked puzzled, and Two Hearts guessed Gifted Tongue found it difficult to interpret what he said. The Mandan shrugged her shoulders, then gestured in signs. "It's good you will be far away in the mountains with Gifted Tongue."

In Kutenai, she said quickly to Gifted Tongue, "I shouldn't stand here talking. I must get food, and find Otter, and get some robes for you. You must be freezing."

"We froze last night," Gifted Tongue said with a nod. "And we ate the last of our rabbit."

"Hide here the rest of the day. Late tonight, paddle up to a high bluff on the left side of the river. Across from it is a creek. I'll meet you there."

Gifted Tongue and Two Hearts welcomed the rest. They nestled in each other's arms. When the sky darkened, they wished to leave but waited for pitch blackness. They crossed the river to paddle past the village. A late rising moon shone on a bluff to their left. Once they reached it, they recrossed the river, and found the tributary.

Two Hearts stiffened at the sight of two figures with Scatterscorn. Gifted Tongue reassured him. "It's Otter and a friend, Juneberries. She chatters more than Scatterscorn."

"Perhaps they will talk the poison out of my foot."

"Or swell your ears as much as your ankle. But we shouldn't joke. They're trying to save our lives."

Despite creaking joints, Otter reached them first to examine the bite. In the dark, she explored with her fingers. "It's cool, but it's swollen. I've got a poultice ready. There's more in this pouch. Keep it dry until you need it, then mix it with warm water. It'll draw the poison."

As Otter stepped back, Scatterscorn and Juneberries took her place. The latter offered a bowl. "Here's corn mush. It isn't hot, but I burnt myself when I tried it earlier. Take some squash, too. It's dry, but after all that pemmican, you need it. I put a supply of cornmeal in this cooking pot."

Scatterscorn laid out two bundles, one a heavy elk skin dress for Gifted Tongue, without decoration. The second bundle, for Two Hearts, held a shirt and leggings trimmed with Mandan designs. "The only small size I could find was a decorated shirt. You'll have to pass for Mandan although you're very dark. Right now you're pretty pale, but that won't last. Not after Otter's poultice. She's the best doctor on the river."

While Otter treated Two Hearts, Gifted Tongue told Scatterscorn about her widowhood and how the intrigue of Roaring Woman had backfired. She and Juneberries stared wide-eyed. Gifted Tongue guessed their silence set a record.

Scatterscorn shook her head and began to speak just as Otter finished. She said, "You and your friend must go. It will be light soon." Otter and Juneberries hugged Gifted Tongue. Scatterscorn held her tightly before she said, "You must leave. May the White Bison watch over you."

A spitting cold rain pelted them as they shoved off. Gifted Tongue sighed in relief at the pot of corn, a parfleche full of pemmican and a bag of the poultice. She tucked the bag along the keel and covered it with the parfleche to protect it from the rain. Juneberries had surprised her with a bison robe.

They pushed off in the last of the darkness, a tear in Gifted Tongue's eye. She would miss her friends. As the eastern sky lightened, Two Hearts said worriedly, "I wonder how fast Weasel is going. We must be careful not to overtake him. He might wait for his lookout to catch up with him."

"He'll probably give no thought to the man," Gifted Tongue said, turning to look at Two Hearts. "Weasel will want to reach Kutenai shelter as soon as possible. I wonder how the Kutenai will feel about feeding extra people for the winter?"

"My guess is that Dakota Next to Sun sent larger dugouts with gifts and food. They'll be behind us. He used those tactics before when he sent warriors up the Mississippi after friends of mine that he accused of treason."

They decided to keep an even pace. At midday, Gifted Tongue took the stern without protest from Two Hearts. He rested a while in the bow. His slumping shoulders told her that the poison tired him.

. . .

Days later, Two Hearts insisted that he take the stern. Gifted Tongue smiled warmly. His eye twitched less, and he kneeled erect. But that night, she discovered the patch in the keel had loosened. Water had soaked the poultice. She said with alarm, "Otter warned me to keep the poultice dry. I've failed you again. It's sopping wet."

"You've never failed me, and I should have watched as much as you. Besides, it's done its work. I'm feeling good."

Gifted Tongue felt reassured until that night when Two Hearts hobbled to shore. She saw that his ankle had swollen, and he grimaced when he helped her lift provisions from the canoe. She tried not to share panic.

That night when they rested in each other's arms, Two Hearts tossed and turned. Gifted Tongue hardly slept. She worried about what to expect once they reached the Kutenai. Weasel would be waiting for them. No doubt, he had promised Kustata wealth beyond measure. She wondered if Left Hand would defy the chief in order to help her.

A few days later, angry clouds unleashed frigid rain that turned to sleet. Gifted Tongue steered to a beach where pine trees offered protection. Two Hearts limped ahead to make a shelter while she unpacked. When she pulled the unloaded canoe onto shore, she heard a shout from downriver, followed by a clash of thunder.

Between the sleet and fading light, she spied two dugouts, each propelled by six warriors. She thought someone must have shouted they had seen her, but a second shout told the other dugout to take shelter.

Two Hearts' lean-to held off much of the rain. The bison robe kept them warm for a decent night's sleep, but in the morning Two Hearts groaned when he rolled onto his swollen ankle. She felt it and found it hot.

"You've got to rest," she said with concern. "Last night I saw two dugouts with a war party. They didn't see me, I'm sure. We can let them pass us."

"I doubt you would have seen them without being seen," Two Hearts said, his eye twitching. "But since they saw only one person, I want you to pack all the food you can carry and flee. From the top of the terrace I can hold them off for the day. After they kill me, they may not even look for you."

"I won't leave you. Besides, you know they'll search for me." She missed her Double Woman medicine that she had left in the canoe. She concentrated on saving Two Hearts. She said decisively, "I'll wait for them, dressed in your Mandan clothes. I'll blacken my face and pretend to be an insane Mandan, bent on killing myself in revenge against the Kutenai."

"It's possible, I guess," Two Hearts said with a breath of hope. "Is your Mandan good enough to fool them?"

"Not if any of them are fluent."

"Not likely. They're probably all warriors."

The two changed clothes moments before the dugouts swung into view. The warriors bent into their paddles, and Gifted Tongue knew they would have been overtaken yesterday had it not stormed. She dabbed her face with mud, added an extra layer over her scars, and hoped the Dhegiha recognized the Mandan sign of mourning.

She started for the canoe to get her Double Woman medicine but didn't have time. She screeched what she hoped sounded like a Mandan death song. The plan seemed to work because one of the Dhegiha spoke warily in broken Mandan to ask about canoes that had passed earlier.

She answered in signs and a few words of Mandan that she had seen no canoes, but that she searched for the Kutenai who had killed her wife. She wasn't sure she spoke deeply enough to sound like a man, so she gestured wildly with signs, mixing their sequence to suggest a crazed mind. She hoped they would come no closer if they believed they had to deal with a madman.

Her trick succeeded. The Dhegiha signed that they hoped the mad Mandan would find his Kutenai victim, and they bolted toward the opposite shore to disappear around a bend.

Gifted Tongue sighed in relief and returned to Two Hearts to tell him that they could rest until his foot healed. He smiled warmly at how she had tricked their pursuers, then said gravely, "You should go on without me. The bite's become infected. The poison couldn't last this long."

"Even if I left you, where would I go? For moons, I've thought we'd be safe with the Kutenai. Now, Weasel has probably bribed so many people I don't know whom to trust, except for my friend, Left Hand."

She decided to rest for a day with Two Hearts. Then she could creep into the village at night to find Left Hand who should know a remote refuge where Two Hearts could recover.

That night, as she held Two Hearts close, her confidence returned. She decided to leave the next day, but the excitement of fooling the Dhegiha warriors and the moons of ceaseless paddling caught up with her. Gifted Tongue slept in exhaustion mixed with a low-grade fever of anxiety.

In the middle of the night, a raging flap of wings startled her. She grabbed a branch for protection before recognizing the sounds of her guardians. They must have come to guide her, but when she took one direction, they drove her back. When she tried another, they forced retreat. She turned frantically, but wherever she headed, owls menaced her. Finally, she realized they were warning her to stay in camp. Untroubled sleep overtook her. The sun soared high before she woke.

She felt recovered, lit a small fire where dense pines hid the smoke, and cooked cornmeal. The next day, she cooked a two-day supply for Two Hearts and prepared to leave for the village, assuming that her owls had meant for her to rest.

She had just emptied the pot when she heard footsteps and muffled voices. Gifted Tongue doused the fire, covered the embers, and slipped to Two Hearts' side. Their well-hidden shelter needed only a few pine boughs to cover its opening.

"I'm sure I smelled smoke," a woman's voice said that sounded familiar to Gifted Tongue.

"A moment ago you were certain you heard voices," another woman said skeptically.

The first voice answered, "You have to admit this pine grove makes an ideal hiding place."

"My sister," Gifted Tongue called, recognizing Left Hand's voice. She darted from the lean-to to embrace her. The two trembled with delight. Good Woman followed Left Hand's example and hugged Gifted Tongue.

"What are you doing here?" Gifted Tongue said, her eyes beaming. "I was about to look for you."

"I thought so. That's why we came. The Dhegiha arrived days ago, and asked if anyone had seen you. We were all puzzled. It took several days before we discovered they hunted you."

"Will Kustata help them?" Gifted Tongue said.

"I thought he wouldn't, until a second party arrived with a dugout full of gifts. He might give you up."

"Can you find us a secluded spot in your valley where my friend, Two Hearts, and I may winter? He's in that lean-to." She pointed with her chin.

"Some hunter would stumble over you in the valley," Good Woman said, shaking her head.

Left Hand spoke quickly but distinctly, "I talked with Works Alone before we left. She guessed you might hide here. She told me the Owl Dance Society can help you over the mountain wall behind you. The other side slopes down to a Kutenai village. Our relatives there will shelter you. They're so isolated from the river that the Dhegiha don't know about them."

"The mountain's a vertical cliff," Gifted Tongue said warily. "Is there a trail?"

"Not one to speak of. That's why the Kutenai village is so isolated," Left Hand said.

Since Two Hearts slept, Gifted Tongue used his name. "A rattlesnake bit Two Hearts. A poultice the Mandan gave me nearly healed him, but we lost the medicine. Now he can hardly walk."

"Tomorrow, I'll bring herbs. My guardian gave me strength to heal," Left Hand said proudly. "Works Alone will bring the Owl Dance Society later in the day to help."

"Don't those women hate me? After I flew east instead of west in my initiation, they must have lost all patience with me."

"They didn't hate you, although you weren't very popular." Left Hand laughed, but then her expression turned serious. "After you left, Fish Weir Woman listened to the other women talk about how hard you worked and how much they liked you. She changed her mind. So everyone will help you escape. After all, we share power."

"We've got to go," Left Hand said, glancing around. "I must gather herbs while Good Woman notifies the Owl Dance Society members. We'll be back by midday tomorrow. You'd be surprised how close you are to camp. Guard your smoke."

Gifted Tongue felt the night would never end. Two Hearts quaked with fever, and a sickening yellow pus oozed around the bite. She worried that Left Hand would be too late. Two Hearts slept until well past sunup. She offered him a little mush, but his swollen tongue refused it, and he lapsed into a trance.

.   .   .

Two Hearts sensed a world of dancing colors where the scars on Gifted Tongue's face changed colors in exquisite patterns on her beautiful face. At times, a shooting pain disrupted the pattern, but the designs became more vivid. A drum throbbed in his head to make colors zigzag behind his eyes.

He wanted the sensation to last, but something cooled his foot and a soothing liquid crept down his throat to quiet the drama of the colors. A wizened woman with an otter skin headdress danced in and out of his view to end the spectacles of reds, oranges, and yellows.

White blurs took the shape of a weaving line of women in bleached elk skins. The last woman held switches in one hand while she whipped the women before her with the other hand. When she struck Gifted Tongue, he battled to consciousness, but his lover only danced more vigorously. He lapsed into a fretful rest. When the drum pulse woke him, he saw the line enter their lean-to, then circle it. He fell into semi-consciousness.

He felt himself lifted to pass through the hut and around it. A sense of soaring elated him, then frightened him. He couldn't tell if the women carried him or if he flew. In his semi-consciousness he decided the women carried him. Then the line passed through the trunk of a large pine. He focused with all his might to see the line ease through another tree. They all soared toward the sun, and its heat made him sleep.

He awoke to a chill. His foot no longer throbbed. When he rose to test it, he felt no pain. Ahead, he saw a patch of snow. He couldn't tell if he had slept days, or if he had been carried up a mountain. He looked for a line of women, but only Gifted Tongue stood beside him. She said with a wry smile, "We've made it up the mountain. It's an easy walk down to a Kutenai village where we'll be welcome. We'll reach it tomorrow."

Two Hearts took a tentative step and couldn't believe how good his foot felt. When Gifted Tongue stepped to his side, he put his arm on her shoulder to enjoy her warmth and support. When he asked how they had reached the mountaintop, she replied that women of the Owl Dance Society had helped. Her wistful manner told him he would never learn more.

He didn't need to. With her by his side, he was content. He stared into her face until she blushed and turned away. He tried to remember the first time he had seen her because he thought the scars on her face had repulsed him. Now he couldn't believe that. Her beauty radiated, and her wondrous smile danced within him. He said, "You are the most beautiful woman I've ever met. Let us go find your family."

"And then we'll look for yours."

"Perhaps we can be married both by Shoshoni custom and Paiute style? Will you marry me, my Shoshoni friend?"

"Yes, my Paiute friend."

The sincerity in Gifted Tongue's answer assured him she had no doubts about marrying a man from a foreign tribe.

THE END

AFTERWORD

I leave it to the reader to decide if Gifted Tongue, Two Hearts, and Owl Dance Society members flew to the cliff top or if music and dance induced a group hypnosis while they climbed the mountain. Before deciding, I urge you to read page 157 of Ethnography of the Kutenai by H. H. Turney High who vividly describes the Owl Dancers' flight, as related to him by trusted informants.

For a general description of Shoshoni and Washo culture, see the ethnography of native North Americans in North American Indians by Alice Kehoe. It links prehistoric and historic cultures. Her discussion of Southeastern tribes is relevant for Mississippian, or what I call Dhegiha, and the Cahokia Mounds' site or what I describe as the Center of the World.

Description of the White Bison Cow Society is based on Robert Lowie's Societies of the Crow, Hidatsa and Mandan Indians. General descriptions of the Plains' Indians note the importance of men's societies. Although women's societies were fewer, they were vital in the ritual round.

For Gifted Tongue's trip to Aztalan, I imposed Menomini

and Winnebago contemporary culture upon prehistoric remains. The ancestors of the two might have been at Aztalan in A.D. 1000 but for now its true occupants are unknown.

I assume the Caddo peoples occupied Spiro because they lived there when Europeans explored. To bring Spiro to life, I used a description of the Pawnee provided by Gene Weltfish in The Lost Universe.

My assumption that the prehistoric people at Cahokia Mounds spoke a Siouan language is controversial. This unique archaeological site, a few miles east of St. Louis, is the most important one in North America but relatively unknown. The people possibly spoke Algonquian, being ancestral to the Illinois tribes or ancestral to the Natchez, who resemble the Dhegiha with a complex political hierarchy.

I believe the people at Cahokia spoke Siouan because of language distribution. A map of Siouan speakers suggests that their homeland centered near the mouth of the Ohio River. Moreover, the early reports of tribes such as the Omaha suggest complex religious and political organizations that could be derived from a complex hierarchy based on intensive agriculture as practiced at Cahokia.

I used the Omaha as a model for the ceremonial life of the Dhegiha, a generic linguistic term for Dakota, Kansa, Omaha, Osage, Ponca, and Quapaw. The related Chiwere is generic for Iowa, Missouri, and Oto. Use of these tribal names as wards for the prehistoric city presupposes the Siouan connection. These tribal names are likely of more recent origin, but Quapaw does mean "downriver" while Omaha means "upriver," both appropriate for a Cahokian origin.

Details of Omaha ethnography are given by Reo Fortune in Omaha Secret Societies. The competition between the Water

Monster Society doctors and the priests of the Long Nose God Society is derived from his observations of competition between Omaha doctors and a society of chiefs comprising the Midewen, a cult the Omaha borrowed from the Winnebago.

My Long Nose God Society is based upon prehistoric traits such as ear spools of a human face with exaggerated nose. Williams and Goggin analyze the trait in "The Long Nose God Mask in Eastern United States," October, 1956, Missouri Archaeologist.

The Dhegiha origin myth that Whirlwind tells Gifted Tongue is taken from James Walker, Dakota Myths, and Ogallala Women by Maria Powers. They serve, too, as sources for Double Woman.

The use of ethnographies to enliven prehistory is cultural anthropology's contribution to recreating the past. The method exaggerates the stability of Indian cultures. Change was persistent in North America, and the Shoshoni ancestors in A.D. 1000 differ from Shoshoni today. However, until archaeology becomes more adept, projecting the present upon the past is the best anthropologists can do.

The archaeological work in the Midwest since 1945 has advanced our knowledge far beyond what anyone imagined possible before World War II. For the past twenty-five years I have observed work at Cahokia from two miles east in Collinsville, Illinois, where I live. I watched Melvin Fowler unravel the secrets of the site, describing his discoveries in Explorations into Cahokia Archaeology and "Late Prehistory of the Illinois Area" in Smithsonian Handbook of North American Indians, Vol. 15.

The Cahokia Mounds Interpretive Center offers an extraordinary introduction to the site. Like the site, the center is unique. The magnificence of Cahokia caught the imagination of the pioneer archaeologist, Warren Moorehead, whose reports stirred Illinois legislators to buy portions of the site, but for many years politics and lack of funds prevented adequate acquisition and allowed almost nothing for a museum. This archaeological gem went virtually unprotected until the 1960s when archaeologists steadily deciphered the evidence for its importance, and the state of Illinois began a program of land acquisition and preservation. It was declared a Unesco World Heritage Site in 1982 and the Interpretive Center opened in 1989. It presently attracts more than half a million visitors annually.

A day spent at the site leads one to hours of imaginative recreating of life there a thousand years ago. We can only hope that archaeologists continue to provide us with more facts so our reconstruction will rely less upon imagination and more upon the reality revealed by excavation.